"I am afraid that if I am discovered here alone with you by Sir Rupert, I will be in great trouble."

"Why should you be?" said Peter with some asperity, as he stepped up onto a portion of the half-fallen wall, extended his hand toward Miss Sterling, and deftly guided her to follow him. "Our being locked in the garden was entirely an accident. It is not as if we had come out here to escape notice and to enjoy a private moment together, is it?"

"Certainly not," said Miss Sterling, now climbing further up onto the rocks. "You are right. Sir Rupert cannot object! After all, it is not as if we had purposely arranged a clandestine meeting!"

"Of course not!" said Peter. "What a ridiculous notion!"

"What reason would we have to do such a thing?" she pointed out. "We are friends."

"Fast friends," Peter agreed. "Very good friends indeed."

At this juncture, a piece of cracked stone shifted on the high pile and gave way, causing Miss Sterling to lose her footing and tumble dangerously until Mr. Gilbough swiftly stopped her fall by scooping her up into his arms.

In just that moment, when he looked into those incalculably deep blue eyes of hers, he felt as if the world had shifted on its axis. What was occurring between them seemed inevitable, and somehow predestined. Almost against his will, he murmured, "I love you, Helen . . ."

THE COUNTERFEIT HEIRESS

Isobel Linton

Zebra Books
Kensington Publishing Corp.

http://www.zebrabooks.com

ZEBRA BOOKS are published by

Kensington Publishing Corp.
850 Third Avenue
New York, NY 10022

First Printing: July, 1997
10   9   8   7   6   5   4   3   2   1

Printed in the United States of America

1

Although receipt of an invitation to Cornell Castle for one of Lady Arabella Gilbough's celebrated summer parties was highly coveted, and a singular mark of social approbation, Helen Sterling was unable to keep her hands from trembling slightly as they broke open the red wax wafer on the invitation's vellum envelope. She ran her fingers idly over the thick imprint of the seal, which bore the ancient Gilbough coat of arms.

Miss Sterling perused the ivory card within, which had been engraved in the finest copperplate. She seemed almost to shake her head, then sighed. She put up her hand, instinctively smoothing her straight, ash-blond hair, and then carefully put the card back into its envelope, and placed it in the top right-hand drawer of her secretary desk, vowing to pen her note of acceptance later in the day.

Father will be pleased, she thought to herself.

She knew why she had been invited, of course. It was

because her engagement to Sir Rupert Fellowes was now quite a settled thing. Sir Rupert, after all, was a well-known personage in London. His father had been a friend of the late Lord Locksley, whose equally magnificent estate, Gordon Park, had lands that marched with those of Cornell Castle.

It had been only a matter of time before things like this had begun to happen—this particular card would be only one of many more to come, for the hand-delivered invitation to Lady Arabella's fortnight of gaiety marked Miss Sterling's first entree into the very highest circles of the ton.

Though not a circumstance Miss Sterling had in the least desired for herself, she could not have been more sensible of the fact that this rise in social status was precisely the gift her father had always hoped to be able to bestow upon her.

Her father's dearest wish had been achieved. That being the case, Helen Sterling sought to find delight in it.

Miss Sterling was, above all things, attached to her father. He was famed as "Black Jack" Sterling, ebony-haired, swarthy and powerfully built, a self-made man who had risen in a single lifetime, by his own merits and the sweat of his brow, from abject poverty to fabulous wealth. Black Jack Sterling's Nottingham cotton mills were arguably the most prosperous mills in all England; he ran his mills with rare fairness, precision, and intelligence, and these attributes paid off in enormous profits.

"Nottingham cotton" or "Sterling cotton" as it was sometimes called, was the most desirable machine-made fabric due to its evenness, durability, and softness. It was the only muslin that compared favorably to Indian muslin, and this was because the spun thread for all the fabric had been imported directly from the Orient: the dyeing occurred in England, as did the weaving, which was done on the finest machine looms. If, as for sprig muslin, white fabric needed to be block-printed after weaving, this could be accomplished in Black Jack Sterling's factories as well. Controlling almost all the basic processes—weaving, dyeing, block-printing—Mr. Sterling produced the finest cotton fabric available in the English market, and every mantua-maker vied for Black Jack's muslin cloth to use for their best customers.

Through his hard work, business sense, and control over so many aspects of production, Black Jack Sterling had made his fortune.

His only child, Helen, was the sole heiress to all of this wealth.

Helen's mother, Mary Dunn as she was before her marriage, had died giving birth to Helen, who inherited her mother's pale blond coloring. She grew up to be the very image of her mother, which further endeared her to Black Jack. By the age of eighteen she had become a lovely girl—she was of medium height, with beautiful blue eyes, straight, pale champagne-blond hair, and skin that was porcelain fair. Her nose was straight, her gaze straightforward, her manner direct and charming.

Since Helen was all the family that Black Jack Sterling had, her happiness and well-being meant everything to him.

No expense had been spared in her upbringing. Miss Sterling had had all the silks and satins and feathers and furbelows a young lady could ever wish for. She had been raised at Barton House, the great London town house Mr. Sterling had taken on a long lease from the ever-indebted Viscount Barton. Helen had lived there for so long that she regarded it as her true home.

The day to day upbringing of Helen Sterling had been left in the hands of Miss Lydia Trenton, who, loving Helen as if she were her own child, was far more than a mere governess. Miss Trenton's kind heart was unequaled, she was to the manor born, and her understanding was quite considerable (her own education had occurred, at considerable expense, at Miss Fanshawe's Select Seminary for Young Ladies in the days when the Trenton family was still very well off).

As a direct result of Miss Trenton's many years of devotion to her charge, Miss Sterling grew up to be everything a fond father could have hoped for. She spoke with an educated, well-modulated accent, her address was genteel and unspoiled, her manner was direct but not at all forward, and she was never described as anything other than very pretty-behaved.

Helen Sterling spoke good French and passable Italian. She played the pianoforte, and sang a very pleasing soprano. She painted and sketched nicely; she could do delicate embroidery. She had been taught to have a decent seat on a horse; she could even drive just a little.

In short, she had all the accomplishments of a young lady of quality save one—Miss Sterling was not a gentleman's daughter. In England, it was a fact that, though a man be as wealthy as Croesus himself—and Black Jack Sterling was nearly that—if his wealth had been acquired in trade, it was tainted.

Pretty Miss Sterling had never been presented at court, for there was no one in her family able to present her. She had received no tickets to the Wednesday night dances at Almack's, for there had been no one, neither family nor friend, who knew a Patroness well enough to request entrance for her.

When she was seventeen and had left the schoolroom, Miss Trenton undertook the role of companion to Miss Sterling, so that she might have a chaperone and go about in society. However, while Miss Trenton's presence lent Miss Sterling propriety and some consequence, she could not be expected to work miracles. Helen Sterling would always be Black Jack Sterling's daughter, whose family riches arose not from the land rents of great estates, but came from the cotton mills of the north.

Miss Sterling knew of the social stigma attached to her. It did not precisely matter to Helen herself that her family lineage harked back only to tenant farmers, and that her father's wealth was not inherited, but she had been made to feel acutely that her precise social status mattered to everyone else.

Helen Sterling, for all her many excellent qualities, her shy beauty, her wealth and education, remained naught but a tradesman's daughter, and everyone in London knew it.

2

It was not more than a fortnight after her receipt of the invitation to Cornell Castle that Miss Sterling, her father, and her dear companion Miss Trenton (their servants and baggage following close behind them) set forth toward northern Buckinghamshire, taking their time, and going on by easy stages.

The party traveled slowly since Miss Trenton, by constitution, was not a good traveler. Even so, by the time the carriage finally entered the tall iron gates that marked Cornell Castle, the pale pasty look on Miss Trenton's complexion strongly heralded the fact that, as usual, she would have to rest to recover from the strain of the journey.

"I'm so sorry, my dear," said her companion, as their carriage made its way down the long drive through the swath of green that bordered the park leading up to the Castle. "I hate to leave you to all to yourself, in a strange place, with persons unfamiliar to you."

"Don't give it a thought," replied Helen in a reassuring

tone. "Father is here with me, and will be my companion until you are better."

"Companion? I?" said Mr. Sterling, looking up from a thick leather ledger. Mr. Sterling was a large, stern-looking man, with curling black hair that held a hint of grey. He had thick eyebrows, and a very determined-looking chin, and his features revealed more strength of character than handsomeness. "Can't be done! Sorry! I have my accounts to do, Helen. If I don't keep abreast of expenditures, down to the very last farthing, things will get lax. Men will get lax. Machines will be neglected. Profits will be lost."

"Father, try a little to disport yourself, keep me company, and engage in some restful activities. It would be good for you for once to enjoy a bit of leisure."

"Leisure? Rest? I? Never, my love! Can you see me lounging around a castle, touring the galleries, strolling through the parks? Bore me to tears, it would, for one thing. Makes me shudder at the very thought! Viewing paintings! Taking walks! Admiring the furniture! Not I, my dear Helen. I'll take you down to dinner, but that's an end to it. For all that I love you, Helen, you'll have to try to amuse yourself until Miss Trenton is herself again."

"Very well, Father," she replied, though the thought of having to make her way amongst so many grand strangers dismayed her.

"You need not feel ill at ease. Don't be shy; I am sure you will make many new friends here. It is a great opportunity for you, and you should make the most of it! Your Rupert will arrive soon, and he will introduce you around. There will be scores of other young people attending, I wager. So pitch in, and do whatever it is that young people do at these things."

"I know no one. I hardly know what is expected of me," Helen said frankly. "I've never been to a country house party before, Father."

"Nor have I, come to think of it. Nothing to it, I'm sure," replied her father. "Is there, Miss Trenton? By the by, you don't look at all well. There are some bushes down the lane—do you need the carriage to stop?"

Miss Trenton shook her head no, and bravely removed the linen handkerchief behind which she had been hiding her face, which had now turned almost ashen. She summoned all her energy in order to state with dramatic certainty, "Summer parties at grand houses are one of the singular delights of ton society! With so many people clustering in a relatively confined space, a house party offers opportunities for intrigue, for advancing one's standing in society, for flirtations, and for match-making such as never occurs otherwise."

"What a daunting circumstance!" cried Miss Sterling. "One must feel perpetually observed, like a fish in a fishbowl."

"Yes, exactly!" averred Miss Trenton, whilst stifling a loud hiccup in her genteel manner. "A proper ton houseparty *is* daunting! It is vital that one realize that at the outset! I am glad that you are a clever girl who is able to see things just as they are, Helen.

"While attending a grand house party is not so expensive nor so exclusive as being presented at Court, it is very similar to that occasion insofar as one's dress, one's conduct, nay, one's very *being* will necessarily be brought under the most severe scrutiny!"

She reached into her reticule, withdrew a fan, and began pumping it in front of her face in a desperate attempt to use fresh air to gain control over her wayward digestion.

"Until I am once again well enough to serve again as your guide through the treacherous shoals of ton society, I beg you will keep a reserved manner, and not go about very much. It is critical to your interests, Helen, that you make no *faux pas* in the time that remains before your marriage."

"I'm sure you know best, and I shall do just as you say," Helen promised.

At this point, the carriage came round a bend, and then passed over a long, gracefully-arching bridge that traversed a long and slender lake, and just at the bridge's end, the road turned again, sharply, and the features of Cornell Castle suddenly came into view.

Cornell Castled lacked a moat, but was massive nonetheless; it had tall stone walls with small windows, and presented a magnificent appearance. What did one call that style, Miss Sterling wondered. Castelated? Yes, that was it.

There were battlements, or rather the semblance of battlements all along the roof line of the main section; sweeping out to either side were yellowing sandstone wings which had been added on later. There were tall triple-tiered windows filled with myriad tiny panes of glass which glistened in the sunlight. There was a pair of odd, turret-like domes that bordered the main entrance, and there was a another pair of larger domes, complete with spires, topping the roofs at either ends of the building.

"I've certainly never ever, been to an affair at such a place as this!" Helen exclaimed, almost in awe. "I shouldn't wonder that I lose my way, wandering around such a monstrous large home!"

"Bit excessive, really, don't you think?" suggested Mr. Sterling. "Only think of all the blunt they must spend on servants, candles, and coal!"

"Father!" chided Miss Sterling, taking hold of her father's arm, and giving him an affectionate squeeze.

"In fact, it would be an interesting exercise to figure out precisely how many servants in a house like this actually are worth their wages, and how many are just useless hangers-on, and how many are just kept on out of respect for tradition, and how many could be let go with no one being the wiser. It would be interesting to determine just how many servants are really necessary to the smooth running of the household. I'm sure there are far too many mouths to feed here—it might just be staff taking advantage of a widow. Come to think on it, I should mention it to our hostess, Lady Arabella. I wager I could save her a bundle of money."

"Father! No! Please, you mustn't discuss such things with anyone!"

"Oh, no, Mr. Sterling, it would be ever so impertinent!" cried Miss Trenton, forgetting, in her horror, her indisposition.

"Would it?" he asked, blankly. "I won't bring it up if you really think it would be out of place, Miss Trenton. You know how highly I value your opinion."

"Thank you, Mr. Sterling," said Miss Trenton, blushing at this compliment.

"Of course you must not mention things like that, Father! I think you do not realize, but it seems to me that all you can *ever* think of is of budgets, pounds, and pence."

"I'm a practical man, my dear," he admitted. "Why, if I weren't, I wouldn't have a feather to fly with, and then, where would we be? Back in Old Hawton, and me trying my best to marry you off to a farmer—*if* I could."

Miss Trenton winced involuntarily. "A farmer? Is *that* the sort of people you come from?"

"Ah, dear Miss Trenton, it was worse than that!" said Mr. Sterling, laughing. "The class of yeoman farmers was a class of persons we, poor mice, *aspired* to!"

Miss Trenton shuddered politely and fell silent, while Helen Sterling merely smiled knowingly and indulgently at her parent, and settled back against the brown velvet squabs to enjoy the last minutes of the ride as they drew nearer to grand entrance of castle, feeling a mixture of excitement and dread.

The last months in London, and now this country adventure, had been rather like a fairy-tale: first meeting Sir Rupert Fellowes at Lady Carteret's rout, seeming to take his fancy, and then becoming singled out for attention by that well-born, well-known, wealthy bachelor. He had quite swept her off her feet.

No one had ever treated her with such fond and deliberate and persevering admiration! Sir Rupert didn't seem to worry a bit about her family background, or about her father's somewhat ungentleman-like speech, which even dear Miss Trenton heard with regret. Her life, after the entrance of Sir Rupert into it, was being quite dramatically transformed.

When their carriage pulled up in the drive, a swarm of servants emerged from the house; they pulled down the stairs, at once, helped the ladies to alight, and quickly ushered the main party into the entranceway.

Once inside the high-ceilinged hall, which gave on to an exquisite sweeping staircase that led up to the next story, they were greeted by the butler, and the housekeeper, Mrs. Flynt, who sent a footman to show them to their chambers, and sent several housemaids and lower footmen to meet their second and third carriages, which held most of their belongings. The carriage with John, Mr. Sterling's valet, along with Miss Sterling's maid, Lily, and a vast amount of luggage, had just pulled up; and another swarm of castle servants appeared, to whisk the luggage up to their suite of rooms.

Helen could hear her own footsteps along the hard marble echoing off the high ceiling; when she looked up at the inner dome, she saw that the ceiling was trimmed with gold leaf all around, in a netted diamond pattern. Faced with such magnificence, she felt tiny in comparison,

as she had when she was a child looking up at the starry
sky.

She followed the footman up the long stairs and then
down several corridors, and up another staircase, until her
party was shown into a lovely suite of rooms that faced
onto the south lawns.

All the appointments of their rooms were just as one
might wish: the long windows were draped in blue silk shot
with gold. The furniture was rather old-fashioned—very
heavy, dark, and ornate—but polished to a deep luster: it
had probably been in the family for many generations.
Her own bed was in a room at the very end of the suite,
and was hung with dusty-rose damask.

Helen went over to her bed, was inspecting it when her
garrulous abigail, Lily, appeared in a customary bustle of
energy, her arms full of band-boxes, her mind brimming
with plans.

Lily Beeton was a petite, attractive brunette; she was also
vivacious, and indomitable, and a well-loved member of
their household. As soon as she appeared, she took charge
of things, saying, "Miss Helen, everything will be fine, do
not fear, for I am here. I have let *all* these people know
that we *cannot*, and we *will not* be pushed around! They
are to bring up all your things at *once*, and I will have every
one of your gowns unpacked, hung, and ironed before
this day is done! Nothing else will do, and so I told them!"

"Very good, Lily. You are a wonder, as ever," Miss Sterling replied with a smile.

"Because, you see, I thought they were trying to put *us*
at the end of the line, and I told them I would not have
it! In particular, I said to that pushy Miss Finton who dresses
the Duchess of Minster, and thinks that just because *her*
mistress is a Duchess, that all the irons and all the fires
belong to *her!* Once they realized that Lily Beeton dresses
Miss Sterling, they all broke down completely, and they

said I could have whatever I want, whenever I need it. That's what you have to do! If you don't get them to respect you at once, these people show their lazy ways, and try to flummox you, and roll over you, and get away with everything!''

"Really, Lily?"

"All those years I spent as a milliner's apprentice taught me just the way to deal with people who try to put themselves first. If someone is haughty to you, you must be *twice* as haughty in return: that puts them in their place, and then they shut up, and respect you. Iron hand in a velvet glove, but mostly the iron hand! Since *you,* Miss Helen, must not put yourself forward (which of course you must not, because it would be unsuitable) then *I* must act on your behalf, quickly and surely—and that is just what I have done!

"So, Miss Helen, you should really take a rest, and then tell me which gown you will be needing to wear to dinner . . . unless you would rather that I choose your gown?'' Lily asked hopefully, for it was her greatest pleasure to turn out her mistress in the finest manner possible.

Miss Sterling recalled Miss Trenton's strictures from the carriage ride, and demurred, saying, "Oh, no, don't bother, Lily—I won't be going down tonight. I thought to ask for something to be sent upstairs. Perhaps you would ask for a cold collation for Father, and some broth for me.''

"And for Miss Trenton? She is ill again? But, of course— she always is ill after traveling!''

Helen nodded, and then Lily exclaimed, "I have the remedy! Plain, hard biscuits! Salt water biscuits and lemonade for Miss Trenton!''

"Do whatever you think best. I know you take pride in your potions, Lily, so I'll leave everything in your capable hands.''

"Very good, Miss Helen. I love staying here, staying at a real castle! It is very large, and very grand, and exciting, isn't it?" said Lily, with starry-eyed satisfaction.

"Yes, it is," said Helen Sterling, thinking again how small and insignificant she felt in comparison to her magnificent surroundings.

"Really, there is nothing I like so much as grandeur!" sighed Lily.

It was no later than half past eight when Helen Sterling pulled the ivory linen covers up to her chin, and snuggled in to the deep, soft bed, waiting for sleep to come to her. Sleep came neither easily nor soon. Too many thoughts filled her mind, each one jockeying for prominence.

"Grandeur," Lily had said, and it was all too grand to be true. The grandeur of the whole occasion was overwhelming—a house-party that was to last a fortnight! No fewer than sixty house-guests, each one selected from the highest circles of the ton!

On the morrow, she was sure to meet the fabulous beau of the ton, Sir Charles Stanton, the famed and feared arbiter of fashion. There would be dukes and duchesses aplenty, and scores of lesser nobles, some of whom she had at least seen in London. She would meet and rub elbows with persons whom she now knew only as legends, like the Season's acknowledged beauties, such as Janet Carteret, Catherine Prowse, and Lady Georgiana Locksley.

Around the great halls of Cornell Castle would stand London's renowned wits and London's wise men. There would be famous politicians, the ones whose speeches were reported in the newspapers. There would be army officers, and naval officers, and she might hope to meet with— or even dance with!—great military strategists, Cabinet Ministers, or Members of Parliament.

As to females, they would all be there in their finest attire, young women and old.

A small fortune would not suffice to pay for the gowns that had been designed for the event by modistes such as Madame Vergere and Madame Fanchon. Rundell and Bridges' whole store could not have provided the fabulous jeweled ornaments that would be brought out and displayed on the ladies at Cornell Castle—heirloom tiaras, ropes of pearls, emerald and diamond sets.

In one place would be gathered the most sought-after hostesses of London: Sally Jersey, Princess Esterhazy, Lady Belleveau, Mrs. Hicks-Aubrey, and the indomitable matchmaker, Louisa, Lady Lacon.

In attendance at Cornell Castle would be all the various and sundry ranks of marriageable girls: the rare beauties, the second-rank belles, the ordinary, commonplace daughters of the gentry, and even the Season's antidotes: poor, pitiable horse-faced maidens; awkward, shy, stammering maidens; sad, fubsy-faced girls.

Each one wealthy and well-born.

Each one well-born save for me . . .

3

"What shall I wear to breakfast, Lily? Shall I wear the sprig muslin with the blue ribands that you laid out? I like it exceedingly," said Helen, as she held up to the light streaming through the long window a gown of fine muslin that betrayed good fashion, superb craftsmanship, and great expense. She brought it over to a long mirror, and looked at herself in it critically.

"I've never worn it, and it *is* quite lovely, and I think very much a la mode. Will this one do, do you think?"

"Oh, yes, Miss Helen! It brings out your complexion, your blue eyes, and your pretty hair. You will look very well indeed, if you will just please hold still long enough for me to make these curls, and pin them back on your head, like this."

Lily's hands moved deftly to shape the curls into an attractive shape.

"Don't move, Miss Helen. I only have a few more to go—do be patient! When we all were having breakfast this morning, I spoke with Miss Finton, the Duchess of Minster's dresser, who is a true high-stickler, and no mistake about it! She said to me that she very much admires your appearance! Can you believe it?"

"You're making it up, Lily, just so that I won't feel so terrified going down to eat with all those tonnish strangers, and no one I know," said Miss Sterling.

"Everyone in the servant's hall heard what Miss Finton said about you, and because of her high opinion, your star is risen very high among the higher servants, Miss Helen! Oh, it is a fine thing to dine as an upper servant—you cannot imagine how fine it is! We have napkins, and good food, and I am so thankful to you, for bringing me with you."

"Thankful? Why should you be? Whatever are you saying?"

"Because, staying here is a wonderful experience for me, Miss Helen. Belowstairs, there is a whole other world, that I had never seen nor hardly even heard of! There are the upper ten, and the lower five, they call them. I don't why they're called that, and I don't think anyone knows, but it is fearful important, and all the servants are to be treated very differently. Because I am your personal maid, I am with the upper ten!"

"Are there ranks of servants?"

"That's just what I am trying to explain! Because of having so many guests, and each one coming with one or two servants, the servants' hall is filled up to the brim, not just with Castle servants, but with all the high and mighty servants of the high and mighty guests! They are each known by their master's names, you see, at least, the male servants are called that way. 'Minster' is the valet of the Duke of Minster, and he, as the servant of the highest-ranking master, gets to lord it over the rest."

"How strange! I can hardly credit it."

"Oh! I almost forgot! Tonight I have to dress for dinner in the servants' hall! If I don't dress up for dinner, I can't enjoy a glass of sherry! We must go to a place called Pug's Parlor. It's a place that's only for the upper servants. Fancy that, Miss Helen! Lily Beeton will be served sherry, just like a lady! Oh, and did I tell you we must each one sink the beer first?"

"'Sink the beer'? Pardon?" asked Helen. "Whatever can you mean?"

"The upper ten leave the servants' hall together, before the other lower servants have finished. If we have beer left over in our glasses, we go through the butler's pantry on the way to Mrs. Flynt's room, and tip out our glasses in the sink. Then we go to the housekeeper's room, and are served sherry, just as if we were the finest of the fine! It is such fun."

Her face fell a little as she added, "Not knowing that such dinners for the servants were the custom, I did not bring a dress, Miss Helen. Of course, I do not even own a dinner dress! Is it asking too much, or is there some dress of yours we have with us, that I could borrow? I don't mean to be impertinent, but I'd hate to miss out on all the fun."

"Why, Lily, of course, you may have a dress! It is fortunate we are almost of a size! Why not wear the green cambric? The color will look very well on you, I think."

"Thank you, miss! It will mean so very much to me!"

Hearing their voices, Miss Trenton made her way slowly in from the adjoining room, then settled herself on the sofa, and wrapped her shawl around herself as tightly as she could.

"You are going to wear the green cambric? Not downstairs to breakfast, I hope," she asked anxiously. "It is far too plain for your first appearance."

"No, Miss Trenton, we were talking about finding a dress for Lily."

"For Lily? Oh, of course, she must dress! I had quite forgotten about the dinners in the servants' halls. This visit will include rather interesting social events for you as well, Lily, but do be careful. You are much more attractive a girl than generally goes into service."

"Pooh! I'm strong, and I know how to take care of myself, believe me. But now, Miss Trenton, see if you approve of this dress for Miss Helen."

"The new white one with the blue sprigs and blue ribands? Yes, that will do nicely. It's so lucky you have such good taste, Lily. I don't know what we'd do without you— I think I should die under the weight of such responsibility. You seem to thrive on it, and you really *never* fail."

"Thank you," Lily replied, with pride.

"One's choice of dress at a party such as this is momentous, to say the least, in order to make the right impression, you see. It must possess a certain innocence, and a certain simplicity—for you are still a young girl, Helen," Miss Trenton explained. "One's gown must be cut according to the very height of fashion—for one must not be regarded as a dowd—that would be fatal to one's chances. Further, to impress upon one's viewer the proper respect for rank and position, the gown must belong to style of a recognized modiste, whose goods cost the moon to procure."

"I think this one will fit the bill, then. May I go down? I can hardly make a misstep at breakfast, can I?" said Helen. "Or do you feel well enough to join me?"

"Sadly, I do not, but I don't really care for your going down to eat all alone," said her companion. "It might be regarded as rather singular behavior."

Miss Trenton's eyes fluttered nervously toward the ceiling. She had twisted her handkerchief into a ball, worried that she might give her charge the wrong advice.

"One can make a misstep at any time, and at any meal, of course," said Miss Trenton, after a minute of careful thought. "However, I *suppose* you may as well go down to breakfast. What are Mr. Sterling's wishes? It would look much better if he went with you."

"Papa is long gone, I fear."

"Gone where?" said Miss Trenton, showing some surprise.

"He asked that coffee be brought to the library. He has taken all his ledgers up there, at any rate, and means to read whatever newspapers there are to be had, which is generally his pattern in the morning."

"I worry about your father, Helen. He works so hard, and has no thought of leisure, and I am just afraid that a life consisting only of hard work and strain will be unhealthy for him."

"He thrives upon it, I assure you," said Helen. "For the most part."

"Well, just as you wish. I wish I could persuade him to take you around for a walk upon the grounds, but I suppose that to be a lost cause. You know him better than I," said Miss Trenton. She appeared thoughtful, and then added, "Very well, Helen. Go down to breakfast, with my blessing. Until I am able to join you, just be civil and polite and careful, and if you feel unsure of yourself, just be silent, and that way you will be sure not to offend anyone!"

This last anxious admonition brought a smile to Miss Sterling's countenance, and she replied, agreeably, "Yes, Miss Trenton. I shall try *very* hard not to make a spectacle of myself!"

* * *

A splendid breakfast had been laid out in the Lesser Gold Dining Room for Lady Arabella Gilbough's guests, in a long hall whose windows looked out onto a pleasant eastern view of the formal gardens. Against the far wall, which was richly hung with old tapestries, was a long mahogany sideboard set up with a series of sterling silver chafing dishes. There were a number of other silver-plate serving dishes laid out as well, topped with gleaming, polished lids that were meant to keep everything warm, but since the distance from kitchens to dining rooms was so long, never worked well.

Someday it would be pleasant to enjoy a hot piece of toast, Miss Sterling mused, *rather than these ubiquitous cold ones.*

Miss Sterling went to one end of the sideboard, and was immediately helped by a footman, who took up a gold-rimmed china plate on her behalf, and placed whatever food Miss Sterling indicated upon the plate, which he solicitously held for her.

She chose some eggs, a piece of bread, some fresh raspberry jam, and requested a cup of steaming hot chocolate. She by-passed the ham, and the sausage, as being rather too rich for her taste in the morning.

When she had come to the end of the sideboard, she turned around, trying to decide where to seat herself. In the center of the hall was a very long table, one that could fit fifty persons, and guests were scattered around it, seated in casual groups of two or three. Seeing no one she knew well, she indicated to the footman attending her that she would like to eat apart from the others, at the far end of the table.

Miss Sterling seated herself, and began to eat. Occasionally, she would look up, trying to make out the identities of the others scattered around the long table. A few of them were slight acquaintances: she recognized Lady Arabella Gilbough, their hostess, who was seated at the head of the table with a tall female with a long, sharp nose, and silver-grey hair, who she thought was Lady Lacon. There was a man of the cloth she had never seen before. She noticed three girls sitting together, whose names she could not quite recall, but whose faces she recognized as having seen before during the past London Season—they were break-fasting, it seemed, with their mothers or other elderly female relations.

Seated nearer to her was a very beautiful young woman with jet-black hair, and dark eyes: this she knew was Janet Carteret, one of the great successes of the Season, along with an older woman Helen presumed to be a companion or relative.

Other than these few, Miss Sterling recognized no one at all.

Helen Sterling felt very self-conscious, and very much alone. She devoutly wished that Miss Trenton's health would improve at once, or that some acquaintance of hers would suddenly arrive in the breakfast-hall, so she might have a conversation, and not feel so alone and awkward and out of place.

Every time she heard a trill of laughter, or a whispered confidence, it made her feel more solitary and more wretched. Every once in a while, she would glance over at another group, and swear she had seen heads turned in her direction that turned around again and pretended that they weren't looking.

Were they looking at her? Were they talking about her? Surely, they were not! It was only her horrid self-conscious-ness that made it seem so.

In truth, however, it was not mere self-consciousness that made Miss Sterling feel she was an object of everyone's attention: she *was* the object of everyone's attention, in fact. The presence of the Sterling heiress at Cornell Castle had become the major topic of conversation at the other end of the long breakfast table, right from the moment the other guests had seen Helen enter the room.

Miss Janet Carteret, when Miss Sterling came in, had interrupted a long, involved conversation with her aunt, Mrs. Partridge, about the latest scandal involving one of the Royal Dukes, and had remarked to her aunt, "Look! I remember seeing that blond girl in London, at Lady Farlow's rout! She's Black Jack Sterling's daughter, isn't she? Sir Rupert Fellowes dropped Lady Georgiana Locksley like a hot coal after he was introduced to the rich Miss Sterling, and they are to be wed, I hear. She is very sweet, and good, and I am glad to have a chance to see her once again. What a surprise that she is so fair, so blond! She has not a bit of her father's coloring, has she?"

"To be sure, she has not! I wonder about it—why is everyone so sure that Mrs. Sterling did not play Mr. Sterling false?" Mrs. Partridge said, with a sharp titter of laughter.

The lovely but very well-mannered Miss Carteret silenced her breakfast-partner with a chilling glare, causing Mrs. Partridge nearly to choke upon her muffin.

On the other side of the long room, Lady Arabella Gilbough was sitting at table with the formidable society matron, Lady Lacon, with three young girls of marriageable age seated nearby: red-headed Lady Georgiana Locksley, Lady Agatha Winslow, and Miss Idona Peterson. The younger ladies were seated a bit apart from their elders, and were deeply involved in their own conversation, while the two ladies were preoccupied with noting down who was coming in to breakfast, how well they were dressed, and where they were sitting, and making other important social judgments.

Lady Arabella Gilbough, hostess extraordinaire, took the opportunity of Miss Sterling's entrance to raise to her eye the small quizzing-glass she affected, and peer down the table to inspect her newly-arrived guests. The Sterling heiress would do, she decided, at least as to her general appearance.

Lady Arabella, the only daughter of the late fourth Earl of Blenton, was a woman of mildly advanced years and rather sagging features, whose rotund figure showed the full effects of a life filled with idleness and indulged self-interest. The death three years ago of her extremely rich, but rather eccentric husband, Mr. Edward Gilbough, had freed her to enjoy life as a modish ton hostess to the maximum: her parties were always lavish, and were sometimes spectacular. She was the kind of hostess who thought nothing of spending a small fortune on decorating a ball room with hot-house roses in the dead of winter, or of ordering two hundred special tarts to be sent up from London at a cost of two pounds apiece.

Lady Arabella was engaged this morning in her usual occupation, that of critiquing her various guests, and pronouncing judgment upon them. To her friend Lady Lacon, she said, "The Sterling girl appears well enough, that's one thing I can say for her; I was rather afraid when I first heard about her that she might not be presentable. She is quite pretty, indeed. However, one must wonder *why* has she come down to breakfast all alone? Where is her companion? Where are her friends? Coming down to eat all alone is a very unusual thing to do, in my opinion. If she don't want to come down with her father—and, after all, why *would* she want to come down in *his* company? If one's father is of *that* class, what can one do but try to hide him away as best one can? However, if she don't want to come down with her father, and has no one else to attend her, I say that she oughtn't to have come down at all."

"Precisely!" agreed Lady Lacon, with a silky yawn. "Shows a lamentable heedlessness, and want of following convention, which is the notorious hallmark of the lower classes.''

The hostess considered her guest's appearance again, and said, ''Can't think of what Sir Rupert saw in her, beyond her looks, can you?''

Lady Lacon raised her chin so that she might look down her long, aristocratic nose at Miss Sterling. After studying the young woman for some time, she replied acidly, ''I should say that Sir Rupert sees in her not merely female beauty, but the rare, compelling beauty of her father's bank balance.''

This answer did not sit well with Lady Arabella, who remarked, ''Why should Sir Rupert have to think of money? The Fellowes family's pockets are not to let! Sir Rupert could have had any girl he chose, even your own goddaughter, dear Georgiana! Sir Rupert and Georgiana spent quite some time together this Season, did they not? I forget why that romance fell through.''

She stirred her hot chocolate meditatively with a tiny silver spoon, and said, ''The thing is, why he is wasting his fine family name on a rich girl with no family? I cannot conceive it. I was quite in shock when I heard about it.''

''You don't suppose it is actually a love match, do you?'' Lady Lacon asked, in a tone of disbelief.

''Lord, Louisa, I hope not! I shouldn't have thought that Sir Rupert was the type to do something like that, but one never knows a man's secret mind, does one? Well, I only hope the chit don't say and do the sorts of things that would embarrass him. He would hate that with a vengeance, high-stickler that he is.''

''She *is* presentable,'' sighed Lady Lacon. ''At least on the surface, she appears to be so. Sir Rupert would not be so lost as to what his duty is to his family, that he would bring into society someone whose manner would reflect badly upon his name.''

"Of course not. Well, I wish them very happy, you may be sure. Shall we go over and say good morning? That would be an admirable thing for us to do on the girl's behalf, wouldn't it?" said her ladyship.

"You go, Arabella," said Lady Lacon. "I'm disinclined to give consequence to a tradesman's daughter, unless I absolutely cannot avoid it."

Lady Arabella Gilbough rose from her seat, and approached the other end of the long table, where Helen Sterling was sitting. Her ladyship held out her two hands as she did so, bestowing upon Miss Sterling a wide, welcoming smile. A footman was instantly at her ladyship's side, pulling out a high-backed mahogany chair so that she might sit down.

"Why, Miss Sterling! How lovely that you could join us at the Castle!" she said, still smiling broadly. "How do you do?"

"Very well, thank you. It was so k-kind of you to invite us," Helen said nervously, not yet feeling capable of making sophisticated small talk with her exacting hostess.

"I could do no less for someone so close to Sir Rupert Fellowes, could I? Has dear Sir Rupert arrived as yet? I had not heard one way or another."

"No, Lady Arabella, but we hope he will come just as soon as he may!" said Helen, trying to assume what she hoped was a bright, convivial tone.

"I see. Will your father be coming down to breakfast today? I long to make his acquaintance, as you must imagine."

"No, I think not," admitted Miss Sterling.

"What a shame!" said Lady Arabella Gilbough, patting Miss Sterling's hand. "I look forward to meeting the real Black Jack Sterling, who has lately become *such* a well-known personage! But, I suppose it must wait till this evening—males rarely enjoy breakfasting, for some reason, unlike we females. Even my dear Peter avoids the morning meal, and he hasn't the excuse other men do of preferring to go out early instead to hunt or to fish. Have you met my son, Peter, as yet, Miss Sterling?''

"I have not," said Helen shyly, desperately wishing Lady Arabella would stop chatting to her, and trying to draw her out.

"You must meet Peter! I shall be sure to introduce you, for it is in *his* honor that this party is being held, did you know that? It has been ages and ages since he's been at the Castle. You should know that my dear son Peter is a prince! A true prince! This whole fortnight is sort of a welcoming home party, you see, for Peter has been taking the grand tour of the continent, as many young gentleman like to do.''

"Oh, has he?" said Miss Sterling with careful politeness. "Lovely!"

"My dear Peter spent much of his time staying in Vienna!" Lady Arabella declared. She paused to think for a moment, then added, "Or was it Verona? Perhaps it was Venice!"

She thought again, but then appeared to give the project up, and said, "It is no matter. It was some one of those odd little foreign towns: they all sound alike. Who can tell one from another? Who would want to? Besides Paris and its fashion, what have those foreign towns to do with us, after all?''

Miss Sterling shot her a nonplussed look, but said nothing, while Lady Arabella went chattering on, saying, "Peter went off to Europe, under sad circumstances, three long years ago. It was just after his poor father's death. Peter went abroad to see great art, for Mr. Gilbough had been fond of dabbling at painting pictures himself, wasn't that singular? It was a pastime both father and son were used to share, and after his father's death, Peter went off to dabble a little by himself at painting, and of course, chiefly, he wanted to enjoy some of the continent's cultural delights, as all the finest young gentlemen do!"

Lady Arabella said decisively, "But *that* chapter of his life is now closed! Now dear Peter has come home, and has come to take up his proper social position, take a proper wife, and settle down at the Castle for good."

"How nice," said Miss Sterling with forced enthusiasm, not knowing what else to say, and beginning to tire of hearing her ladyship sing the praises of her son. "How very nice."

" 'Nice'? 'Nice,' Miss Sterling?" exclaimed her ladyship. "Why, nice is not the word!"

Helen Sterling took a wry, private moment to wonder just *what* the word might be, but was interrupted when Lady Arabella continued with her monologue.

"It is what I have dreamed of, to live long enough to see my son take up his father's place. Why, as I said to the Duchess of Minster just yesterday, one really *must* have a male living at home, acting as the head of one's family. Otherwise, the world, the servants, one's relatives—they take terrible advantage of a lady alone. One always feels so cheated and neglected, somehow. The accounts never seemed to balance properly once I was all alone. You will learn when you have your own household, precisely what I mean. At all events, I am so happy to have Peter back with me that I must hold a great party to celebrate! That being the case, I'm afraid I must be off now—there is so much to do! I hope you enjoy yourself during your stay. So good to see you, Miss Sterling. Good day."

With this abrupt dismissal, Lady Arabella swept away from Helen, and then began taking a grand tour of the whole table, stopping here and there to give a smile or a comment to a guest, or to listen to *on-dits* she had not already heard.

Miss Sterling watched her with awe—she had never watched anyone make such a theatrical performance of the simple act of saying hello. Traveling in these rarefied social circles would surely take some getting used to.

Taking her time, collecting some gossip here, and passing it on to the next person, her ladyship eventually completed her long round of well-wishings, and made her way back to her own seat, where Lady Lacon waited.

"Well?" asked Lady Lacon. "What did you think of the Sterling heiress? Has she any address?"

"No, not at all—she's too shy, and has hardly *any* conversation, offers hardly any opinions, whatsoever," said Lady Arabella decidedly. "Miss Sterling behaved like a girl right out of the schoolroom! Why, one could almost *see* her governess at her side, telling her to hold her tongue, lest she make a spectacle of herself! She had no real style, no air about her, which is *so* important when one must present a figure in society. I thank my stars that Peter never conceived a fancy for some care-for-nothing female while he was abroad. Who knows *who* he might have brought home? One shudders to think! Do you recall that short, lisping Spanish creature Lord Dunton's second son tried to fob off on his family? *Completely* unsuitable! He couldn't take her anywhere! They had to go back to her country to live, in the end! But of course, my dear son would *never* be so unfamilial."

"Certainly not! Speaking of which, Arabella, what about the arrangements for Peter and Georgiana?" asked Lady Lacon.

"Which ones, Louisa?" replied Lady Arabella, signaling to the footman to pour more hot chocolate into her cup.

"Whether the wedding should be held at St. George's,

Hanover, for example, or in the country. Decisions must be made!''

Lady Arabella Gilbough looked thoughtful.

"I think Georgiana fancies being wed in the country, somehow, rather than in town. I don't know what Peter's wishes are. He probably doesn't care—he's so generally amenable, you know. Such a complaisant young man.''

"A fine boy, Arabella. He'll make Georgiana the perfect husband, I am sure. It was a very good idea of yours, that they should make a match of it.''

"I can't imagine why I didn't think of it before. There are few young girls I would trust to be mistress of such a grand establishment as Cornell Castle, with its long history and all its ancient valuables, and with such a very large staff to oversee, but Georgiana is a girl after my own heart. She thinks as I do upon every issue of household management.''

The thoughtful look returned to her face, as she added, "I can hardly wait until they wed, and she presents the family with a son and heir. What a relief that will be! As it is, for all three years of Peter's absence, I have had to lie awake nights tossing and turning, worrying myself sick that he might die in some dreadful foreign place, and that my Castle, my beautiful Castle, would devolve upon Cousin Raymond!''

"To think of Cornell Castle in the hands of a country vicar! It would be *such* a waste!'' declared Lady Lacon. "Raymond Dulles wouldn't have the slightest notion how to manage it. His tastes are far too simple. The whole place would go to rack and ruin in a year.''

"And the worst thing, the thing that truly makes my blood run cold, is the idea of my having to move into the Dower House!'' Lady Arabella said with a shudder.

"Unthinkable!'' averred Lady Lacon, wrinkling her long

nose in disgust. "We must see to it that such a thing does not occur!"

"Once he moved into the Castle, I could never again give a party, for you *know* that Raymond would think it frivolous! In the Dower House, of course, I would have no space for such a thing! And, as to money, my jointure is nowhere near enough! My son Peter has been very kind, letting me keep the income I was used to when Mr. Gilbough was alive. Without my parties, I could not exist! I should rather pine away and die without my parties, for I am naturally a creature of a social disposition, and being a hostess is my true talent in life."

"On the other hand, Arabella, if Peter has been so kind as to let you live here, and has kept your income just as it was, why should things not go on as they are?" inquired Lady Lacon. "Raymond Dulles cannot come here unless and until he inherits. Are things really so desperate for you?"

"Yes, of course they are. Peter is home now, and it is time to act! It is not only in foreign parts that people die a sudden death! Look at Peter's father! He was in the prime of his life, and if it hadn't been for that wretched horse of his that he *insisted* upon buying—though I advised him most sincerely *not* to—he would still be alive now! I was married one minute and widowed the next! Just because Peter is young, it does not mean that something dreadful cannot happen to him as well, and then what do I do? I hate to speak like a prophet of doom, but I have seen terribly unjust things occur in my life, where by some mischance or sudden misfortune an inheritance descends upon unsuitable persons—and so, I shall not rest secure until Peter is safely married off to someone I approve of, and becomes the father of an heir—or, better yet, the father of more than one of them, just to be safe."

"Too true, Arabella. The Grim Reaper stands waiting

in the deep shadows behind each one of us. Think of poor
Georgiana's mother—I never thought that *she* would not
last long enough to see her daughter wed. After Lord
Locksley's death, she was so broken-hearted, she began
pining, until she just withered away—poor dear! That kind
of sentimental behavior, while understandable, even
touching, cannot find our dear girl a husband, which is
really all that she needs!" Lady Lacon said with a sigh.
"Have you mentioned our scheme to Peter or Georgiana
yet?"

"I thought you should tell Georgiana, and I should tell
Peter, and then we might announce their engagement
toward the end of next week."

"They won't make a fuss about it, I trust."

"No, I shouldn't think so. Peter is always so generally
amiable, I can't imagine he would protest. He has such a
good nature! So kind, so charming! I can't recall the last
time he disagreed with me, much less acted against my
wishes, so I believe his acquiescence can be taken for
granted. As to Georgiana, although she has been universally admired, this is already her second season, and none
of her suitors has come up to scratch. It's time things were
settled—I think she will welcome it. She would dislike
being thought on the shelf. It is a very good position for
her, all things considered. Georgiana will like very much
to be the mistress of a grand establishment, with a great
deal of pin money at her disposal. Georgiana is like me—
she will enjoy above all things, having the means to be the
grand hostess of society. I don't foresee any problem with
either one of them. Besides, the two of them played
together as children, did they not? If they got along as
playmates, why should they object to being wed?"

"Precisely!" agreed Lady Lacon, with a smile.

"I had a mind to announce the engagement this evening, thinking it would make a far more festive fortnight

for everyone—to celebrate both Peter's return *and* his engagement to be married, but then I realized that Peter and Georgiana haven't even *seen* one another since they were ten or twelve, and making an announcement of marriage, coming right out of the blue, might not be the prudent thing to do."

"It *would* be awkward," her friend agreed. "I think we really *must* tell them, first."

4

Breakfast had come to an end, and almost all the guests had gotten up from the table, and were milling about, seeking a bit of conversation here and there, prior to leaving the room entirely. The three fashionable young ladies who had sat at the far end of the table rose *en masse* and swiftly advanced towards Miss Sterling, intent upon having speech with her just as soon as they might.

As the trio approached her, Helen was able to put names to two of their faces: they were Lady Agatha Winslow and Miss Idona Peterson, two young ladies whom she had come to know slightly in the course of the past Season, and who had previously shown her nothing but hauteur. The third young woman was very handsome rather than pretty, a tall, rather thin girl, with a shock of red hair, piercing green eyes, and a distinct air of self-satisfaction about her. Helen believed that this girl must be the renowned belle, Lady Georgiana Locksley, and her surmise was confirmed to be true within seconds.

"How do you do, Miss Sterling?" said Lady Agatha, with what Helen thought was a particularly false pleasantry. "How nice to see you here, I'm sure! Are you well? You look lovely!"

"I am very well, thank you," replied Miss Sterling, already summoning her reserve of forbearance.

"I believe we two have not met, formally," said Lady Georgiana, extending her hand as she smiled, revealing her perfect white teeth. "I am Georgiana Locksley."

"How do you do?" said Helen, who was uneasy, but trying hard to hide it. "I believe we must have met, once or twice, last season in London."

"Oh, have we?" asked Lady Georgiana, showing scant interest. "I cannot recall so doing. I am, I believe, very well known in town, so I would be more surprised if you had never seen me. I have an extremely active social schedule, of course. It is so weary-making, don't you know? Or perhaps you do not. Do you go about much in society, Miss, uh, Miss Sterling?"

Wishing that Miss Trenton were at her elbow to advise her, Helen replied, "I am not quite sure how to answer that."

"Oh, aren't you?" said Lady Georgiana with a small smile. "I wonder why ever not. I was merely trying to determine your social circle, you see. Who you know versus who I know, that sort of thing. Did you know that my godmother is Lady Lacon, the sister of the Duchess of Minster?"

Helen Sterling began to feel a blush of irritation, but made no comment.

"I am sure that we must have acquaintances in common beyond Lady Arabella, must we not?" asked Lady Georgiana. "Or perhaps our social circles are widely different? My late mother was related to Sir Charles Stanton. I'm sure you've heard of *him*—'the arbiter of fashion' everyone calls him—have you made his acquaintance? Shall I introduce you? I'd be very happy to do so. I'm sure he will be delighted to make the acquaintance of Black Jack Sterling's daughter!"

At this, Lady Agatha and Miss Peterson, looked at one another and began to giggle.

Helen felt her anger rise in earnest, and thought to herself, *this is unbearable! She is deliberately baiting me! Why should she do so?*

"You are a friend of Sir Rupert Fellowes, I believe," continued Lady Georgiana.

"Yes, I know him," said Miss Sterling noncommittally, wishing to reveal as little as possible to this trio.

"Oh, don't be so shy, Miss Sterling," said Lady Agatha. "What damage can result from a little harmless conversation among friends?"

Miss Sterling said nothing, and she began to understand why her companion had been so hesitant to allow her to venture into such company without a protector.

"I met Sir Rupert during the season at Almack's, in May. We danced together several times. Perhaps that is where you saw me?" said Lady Georgiana. "I believe I was wearing a dress of gauze over cream sarcenet—I am sure if you had seen it, you would remember it. It was thought to be very fine—it was done by Madame Vergere exclusively for me. I remember that at the time I thought its price terribly extravagant, but of course if one wants to wear the very best, one must be prepared to pay the price! I liked that gown excessively, and everyone complimented me on my taste. Particularly Sir Rupert. Of course, I could only wear it on one or two occasions, and then I gave it to my abigail. I don't like to wear gowns more than once or twice, and, happily, I don't have to."

Miss Sterling made no reply to this display of conceit.

"But, oh, dear, I have made such a *faux pas*, Miss Sterling, you must forgive me!" Lady Georgiana said disingenuously, adding in a disdainful tone, "Oh, no, what have I done? So sorry, I forgot! How foolish of me! You *wouldn't* recall our having met at Almack's, of course, for *you* may not go there, may you?"

All three young ladies began to giggle and whisper together, as Helen Sterling, despite herself, blushed beet red at receiving such a set-down. It came as no surprise to her that they would behave so uncivilly. In Miss Sterling's experience, sooner or later at these sorts of gatherings, someone always showed her their contempt, which is why Miss Trenton felt so strongly about not letting her charge go about in society unaccompanied.

Dear heaven, I should not let it matter to me! It does not matter! It is the sheerest, most superficial nonsense! Helen thought to herself.

She replied with as much dignity as she could muster, "That is so. I could *not* have met you at Almack's. What a terrible disappointment for me, I'm sure! Now, if you will excuse me, I was just on my way back to my suite. Good day."

"Oh, please, do not go!" said Lady Agatha, blushing and simpering. "We must ask you a question first! We were all wondering—do you know precisely when Sir Rupert Fellowes might be arriving? We *long* to see him again!"

Steeling herself, Helen replied in what she hoped was an even, neutral tone, "I expect him to come very soon, Lady Agatha."

Lady Georgiana Locksley then stepped up so closely to Miss Sterling that Miss Sterling felt she must step back a pace, and her ladyship said in an imperious, insistent tone, "You do *not* know precisely when he will arrive, Miss Sterling?"

"No, your ladyship, I'm afraid I do not know the precise time of Sir Rupert's arrival!" Miss Sterling snapped, her patience at an end. "Perhaps, if you require such precision, you could ask Lady Arabella's butler to stand guard on your behalf, and keep you informed?"

Lady Georgiana's eyes betrayed a flash of temper for an instant.

"I'm sure there is no need to be uncivil, Miss Sterling. I had thought you, being such a *close* friend, would of course know all about Sir Rupert's plans, but I can see I have been misinformed. How singular, I'm sure!" replied Lady Georgiana with a smile of triumph, as she and Lady Agatha and Miss Peterson exchanged surprised glances.

Lady Agatha gave forth her loud, hooting, horsy laugh, and fairly slapped Miss Sterling on the back.

"Men! They never let a girl know what they're up to!" she chortled. "Slippery chaps—but we can't live with 'em, and can't live without 'em, eh, Miss Sterling?"

Helen Sterling, horrified, made no reply, but a slight shake of the head, wishing them all at Jericho, and herself safe in the confines of her room. In a clipped voice, she again wished them all good day. She left the room vowing to avoid them in future, thinking that if such insulting interchanges were to be the hallmark of this house party, it would be completely insupportable!

In Miss Sterling's wake, and behind her back, the three inquisitors were left perfectly free to criticize the demeanor of Black Jack's daughter, and the young ladies of quality at once threw themselves wholeheartedly into their task.

"Well! *She* doesn't even know what day he is coming! Sir Rupert and Miss Sterling are not exactly smelling of April and May, Idona, are they? I knew it would be so!" said Lady Georgiana smugly, twirling a golden wristlet. "I think Rupert will be *very* sorry he ceased his attentions to me, which were become quite particular, and took up with that upstart!''

"I'm sure he will be!" agreed Lady Agatha Winslow.

Miss Idona Peterson looked doubtfully at her friends, and shook her head, pointing out, "I'm not so sure, Georgiana. It is widely said that a marriage between Sir Rupert and Miss Sterling is quite a settled thing."

"How can it be?" asked Lady Georgiana. "The announcement hasn't even appeared yet in the Gazette, and I read every issue, as soon as it arrives from London! If the marriage was settled, I'm sure that wretched *parvenu* would have been telling everyone and his brother all about it. I, for one, cannot believe that Sir Rupert would offer for *her,* when he did not offer for *me!* She's just a rich nobody, and I'm a Locksley! I'm prettier than she is, and I have just as big a dowry as she!"

"Are you certain about that?" said Miss Peterson, looking doubtful again. "Black Jack Sterling is as rich as Midas. Or is it Croesus? Anyway, he's overflowing over with blunt. My father said so! Everyone in England buys Black Jack's Nottingham cotton! It's all the rage!"

"Well, so what!" said Lady Georgiana with a cross look. "I can't have *so* much less in my dowry, compared to whatever that tradesman father of hers promised to settle on her! I tell you, it's not fair! Everyone says I'm the Belle of the Season, *everyone* said so! So why has no one yet come up to scratch?"

"Hush! Not so loud! You know Mama disapproves of cockfight cant, Georgiana. She says it's vulgar," said Miss Peterson, looking around the room nervously.

"It's not vulgar if *I* use it," said Lady Georgiana with great confidence. "When *I* use it, it's all the crack!"

"Hush! If Mama should hear you, I'll be in terrible trouble, and she won't let me be your friend!"

"Stop sniveling, Idona, won't you? You have no courage!

I have courage, and what I am going to do is to take my troubles in hand, because my reputation is at stake! Someone should have offered for me by now, and I swear, I will see that it happens, one way or another. I want to be a married woman!" declared Lady Georgiana. "I *will* be married before this year is out, I promise you! I will *not* become an old maid like Amanda Fitzmorton, who had two full seasons in London, did not take, and is now on the shelf for ever!"

"Calm yourself, Georgiana, someone will hear you!" said Miss Peterson.

"I don't care if they do! I'm very upset, and I hate that Helen Sterling! I'm *better* than she is, I'm prettier than she is, I come from a decent family, nay, an ancient family, and did you *see* how disrespectful she was of me? How *dared* she speak to me in that insolent manner! Just who does she think she is? I'll put her in her place before this fortnight is over, just you see if I don't!"

"Whatever you say," said Miss Peterson, fearing that her quick-tempered friend was well on her way to doing something unfortunate.

5

Miss Helen Sterling was under the happy impression that she was finally alone, when, just as she turned into carpeted hallway, she felt a light tap upon her shoulder. She started, turned around quickly, a shocked expression on her face, and beheld a gray-haired gentleman in clerical garb who seemed to have appeared out of nowhere, and who was a perfect stranger to her.

"Pardon me?" she said, with an uncharacteristic touch of annoyance. "I don't believe we've met."

"Oh, dear! Oh dear!" lamented the stranger loudly, wringing his hands. "Forgive my impertinence, Miss Sterling, but I believe I really must take the liberty of introducing myself: I beg you will forgive me! I trust I do not intrude too much! My dear Miss Sterling, I am Raymond Dulles, a cousin of the Gilbough family, and a great and sincere admirer of your father's. I do hope you find Mr. Sterling well?"

"Very well, thank you," she replied, still with a hint of

coolness. "How do you do, Mr. Dulles? I am glad to make your acquaintance. How do you know my father?"

"Oh, I am a vicar with a living near Hadleytown, and through my friend, Mr. Elroy, with whom I went to Oxford, I learned of your father's generosity, which is now legend. Your esteemed father made it possible for an astonishing number of poor boys from Hadleytown to have proper schooling, and to enjoy the equivalent of a gentleman's education under the tutelage of my friend Elroy, and as I have come here to Cousin Arabella's party, and I discovered to my great delight that your father is here as well, I wanted to take this opportunity to thank him in person for everything he has done for our young men! It has meant so much to our parishioners, you cannot conceive it! The largesse! The open-heartedness! Such condescension! It will transform their lives forever."

"I had no idea my father did such things," she replied simply. "I am very glad to hear it, however. Education is a wonderful advantage."

The vicar looked around hopefully, and asked, "Is your father staying with you at the Castle, I hope? If so, would you be kind enough to introduce me to him?"

"He did not come down with me to breakfast, but I believe you may find him in the library. You need not have me introduce you—you must feel free to go there, and meet him yourself. He does not stand on ceremony."

"I-if you think it will be all right?" he asked uncertainly.

"You may tell him, if you wish, that it was I who informed you of his whereabouts."

"Oh, dear! How kind! Thank you so much," said the vicar, backing away with a slight bow. "I won't bother you further. Thank you again."

Practicing charities in secret? Father can really be very mysterious, thought Helen to herself. *I wonder what other tricks he has up his sleeve?*

* * *

Lily was upstairs carefully nursing Miss Trenton, coaxing her into trying to finish the last of her chamomile tea and plain water-biscuits. She had already brought Miss Trenton a shawl, nestled her into it, and tucked the edges all around, for she felt the best medicine was fond cosseting. Miss Trenton was a particular favorite of Lily's, who would not rest until she had made Miss Trenton perfectly comfortable.

Part of Miss Trenton's indisposition was due to the after-effects of the relentless rocking motion of the carriage as it went from London to Buckinghamshire. However, perhaps the greater part of her indisposition—which was something that Helen Sterling knew nothing of—was that Miss Trenton was quite distraught.

Poor Miss Trenton's eyes were red-rimmed from weeping, and she made no objection when the attentive Lily replaced one soaked-through linen handkerchief with a fresh one.

"Thank you so much, Lily—I don't know what I'd do without you, really, I don't," she mumbled. "Too kind, too kind."

She blew her nose delicately once again, and dabbed at her eyes.

"I know I'm being silly as a goose about my whole predicament. I'm sure nothing is as bad as it seems—it's just my delicate nerves that make me think the worst will happen!"

"Shh! Don't talk like that! Try to rest while Miss Helen is at breakfast!" said Lily.

"Rest? I cannot rest until I have secured my future! How can I? I tell myself ten times a day that after Helen marries Sir Rupert I will certainly be able to find myself a place in some other very nice family. I can place an advertisement in the *Times*. I can answer advertisements. I can go around

to agencies. Mr. Sterling will surely give me a good refer-
ence—there really is nothing to worry about!''

Lily chafed her hands, and tried to quiet her, but Miss
Trenton would not be consoled.

"I knew this day had to come someday, after all. It was
only a matter of time. It happens to all governesses eventually, does it not? Sooner or later, one's services are just
not needed. One comes to a family, teaches and takes
charge of a child, and eventually the child grows up. I was
very lucky that Mr. Sterling was kind enough to have me
serve as Helen's companion when she grew out of the need
for a governess. Other families would not have allowed it,
and I would have been already gone. No, I have been very
lucky indeed. I have stayed with the family to whom I am
deeply devoted, and now it is all at an end! In a month or
two I shall see my dear Helen sent off as a happy bride.
Then, it's all over. I am finished, with nothing more to be
said. I shall never see them again, and why should I?''

"There, there, Miss Trenton," said Lily. "Don't be sad!
Something will work out for you."

Miss Trenton blew her nose once more, and leaned her
head back on the sofa; she stared absent-mindedly at the
ceiling, and began counting the golden leaves that decorated the cornice, desperate to distract herself somehow
from her miserable stream of thoughts.

"Seven, eight, nine ... It's just that I have been with
them for so many years! I feel as if I were part of the family!
Of course, I know I'm *not* part of the family, I'm just a
paid companion, but my heart loves them both, just the
same. Barton House has been my home for so many years
now, and dear Helen has been my charge for so many
years ... she is been my pride and my joy! Without a
mother of her own, I gave her all that I could in the way
of tenderness, and when I think that soon I must leave
her, I just c-cannot b-bear it!''

Miss Trenton gave a few more sobs, and relinquished her newly soaked handkerchief to the ever-ministering Lily, who swiftly replaced it with another fresh one.

"Oh, Lily! Whatever shall I do? Whatever is to become of me?" she said in despair. "I have no money! I have no income of my own! I have no family! I am just a poor thin, wizened woman, with not a stick or a stone to call my own!"

"Hush, hush," she replied in a soothing voice. "It will all work out for the best, Miss Trenton."

"Do you really think so? Why should it work out?"

"Why should things *not* work out, Miss Trenton?" said Lily sensibly.

"I s-suppose you're right," she sniffed. "C-c call me Lydia, won't you?"

Lily considered this briefly, then shook her head, saying firmly, "I think not, Miss Trenton. I believe it is best to maintain the distinction of rank."

"Lily, you are the *most* amazing c-creature!" cried Miss Trenton, momentarily startled out of her misery. "Whatever will I do without you?"

It was very late by the time that Helen Sterling was finally able to retreat to the suite of rooms that had been reserved for her party's use. Helen poked her nose into her father's room, but it was empty save for a tall pile of Mr. Sterling's ubiquitous leather-bound ledgers. She took this to mean that her father must still be reading in the library.

A look into the inner sitting-room revealed an occupant: Miss Trenton, still red-nosed and clutching a handkerchief, but no longer weeping, was sitting on the sofa, wrapped in a shawl, sipping weak tea and nibbling on what appeared to be some plain and uninviting kind of biscuit.

"Oh, Helen, there you are at last!" cried out Miss Trenton, deeply relieved to see her young charge again. "Do tell me! How was breakfast? How was it served—was it all in the very first style? Was the silver very handsome? How many servants were in attendance? Was there any scandal being discussed? You must tell me if there was any gossip, you know, because then we can try to deal with it! Was everyone civil to you? Did you know anyone? With whom did you sit? With whom did you speak? Tell me at once, my dear! I feel it is so remiss in me not to accompany you everywhere, I am ready to expire from guilt!"

"Calm yourself, Miss Trenton," said Helen with a smile, "Everything went very well, I'm sure."

"That won't do, passing it all off like that. You must answer my questions, and tell me everything that happened, in detail! Come and sit by me."

Miss Sterling did as she was told, and seated herself at the other end of the sofa.

"The first person to speak with me was Lady Arabella Gilbough, and she came over to where I was sitting to greet me, and she was very civil, and she asked after my father. I met two—no, three—young ladies whom I had met in London—they were ones whom I did not like, and who certainly did not like me!"

"Oh, no! Oh, dear! Who were they?" Miss Trenton asked in alarm. "This is how bad things begin! What if one of them does you a mischief?"

"Oh, surely not, Miss Trenton. They were just trying to be spiteful and mean."

"Helen, if there is one thing I can teach you about society that should stay with you forever, it is that you must never underestimate the power of girls who wish to marry well! It is perhaps the most potent motivation known to woman! Most women will stop at nothing to snare the man of their dreams, or at least, the man whose income fits their dreamed-of requirements. You will have competitors for Sir Rupert until the moment that golden ring is on your finger—mark my words! Protect yourself! Now, think, Helen—what were their names? What did they look like?"

"One of them was pretty enough, ginger-haired, thin, of medium height, green eyes, good complexion, good address—but with rather an air of artificial gaiety, and a sneaky, simpering manner. Her name is Lady Georgiana Locksley. Do you know her?"

"Of course I do!" said Miss Trenton, who prided herself on her grasp of the ton.

"They were not very nice to me, particularly Lady Georgiana. They asked me when Sir Rupert was coming, and I said I didn't know, and when I said that, they looked strangely happy at my ignorance. That is when I began to dislike them in earnest."

"Very proper, my dear. Certainly your social instincts are all intact. Make no mistake about it, there are those, even now, who would try to fling themselves at Sir Rupert, and fling you out of the way, if they can."

"How very distasteful!"

"Just because one is *counted* among the Upper Ten Thousand does not mean that one is *actually* well-bred," Miss Trenton said with a sage nod of her head.

"I suppose not," said Helen. "I won't seek out their company, you can be sure, and I'll never go down to breakfast without you again. Would it be all right if I walk around a bit this afternoon, walking on the grounds, or going through the galleries? In my guidebook, it says that there are many masterpieces to be seen here, and that the parks and gardens are particularly well-kept."

"As to that, I think surveying the galleries would be a fine thing, for no one else will think to do it, I assure you. Walking outside I would avoid just now, for in the first place, it is rather overcast, and I think overcast days can have a deleterious effect on one's complexion. In the second place, this is just the beginning of the house party, and for those who do choose to venture through the grounds, I wager there will be a great deal of conniving going on. I would avoid the grounds just at this point—one is all too easily seen in the gardens, and tongues may be set wagging," said Miss Trenton, who weighed the various options with the care of a general planning a military offensive.

"If you insist, I will do as you say, then, with pleasure. Will you be able to come down this evening, do you think? I am persuaded I should not mingle with these people by myself."

"Heavens, no! To join in dancing at a house party is even more dangerous than going on picnics or taking walks in the park! I shall not fail you! I shall be dressed and come down during the dancing after dinner tonight, Helen," declared Miss Trenton, "If it is the last thing I do in this life! At any cost to myself, I shall do whatever is necessary upon your behalf, my dear! Do go around now, explore the Castle at your leisure, and we shall pray that Sir Rupert comes quickly, so you may have him as your escort and a protector!"

6

"Mad as a meat-ax!" declared a cheerful male voice coming from behind Miss Helen Sterling, who, in the course of exploring the various historic treasures of Cornell Castle, had been scrutinizing a painting in the west gallery, and consulting a popular guidebook. "Mad as a meat-ax!"

"Pardon me?" replied Helen, flustered.

She turned around at once, and she found herself facing a very handsome young gentleman whose dark blue eyes were filled with merriment.

"I wasn't calling *you* mad, my dear, if that's what you thought. I was merely taking the liberty of pointing out to you the dark gentleman in that portrait. He is Henry Gilbough, and he was as mad as a meat-ax."

"I see," said Miss Sterling carefully, unsure what to make of this intelligence.

"I'm Peter Gilbough, by the way," said the young man, bowing politely, glad of any opportunity to converse with such a pretty girl, particularly one who had, he now began to realize, the very face and coloring of a Botticelli angel. "I have not yet had the pleasure of making your acquaintance. May I know your name?"

Helen Sterling's diffidence was overcome by the frank charm of Mr. Gilbough's address. Favoring him with an attractive blush, she made him a curtsey, and extended her hand toward him, saying, with a smile, "I am Helen Sterling."

"How do you do, Miss Sterling?" he said pressing her hand briefly and warmly. "Are you come here to attend my mother's party? I must assume you are! At least, I hope so! Are you a great friend of hers?"

"Oh, no, sir," she replied at once. "L-Lady Arabella and I have only recently met, in London during the past Season, and she was k-kind enough to invite me to come up for the fortnight."

So this is Lady Arabella's darling Peter. He seems a much more agreeable fellow than one might have thought from his mother's vapid acclaim.

"Excellent! I'm sure you'll have a splendid time! Mother's summer house parties are famed for being bang up to the mark!"

Miss Sterling suddenly became self-conscious, and colored, remembering Miss Trenton's strictures, and not knowing what to say next.

Peter Gilbough, who was nothing if not a gentleman of the world, at once noticed Miss Sterling's hesitant discomfiture, and, with the kindness that was second nature to him, decided to take the lead for her.

Indicating the unusually tall windows lining one side of the high, vaulted gallery, and the vast view of the gardens beyond them, he inquired, "What do you think of the Castle? Have you seen much of it as yet?"

Helen Sterling said, "I arrived only yesterday, and so I've seen but little, but it is obviously an ancient and splendid place. One can easily see why it is described in all the books as one of the most fascinating sites in all of Buckinghamshire!"

Without hesitation, Mr. Gilbough replied, "Don't waste your time with guidebooks, Miss Sterling! They can't tell half the story of the house, I assure you. As a castle belonging to an old family, our ancestral home offers all the requisite accompanying features: a panoply of family portraits including our most eccentric relatives, various concealed staircases, even a perilous dungeon or two. Everything a visitor might wish for one may find here at Cornell Castle, and it is all at your disposal, at your command! Do let me serve as your guide."

"That would be so kind!" she said, feeling very much put at ease, relieved to be in the company of such an amiable gentleman. "I have a particular fondness for eccentric ancestors, for I have none!"

"No ancestors?" he asked, raising a single eyebrow in disbelief.

"No eccentric ones—that I know of, at least."

"What about dungeons?" he inquired.

"Alas, no dungeons, either."

"I see," said Mr. Gilbough with a smile. "Are you then interested in touring our dungeons?"

"I take a deal of interest in touring dungeons, sir, but that is, I believe, best done in thunderstorms," opined Miss Sterling, keeping a perfectly straight face, and thoroughly enjoying herself. "So that one may experience them in all their thrilling gothic splendor."

"A good thought! Since the weather is clement at present, let us ignore the dungeons for the nonce, and discover the family eccentrics. We'll begin with old Henry, then, shall we? By the way, I should point out that this portrait of Great-uncle Henry was painted by my grandfather, after the style of Gainsborough. Painting happens to be a talent that runs in the family," said the young man, gesturing toward the portrait of a wild-looking man, who was portrayed surrounded by hunting dogs, wearing a tartan kilt, and carrying a gun.

Mr. Gilbough went near the portrait, and struck a playful pose, asking in a teasing manner, "Do you see any family resemblance?"

Miss Sterling nodded, for it was perfectly obvious. The two men shared the same unusual dark blue eyes, and a crop of tousled brown hair, naturally wavy. Both had powerful, broad shoulders, and looked to be well above average height.

"You resemble him, outwardly, to be sure, but you said Henry Gilbough was mad, did you not?" Miss Sterling asked with feigned innocence. "Are you like him in that as well?"

"Am I mad as a meat-ax, do you mean?"

Miss Sterling nodded mischievously.

"Well! What a question! I fear my mother thinks so, but let's see—for one thing, I do *not* insist upon keeping chickens in the Great Hall, as Henry Gilbough did, nor do I dress in green silk in all seasons of the year, as he did, nor do I insist upon a keeping to a strict diet of raw green vegetables, fresh eggs, and under-cooked rice."

"What a singular forbear you have! A strict diet of raw green vegetables, fresh eggs, and rice sounds very intimidating, not to say drear. Why did he adopt such a diet? Do you know?"

"I suspect he might have wished to gain a fame that would outlive him, by making a name for himself as an oddity, in which case he succeeded very well, for that is precisely how he is known to this day!"

Miss Sterling giggled.

"Eccentric is how he shall always be remembered, and I assure you, Miss Sterling, I do not take after him in the least. I allow no live fowls to be kept in the house, I keep to a proper English diet of over-cooked beef, and I dress in what I hope you find an unexceptionable way."

At this, Miss Sterling let herself contemplate Mr. Gilbough's style of dress. He was a most attractive gentleman, with broad shoulders that fully filled out his well-tailored coat of hunter green superfine. He had the air not of a London dandy, but that of a country gentleman. His breeches were biscuit colored, and sufficiently well cut that they showed off his muscular legs to great advantage. His top-boots were buffed to a shiny brightness; his hair was tousled carelessly, his cravat starched snowy white, but was turned to a medium height that came up just beneath his chiseled chin.

"To be sure, you do," Miss Sterling acknowledged.

"I think Great-uncle Henry's seeming eccentricity may well have been due to a vain wish to carve a unique place for himself in the world."

" 'Vanity of vanities!' " sighed Helen, shaking her head. " 'All is vanity, and a striving after wind'?"

"Just so. In the eyes of high society, one's empty image is all and everything. For example, consider Lord Byron, who subsists on soda crackers and water," said Mr. Gilbough, "Just in order to keep his figure."

"One hears all too much about Lord Byron, I think," said Miss Sterling, looking disapproving, "And most of what one hears, one may not even mention! I think it very disobliging of him, the way he carries on, creating such a great deal of priceless material for gossip, which then must needs be *wasted* since it is so very shocking, that it is too shocking to divulge at all! At least, the man could have had the goodness to confine his wild escapades to what might be *openly* savored and discussed amongst polite society!"

Mr. Gilbough burst out with appreciative laughter. "And so I shall tell him!"

Miss Sterling colored prettily, and asked, "Is he an acquaintance of yours, or are you jesting?"

"I took a tour abroad, after my father's death, and spent time in Italy and in Greece. I met Lord Byron there, in Athens. We are not close friends, but are acquaintances. I do not like his style of life, but I do admire his work."

"Nevertheless, I must apologize for my wretched tongue! You have put me to the blush!"

"Miss Sterling, you mustn't blush, you know," said Mr. Gilbough, beginning to relish with an artist's eye the sight of his fair companion. "Blushing only makes your fairness even more fair, which is not fair at all!"

Miss Sterling's color increased even more, and she said, "Really, Mr. Gilbough, are you flirting with me? You must stop!"

"Why must I?" he inquired civilly, not waiting for her answer. "I am certainly trying my best to flirt with you, to be sure, in my own well-bred fashion. This party centers around me, I'll have you know. I'm under strict orders from my mother, your hostess, to meet as many of our guests as I can, and make myself agreeable to them. I prefer to concentrate first upon our young lady guests."

"You are certainly talented in *that* regard," said Miss Sterling, giving him a sly glance.

"Thank you for the compliment! I hope it was one?" he inquired.

"It was indeed, sir. Your address is such that one cannot help but feel charmed by your presence. Tell me, why does your mother wish you to seek out so many guests? Wouldn't one, or perhaps two, suffice?"

"No, and that is because my mother says that since I have been abroad and out of circulation for some time, I must work hard to re-establish myself in society once again.

I have been on the continent, availing myself of art and music and the higher amusements of every sort."

"On the continent? However did you go? It must have been dangerous!"

"Not at all. I traveled to Italy by way of the Mediterranean. I spent a very long time there, nearly three years, living in Venice, Florence, and Rome. I visited Greece, came back through the mountains into Switzerland, and into Germany, Denmark, and came back by way of the Netherlands. It was certainly not the normal Grand Tour, but there were a few things I very much wished to accomplish. That explains why I spent such a long time in Venice—I was studying painting under a great master. Are you interested in such things?"

"Very much so, although I am not knowledgeable."

"My father liked to paint, you see; he worked both in watercolors and in oils. I inherited that artistic tendency from him, much to my mother's dismay, for she never approved of my father's paintings. She is the daughter of an earl, and thought it rather *declasse* for Father to take what ought to be a mere gentlemanly hobby so seriously. In the end, he had to build a little cottage where he was able to work, for Mother said she could not bear the smell of linseed oil and turpentine. My fondest memories of my childhood came from the White Cottage: I used to spend hours there with him, looking on as he worked. When he died, I felt impelled to go abroad and visit the places he always talked about, and to see the original works of art that had most impressed him when he had done the Grand Tour, as a youth. I also wanted to be able to study in peace, and in a more serious manner than I can at home."

"Now that you are come home, what will you do?" she asked.

"If you have the time, come with me now, and I will

show you. I have a small room where I work, up in the attic of the west wing."

It was a good ten minutes' walk to the older portion of the castle, and then to ascend the innumerable drafty stone staircases, following so many twists and turns that Miss Sterling could hardly keep up with them, but they finally reached a little stone room in a corner of the Castle, with a thick, elderly wooden door. Mr. Gilbough opened it, and Miss Sterling walked within.

She was charmed by what she saw. There was a profusion of canvasses and easels, finished and half-finished oil paintings, mostly of landscapes, but with several portraits among them. There were bottles of linseed oil and turpentine, piles of colorful old rags, and stacks of canvases laid upon stretching frames.

On one side were a series of watercolors with a subject that looked familiar to her. It was the view of the lake she had seen the first day they had driven in.

She moved closer to it to judge the brushwork; it was very fine, and done in a technique she had never seen before. Somehow he had managed to capture just the right sense of country light, one which presented a feeling of rustic serenity and rural contentment.

"Your work is wonderful, Mr. Gilbough," Miss Sterling remarked. "I envy you, more than I can say!"

Mr. Gilbough said nothing, but was clearly pleased at the warm reception Miss Sterling gave his work. She moved from painting to painting, slowly and carefully admiring each one.

Giving light to the studio were two high windows that gave out onto wonderful views of the gardens and parks. To one side of a window was a sketch done in charcoal, partially complete, of another view of the countryside.

"You are so lucky!" exclaimed Miss Sterling, comparing the sketch to the view through the window "How I should love to be able to do something like this, and to do it so well as you do!"

"I am afraid my mother does not approve. I fear I am something of a disappointment to her, for my heart is in this room, and not in the world of society which she so happily inhabits."

"How could a son who produces works like these ever be a disappointment to anyone?" she replied, her eyes sparkling as she went round the room.

It was perhaps the way the slant of light had fallen on her hair, giving it a warm, celestial glow, but it was at that moment that Peter Gilbough knew that he really must try to capture Miss Sterling's unusual beauty.

"Miss Sterling, forgive me if I seem a bit forward or encroaching after our comparatively short acquaintance, but I cannot restrain myself. There is something I must know: will you allow me to do your portrait? You really do possess the most extraordinary face, you know!"

"I?" she cried, genuinely shocked, and immensely flattered.

"If you wouldn't mind too much, I wonder if you would sit for me, during your stay at the Castle. Would you mind?"

"You are embarrassing me, Mr. Gilbough," said Miss Sterling, coloring again. "We have only just met. I do not know what to say."

"I did not mean to embarrass you, I assure you."

There came a commanding knock on the door, and the latch began to lift well before the knock could be answered.

"Peter!" called out Lady Arabella, barging into the studio with no word of greeting. "I have been looking for you everywhere! I *wish* you will stop spending time up in this horrid little attic, bringing that horrid lingering smell downstairs with you. You really must give it all up! After all, you're a grown man now; there are important things to be done in your life. Oh, good day, Miss Sterling. Whatever are you doing up here?"

"Mr. Gilbough was kind enough to be my guide for some of the family portraits in the gallery downstairs, and then he offered to show me his studio, where he works," said Helen, feeling rather embarrassed.

"Work, do you call it?" sniffed Lady Arabella dismissively. "Famous! Hardly the occupation that a gentleman should be engaged in!"

"My father engaged in it, and he was a gentleman," said Peter, not bothering to mask a slight edge in his voice.

"No need to speak ill of the dead, I'm sure. I asked your father many times to give it up, but he never did, and that's all there is to it—such a stubborn man! Peter, I need to speak with you on a topic of the utmost importance. Would you come downstairs to my chambers, so we may be private? You have many family obligations which yet remain to be fulfilled," said Lady Arabella pointedly.

"I shall come at once, Mother. But, before I do, as I hope you may have some influence with Miss Sterling, would you be kind enough to convince our fair guest that she should consent to sit for me?"

Lady Arabella gave Helen a narrow look, taking measure of the clear blue of her eyes, the pale blondeness of her fair and the sweetness of her features, and deciding that it would be well to inform her son at once of how things stood with Miss Sterling.

"Convince her to sit for you? What, for a portrait? No, Peter, I will do nothing of the kind!" she said in an appalled voice. "I am sure that Miss Sterling's fiancée, Sir Rupert Fellowes, would not at all approve of such a thing! I saw the news of their impending marriage just a short while ago, when someone brought in the latest newspapers from London, and I happened to read the notice that appeared in the Gazette. I'm sure I wish you joy, Miss Sterling."

"Thank you," Helen said shyly. She was flattered to note that Mr. Gilbough received the news of her engagement with obvious regret.

Mr. Gilbough said at once, politely, "Let me extend as well my best wishes for your happiness, Miss Sterling. Sir Rupert is a very lucky man."

Lady Arabella chose to ignore her son's warm response, and stated baldly, "Since Miss Sterling is now officially engaged, you must realize that it would not do for her to sit for you: Sir Rupert might not like it, and already it looks a little odd for the two of you to be up here in this room all alone. Besides, Peter, I thought you were done for once and for all with your paint-dabblings. I wish you would just burn those brushes and pots—I can't think why you do not! Now, Miss Sterling, if you will be so kind? We really must all return!"

Mr. Gilbough gave her the most polite of bows, an appreciative smile, and led the way back downstairs.

What an extremely charming gentleman! Helen thought to herself, as she followed him down. *Truly charming!*

7

At precisely one o'clock, Lily Beeton went down to enjoy lunch in the company of the upper ten servants. She returned precisely one hour later to her mistress's suite, quite unable to contain herself. She was bubbling over with new *on-dits,* and a hundred different tales of backstairs and upstairs gossip and intrigue.

"Oh, miss, you cannot imagine what it was like! All the servants who are in service to anyone who is *anyone* were there! There was so much gossip, it was exhausting! Everyone swore that His Royal Highness the Duke of Cumberland will certainly not be coming to Cornell Castle just now, because he has involved himself in some kind of terrible scandal, and when the word comes out about it, he will be quite in disgrace."

"None of the Patronesses who had accepted their invitations is coming down for the party, because they somehow insulted one another, and they aren't speaking anymore! Lady Arabella is very peeved with them, and said they were just being childish as usual, and that if they are going to behave in that way, they can just stay in London, and be hot and sticky, and she don't care a whit! She told her abigail that if she had thought Princess Esterhazy or Silence was cutting her on purpose, she would never invite them anywhere again, and that would serve both them right!

"Sir Charles Stanton asked Miss Carteret to marry her again, and she has refused him, again, and asked that he try not to ask her so often.

"Captain Prendergast has been promoted, and Lady Agatha Winslow is very hopeful that his new rank will make her mother think more kindly on his offer of marriage.

"Mrs. Hicks-Aubrey has dismissed her new maid, after discovering she was not French, as she claimed to be, but came from Yorkshire, which was too much for madam to bear. Lady Belleveau immediately offered her a position, saying that she didn't care if the girl came from Yorkshire or Hampshire or Worcestershire—she had a good eye for fashion, and deserved a post!

"Oh, and I talked to Miss Finton again, the dresser for the Duchess of Minster. She likes me very well now, because I gave her some very particular information about how to procure some French fabric she needed to buy, that I can get very cheap through some shops I was used to deal with when I was in London. Being a milliner's assistant made me so many useful friends!

"With so many servants gathered together for the party, and all of them putting on airs and trying to out-do one another, it is the funniest thing imaginable! And the stories they tell! Some of them would truly put you to the blush, and so I won't tell any of those, but really it is quite shocking what goes on—upstairs and downstairs! The servants all say they would never stoop to gossiping about their betters, but of course they do it all the time!

"I even met Sir Charles Stanton's valet, Jeffers Pym!"

Lily added with great excitement. "Yesterday at dinner, someone told me that Pym is as haughty as his master, but to me he was very well-mannered, and really very kind and nice."

"I feel sure that he was kind and nice to you because you are so very pretty, Lily," Miss Sterling explained.

Lily blushed again, saying, with a coy smile, "Jeffers said as much to me. He paid me many pretty compliments, as no one ever did before."

"If so, then you must be careful, Lily! The castle is large, and the servants' hallways are long and dark. It is all too easy for a girl to be caught, and kissed. And if a couple does get caught, it is the girl who is always sent packing."

"Don't worry, Miss Helen—I wasn't born under a cabbage leaf, and I know how to go on, I promise. Now, as to Jeffers Pym, here is the most wonderful thing, if you can credit it—he has a brother called Jeffries Pym, who is in service to Sir Rupert Fellowes, of all people! And they are twins! Jeffers and Jeffries! They are the *perfect* image of one another! They are both in service to baronets! Sir Charles and Sir Rupert! What a coincidence, don't you think? I had heard of twins, but in all my life, I had never *seen* identical twins before—it is the very strangest thing! In looks, they are perfectly alike, and yet the two brothers are very opposite in their manners and in their dress! Jeffers Pym is quite meticulous and fashionable about his dress, just like his master Sir Charles, while Jeffries Pym is rather old fashioned."

"You're right—so much information, it is too exhausting!" commented Miss Sterling. "Thank you, Lily, I believe that will suffice for the moment. I don't wish to excite myself excessively before dinner—too much intrigue is bad for the digestion."

"Too true," said Miss Trenton, joining them.

* * *

The remainder of the afternoon at Cornell Castle passed by uneventfully for Helen Sterling and her party. Mr. Sterling was nowhere to be found, which was not unusual in him—he preferred to spend whole days at a time in the quiet of his own library, unless he had to take a trip to go up to his mills, and inspect their working personally, which he did very often.

Helen wrote a few personal letters, did a bit of embroidery, read a book by Maria Edgeworth, and then slept for an hour and a half. Miss Trenton, steeling herself for the long evening to come, had some hot chamomile tea, and then she took a long nap as well.

Lily busied herself with sewing and inspections, making sure that all the fastenings on her mistress's gown were just as they should be, and that each and every gown was properly hung, and perfectly free of wrinkles and dirt. She had just enough time to polish every piece of jewelry that Miss Sterling had brought with her, and to check every other article of clothing for tears or weakened seams.

It was fully four o'clock when there was a knock on the door, and Lily opened it; she admitted the perfect picture of a gentleman's gentleman. The valet she beheld was dressed in a severe black suit with a high, starched white cravat. He had an extremely puffed up appearance; he was short on hair, he was short of stature, but he was very wide of girth.

"Why, it's Mr. Pym!" said Lily with delight, clapping her hands. "How nice to see you again, Jeffers!"

At this, the valet's face turned dark and stormy, and he said, with some asperity, "There must be some misunderstanding, Miss Beeton. While my last name *is* Pym, I think we two are not as yet properly acquainted. I am *Jeffries* Pym, and am known to all as Jeffries. You mistake me for my brother, Jeffers, I believe, whom I closely resemble."

"Forgive me, I'm sure!" said Lily, surprised, and she stood aside to allow Jeffries to come in.

"I have a message for your mistress, Miss Beeton, from Sir Rupert Fellowes."

"Miss Sterling is within," said Lily. "Come with me."

He waited patiently until Lily led him into the sitting-room next door where Miss Sterling and Miss Trenton were occupied with some embroidery.

Jeffries Pym bowed deeply to both ladies, and, in the stentorian tones worthy of a butler announcing a ball said, "Good afternoon, ladies. I am commanded to speak with Miss Sterling."

He looked around the room until Lily confirmed by a gesture of her head the young lady to whom his message should be addressed.

He bowed deeply once again to Miss Sterling; Helen inclined her head, wishing the man would get on with his message. Sir Rupert's valet seemed to be a droll fellow, and one who was memorably pretentious!

In tones which conveyed a sense of the very greatest self-importance, he announced, "My master, Sir Rupert Fellowes, wished me to convey his warmest greetings to you, Miss Sterling, for we have just now arrived from town. Sir Rupert inquires very solicitously after your health, and he inquires very solicitously after that of your esteemed father, and takes the opportunity of sending myself to your chamber, in the greatest hope that he may he may have the honor of your hand this evening, should there be dancing after dinner."

"And you are—?" inquired Helen.

"I am Jeffries, madam. Sir Rupert's man," he said, bowing once more.

"How nice. Well, Jeffries, please be good enough to

convey to your master our greetings, and tell him that my father and I are indeed in good health, and that we hope his trip was pleasant, and that I will of course reserve a dance for him this evening."

Jeffries continued to stand as he was, stock still. Miss Sterling wondered idly just how long the valet was prepared to stay there in one place, looking like nothing so much as a human end-table, but she decided it would be kinder not to put him to the test.

"That will be all for now, Jeffries," she said, dismissing him.

He bowed again ceremoniously, and finally took his leave, backing out backwards toward the door, as if honoring royalty.

Once the door had closed behind the messenger, all three women had let loose the laughter that had been building within them during the visit of the pompous valet, and after their laughter had died down, Lily cried out with excitement, "He is, you will note, one of the twins I spoke to you about! His brother Jeffers Pym, is the elder brother, and as a consequence of their difference in order of birth, the two of them have been at dagger's-drawn since they were in leading strings!"

"Remarkable! And you say the other one has a very different personality?" asked Miss Trenton.

"Oh, yes! The two are as different as night and day!" commented Lily.

"I have never seen such a thing in my life," said Miss Trenton, "And I'm not at all sure that I wish to begin now. It seems too much like sorcery."

"No, really, you must try to see the two of them together, for it is the very strangest thing imaginable! They are just as like as two peas in a pod, and if they were dressed alike, which thankfully, they are not, no one could tell them apart. Of course, the other one is most pleasant and engaging while this one, as you have seen is just as silly and puffed up as can be."

"I wouldn't call him silly, precisely," said Miss Sterling, considering the matter carefully. "I'd say he was stiff as a board."

This made Lily giggle, and she disappeared into the dressing room once again to continue her search for the perfect gown for her mistress to wear this evening at her first formal appearance at Cornell Castle.

It took nearly an hour for the abigail to emerge with her selection, for Lily had brought every gown her mistress owned, and she owned many. Lily chose for Miss Sterling's approval a particularly lovely high-waisted gown fashioned from light blue silk, with a line of twisted seed pearls sewn upon the circle of the waist, and with similar twists of seed pearls decorating the hem on which were sewn a series of deep flounces. The gown's puffed sleeves were ornamented with smaller, similar flounces, and was decorated with similar twists of pearls. The bodice was cut attractively low, but without being overly revealing.

All in all, Lily thought, the effect would be enchanting.

Two hours and a great deal of fussing and primping later, with minor adjustments being made according to Miss Trenton's sage advice, the magical look that Lily had sought was actually effected.

Looking at herself in the long mirror with a distinctly critical eye, Helen Sterling felt pleased and happy. Helen thought she looked quite well, considering, while the doting Miss Trenton and Miss Sterling's devoted abigail thought Helen looked the perfect pattern-card of a princess.

A comb of diamonds had been threaded through her upswept blond hair, which Lily had curled laboriously so it hung down in ringlets at the sides of her face, framing it charmingly. She wore matching diamond circlet earrings, and a delicate diamond necklace. The celestial blue silk gown looked made Helen seem at once alluring and enchanting.

Helen's father burst in the door, followed closely behind by his man, John Snow, who was attempting to get his master to stand still for just a moment so he might tie the cravat in a proper knot. Only the most piteous entreaty by his faithful valet finally slowed down the energetic Mr. Sterling, who strenuously objected to the effect that he had no time to waste on miserable pointy-collared cravats, and that it was high time he took the ladies down to dinner!

Mr. Sterling stood still just long enough to look at his daughter Helen. At once his entire expression changed from a look of exasperation to one of infinite warmth.

"Oh, my dear, you do look wonderful! How I wish your mother had lived to see this day! To see our daughter Helen transformed into such a beautiful lady, who is about to become a baronet's wife!" said Mr. Sterling with a wonderful smile on his face. "She would have been so very proud!"

"Thank you, Father," said Helen, kissing him on his rough cheek.

Mr. Sterling then turned his attention toward Miss Trenton, who was dressed in a round gown of chestnut brown, suited to her position in its muted color and simplicity, but nonetheless expressing Miss Trenton's innate sense of style and good taste.

"You look very well, as usual, Miss Trenton. I am glad to see you feeling better. Will you be coming down with us?" he asked.

"It would not be quite the thing, sir. I will take dinner in my room, and join you briefly after dinner."

"I have to say I find some of these high society rules

and regulations truly vexing, and unintelligible, but I trust your judgment in all things, Miss Trenton, as to what can be done, and what cannot, and I shall defer to it, though with regret. I shall see you after dinner, then."

His man found just enough time to slip his master into his black Scott-cut coat. Mr. Sterling bowed deeply to Miss Trenton, and then gave his daughter his arm to escort her from their suite down toward the parlor, where they and the rest of the guests would await the bell that would signal the time to go into dinner.

No one but Lily noticed that whenever Mr. Sterling spoke to Miss Lydia Trenton, Miss Trenton's cheeks were suffused by a rosy blush.

Miss Sterling could not have made a better entrance. When she came down the main stairway on her father's arm, most of the house guests were already gathered in the hall, waiting to be summoned into dinner.

It was then that she saw Sir Rupert. He was easy to pick out in any crowd, for he was a full head taller than most other gentlemen, and his black hair, so like Helen's father's, was unmatched by any other guest. His shoulders were broad, his laugh deep and mellow: seeing him, Helen could feel nothing but excited happiness and real pride.

Her father left her on an upper landing, and she stayed there for a few minutes, enjoying her excellent view of the crowd, and trying to pick out familiar faces. While she was there, watching the guests, Sir Rupert turned around, as if he had instinctively sensed her presence. Catching Helen's eye, smiling, he indicated that she should come down to him, and she responded at once. He threaded his way through the crowd to her, swept her a deep bow, took up her hand, and kissed it tenderly.

"You look very well, my dear," he said genially. "Is your

father in good health? I must pay him my respects. Where
is he?"

"He's just over there, talking with Lord Winterspoon,
and Raymond Dulles, the vicar," said Helen, indicating
with her fan. "Lord Winterspoon has an interest in the
plight of the millworkers, and Father is trying to explain
to him his own theories on management, as well as those
of Robert Owen."

"Is that so? Well, I won't interrupt them, then, for the
moment," said Sir Rupert, and then said nothing more.
When the silence began to be uncomfortable, Helen
thought to ease it by asking her fiancée if he had a pleasant
journey from London.

Sir Rupert told her that the journey was fine, and then
asked about the weather they had been having, as it had
been quite humid and inclement in London of late.

"Here, the weather has been very fine indeed. We have
had no rain at all so far, I am glad to say," Helen reported.

There was then another silence between them, while
they waited for the doors to be opened. Helen began to
wonder how long it was going to take for such a large
crowd of persons to be seated.

*I should have listened when Lily warned me I should take some
food before dinner,* Helen thought to herself. *I thought she
was being silly, but she was right. With so many guests, and such
a complicated order of precedence to be followed, everything seems
to take forever!*

"Have you met our hostess?" ventured Sir Rupert.

"Yes, Lady Arabella and I have met and spoken twice,
briefly. I have also met her son, Mr. Peter Gilbough."

"I cannot quite recall her son. He has been away on the
Continent for several years, I am told."

"I believe he said as much," said Helen. "He seems a
very nice young man, and very talented."

Their conversation lagged once again, making their time

together seem very awkward. Helen began inwardly to berate herself for not possessing that talent for light, bantering conversation that was such an advantage in society.

"Your rooms have been comfortable, I hope?" asked Sir Rupert, after some time.

"Very much so," she replied, wishing she felt more at ease.

"Good. Good," said Sir Rupert, vaguely. "That is good."

A sudden, desperate silence fell over the pair that seemed to Helen Sterling to be very uncomfortable. This was not at all going as she had hoped! She had been looking forward to Sir Rupert's arrival as if he were an old friend like Miss Trenton, or Lily, someone with whom she could speak freely, and with whom she might share her thoughts.

In reality, being with Sir Rupert was not like that at all! In fact, she felt just as uncomfortable in his presence as she had that morning at breakfast, when everyone was teasing and quizzing her so. At once, she realized that the person she was betrothed to and now stood next to—so closely that she could smell the aroma of tobacco on his breath—was more or less a perfect stranger.

Sir Rupert Fellowes was a well-mannered gentleman whom she had met on a few occasions, and danced with, and found genuinely attractive—so it was, and no more than that. She really hardly knew him.

It was not, she knew, an unusual thing in London society for a girl to become engaged to a young man after a comparatively short acquaintance, just as she had become engaged to Sir Rupert. It was very much the thing, in fact.

Sir Rupert and Helen Sterling had laid eyes on one another for the very first time only a month previously. Then, only two weeks after that first meeting, Sir Rupert had asked her father if he might pay his addresses to her, and her father had given his permission.

The thing was, that although he had courted her in the prescribed manner, and attended various socially prescribed events with her, bringing her refreshments at balls, and taking her out for carriage rides, and done everything that an ardent suitor was expected to do to woo and win his lady, Sir Rupert hardly knew Miss Sterling, and Miss Sterling hardly knew the man she had agreed to marry.

In a situation like this one, where they were thrown together with nothing in particular to do, it became all too obvious that they had little in common. Miss Sterling felt she didn't even know Sir Rupert well enough to feel comfortable trying to coax him into conversation. What were his tastes? What were his interests? Suddenly, she felt shy and awkward and girlish and painfully self-conscious, all this in the presence of the man with whom she had consented to spend the rest of her natural life.

A deep blush spread over her features, which was succeeded by a feeling of faintness.

Noticing that his partner had paled suddenly, Sir Rupert said, "Are you quite well, Helen? Somehow, I feel that you are not. Would you care to sit down, or may I escort you to a less crowded room?"

"Oh, no, not at all. I was just wondering what I am supposed to say to you," she admitted ingenuously. "I felt frightened, suddenly."

"Pardon?" asked Sir Rupert, uncomprehending. "I don't think I quite understand what you mean."

"N-no, n-no, it is n-nothing," she stammered, embarrassed by her own directness. Things were not going on very well at all.

Sir Rupert gave her a puzzled glance, and forbore to speak.

There fell another silence between them which was broken when a cheery voice hailed them, saying, "Miss Sterling! There you are!'' as Mr. Peter Gilbough approached the couple.

Sir Rupert stiffened slightly, and gave his fiancée a rather possessive glance; seeing this, Mr. Gilbough sought to introduce himself.

"You must be Sir Rupert Fellowes—I am Peter Gilbough. How do you do?'' he said in his usual cordial manner, extending his hand.

"Of course, you must be Lady Arabella's son. How do you do?'' said Sir Rupert without much enthusiasm. "Our fathers were acquainted, I believe. Same London club, as I recall, similar interests. I can't think why we haven't met before, in Town. I feel sure we must have, somewhere. In general, one meets the same gentlemen over and over again.''

"Indeed! Bit of a bore isn't it?''

Sir Rupert shot him a puzzled look, as Mr. Gilbough went on to explain genially, "I've been away from town and country, studying on the Continent for some time.''

"Have you?'' said Sir Rupert, betraying no interest and idly wondered how long it would be before dinner was over, and cards could begin. Like his own father before him, finding a good game of cards was really the only reason Sir Rupert bothered to go about in society—finding wealthy partners ready to take high risks were as necessary to him as breathing.

"Do you play cards, Mr. Gilbough?'' Sir Rupert inquired, hoping against hope that Gilbough would prove a good match at the card-table.

"Alas, sir, I do not,'' he admitted.

A look of disappointment mixed with boredom passed over Sir Rupert's features, as he replied stiffly, "What a pity! I enjoy cards and gaming exceedingly. It is always so kind of your mother to provide such an opportunity for her guests.''

"Mother's summer party is the social highlight of her year. She likes to set a stage where her guests may enjoy themselves."

There was another silence.

"You are acquainted, I see, with my *fiancée*, Miss Sterling?"

"Yes, we met earlier today, I had the pleasure of giving Miss Sterling a tour of the west gallery. She particularly admired the portrait of Henry Gilbough that was painted by my grandfather, Bertram Gilbough."

"A *very* interesting personage, Great-uncle Henry," said Miss Sterling confidentially. "Mad as a meat-ax."

"Helen!" said Sir Rupert in disapproving tones. "How can you say such a thing? Do apologize, my dear!"

Mr. Gilbough laughed, and added, "None is necessary: the family is quite ready to acknowledge his eccentricity, I assure you. Now, perhaps I might take this opportunity of our meeting again to solicit your help, Miss Sterling. I have a special project in mind, and if it would not inconvenience you, I really would like you to sit for me."

"Very well, Mr. Gilbough," replied Miss Sterling, favoring him with a lovely smile. "I suppose I must, if you insist."

"Sit for you? I say, do you mean, sit for a *portrait?*" said Sir Rupert, not bothering to conceal his shock and distaste. "Are you an artist or a gentleman, Mr. Gilbough? Do you mean to say that you receive . . . money . . . to *paint?*"

Peter found himself uncharacteristically flustered, and replied, with unusual asperity, "No, Sir Rupert, I do not *'take money'* for my paintings, but I have studied for several years in Venice working directly under maestro Paolo di Capoletti, and I certainly consider myself a serious student of the medium."

"Do you?" Sir Rupert replied with polite disdain. "I am so sorry to hear it. At any rate, Helen's sitting for you is

entirely out of the question. Why, I believe I hear dinner being announced. Where is your father? We should all be going in to dinner: our hostess has already set the order of precedence."

"Just one moment, Rupert," said Helen, putting her hand on his elbow. "How do you mean, my sitting for a portrait is 'out of the question'?"

"I mean, my dear," said Sir Rupert, with a show of great patience, as if explaining something extremely simple to a small dull child, "Just precisely what I said. It is quite out of the question for you to sit for Mr. Gilbough, or for anyone else, until such time as we are ready to order an official family portrait, one which will be displayed in our home, in the family gallery, and will seen by our family and friends alone. For you, who are to be my wife, to have your visage and image bandied about here and there, for anyone at all to see, is unthinkable."

"I am not your wife just yet," Helen whispered testily, surprised and angered by her fiancé's high-handedness.

This uncensored comment was received by Sir Rupert with a black glare and a frigid command, "That will do, Helen!"

Sir Rupert's imperiousness froze Helen in her tracks, making her feel completely mortified.

Uneasy to be witnessing this lovers' quarrel, Peter backed away from them, saying, "It was of no great import, really. Let us leave the matter for now, and perhaps we might discuss the question at some other, more convenient, time?"

"At no time, Mr. Gilbough, thank you so very much," said Sir Rupert said with cold correctness.

Peter made Miss Sterling a polite bow, and left to join his mother's party. The other guests had already begun going in to dinner, and he had to seek out the lady who had been assigned to him.

Sir Rupert offered Miss Sterling his arm to escort her to either her father, or to the gentleman with whom she would go into dinner, but though she accepted his arm, she was unwilling to leave off their conversation, and said, "Rupert, you need not have treated him like that! You were uncivil!"

Rupert turned on her at once, and said in an outraged whisper, "My dear Miss Sterling, it is not for you to tell *me* how I should have treated him, or anyone! You must learn to keep your criticisms to yourself. It is unseemly to do otherwise, and is most certainly *unladylike!*"

Stung to the quick, furious, Helen ceased to speak at once.

When Sir Rupert walked her to the door, and gave her over to Mr. Sterling, she breathed a sigh of relief, but at the same time she was all too conscious that her behavior and her feelings were not at all what they ought to be.

Helen Sterling was feeling nothing but irritation toward the gentleman she had solemnly promised to marry.

8

Miss Sterling and Sir Rupert Fellowes were parted coming into dinner. Sir Rupert led the wife of a baronet in on his arm, while Helen had to be content with going in long afterwards on the arm of a certain Mr. Twickenham from Bath. Luckily for Helen, Mr. Twickenham proved to be a bore of the first degree, capable of holding both parts of a dinner conversation by himself, which happy circumstance left Helen to follow her own train of thoughts uninterrupted.

Her black mood was lifted for a moment as she became conscious of the vast scope of the Great Hall at Cornell Castle in which tonight's dinner was being served. It was located in one of the older, stone portions of the castle; the hall was two stories high, with a great fireplace at one end with a raging fire in it, looking barely contained.

There were two very long tables set in parallel lines, with very complicated settings upon them. The napery and china and silver were all set out in exquisite order; there were two wine goblets offered at every place.

Once the guests were all finally seated, a platoon of bewigged footmen in shining navy blue and grey livery entered with great stateliness, bearing a variety of silver dishes borne in on silver trays carried high above the footmen's heads—Lady Arabella was very exacting as to the manner in which she wished her dinners to proceed.

The trays were first placed on sideboards, and then the silver serving dishes were quickly uncovered and whisked to the tables, and placed there, at small intervals. It was also part of Lady Arabella's aesthetic to include a wide aggregation of foods, so as to provide her guests with a sense of abundance at the very least, and untrammeled extravagance at best.

However, this hardly appealed to Miss Sterling.

Her thoughts at dinner remained bleak, to say the least, and she soon longed desperately to escape from the table and retire to her chambers. Miss Helen Sterling stolidly made her way through the interminable removes of dinner, heaven only knew how. There was pea soup removed for a joint of beef, which removed for glazed ham, which removed for turbot with French sauce, which removed for cheese, which removed for pudding. It was an endless succession of viands she had no desire even to see, much less consume.

It was her own inner dialogue that consumed her. Helen Sterling had been engaged to Rupert for nearly two weeks; she had known him for nearly a month, and tonight was the very first time they had quarreled!

She wanted nothing more than to retire to her rooms to have Lily and Miss Trenton comfort her, and tell her that everything would work out in the end.

However, this was not to be.

Helen knew she would have to remain at dinner, in the

glare of the harsh light of the ton, till every course had been cleared and served, and she would have to remain with the ladies, making the best of it as they withdrew, and only later, much later when the music began for dancing, perhaps she would be able to slip away.

But she remembered she had promised to dance with Rupert! Of course she had! Any time she remembered it, she felt resentful, for he was quite in her black books at the moment. It seemed so wrong to get upset over a little thing, but, at the same time, she felt it was no little thing at all!

Helen felt both irritated and misunderstood, and she felt blameworthy about feeling angry, and wondering why at the moment she felt no favorable feelings toward the man she had promised to marry; all in all, she felt very much alone.

She managed the appropriate nods of her head and agreeable smiles for her left and right table-mates, and was successful enough that no one, save perhaps the footman who took her wholly untouched plate away, was aware that things were not quite as they seemed.

Miss Sterling was relieved when, at last, it was time for the ladies to withdraw to the parlor, but soon learned she had a further price to pay: none of the high-born ladies would leave her alone, but in a long line came by to pay their respects to her, for the word was out that the announcement of her engagement had finally appeared in the papers.

She was no longer the tradesman Black Jack Sterling's daughter, but a wealthy young lady who was promised to become the wife of a wealthy baronet, whose eminence in society would be unquestioned. All past snubs against her must needs be forgotten, and all mention of her low-born origins must now disappear, for Miss Sterling was to soon be anointed into the ranks of the ton, as Lady Fellowes.

Her nemeses from breakfast descended upon her in a trice: Lady Georgiana Locksley and Miss Idona Peterson appeared, very full of themselves, and full of talk about Sir Rupert Fellowes.

"Doesn't Sir Rupert look wonderful tonight, Miss Sterling?" sighed Lady Georgiana. "I hear it's all settled, and announced in the papers! Congratulations! You are such a lucky girl, aren't you?"

Miss Sterling, who still simmered with such feelings against her fiancé that she did not feel lucky at all, merely gave Lady Georgiana a dark look.

"Well!" said Lady Georgiana, nonplussed "You don't have to stare at me like that, Miss Sterling! I meant nothing inapt by my remarks!"

"We just came by to wish you joy," said Miss Peterson, laughing loudly.

"Did you?" asked Miss Sterling, rather bluntly. "Why did you?"

Miss Idona Peterson had the grace to blush, and it was Lady Georgiana who defended her friend, saying, "Why were you so coy about mentioning this morning how things stood with Sir Rupert, Miss Sterling? My godmother, Lady Lacon, has informed me that news of your engagement has just now appeared in the Gazette."

"I see your strategy, Lady Georgiana. Now that we are officially a couple, you are trying to make amends for your uncivil behavior this morning. I wonder that you even bothered to try. There must be some favor Sir Rupert can do for you for which you could use my backing. Why don't you just tell me what it is, and I'll see what I can do about it?"

"I'm sure that I had no such thing in mind!" said Lady Georgiana, incensed that this cit's daughter should speak with so little attempt at civility, but she knew that, unlike their meeting at breakfast, now it was vital that she hold her tongue, since Miss Sterling, as Sir Rupert Fellowes' acknowledged *fiancée*, held a position in society which could not be dismissed, and had to be reckoned with.

Therefore, making a great effort, Lady Georgiana took a deep breath, spun her fury into a semblance of complacency, and did something that cost her dearly—she actually apologized to Miss Sterling.

"Please believe me, Miss Sterling, if our behavior this morning was in any way offensive to you, we are heartily sorry for it. Can we not make amends?" said Lady Georgiana, attempting a friendly smile. "Just a short while ago, our hostess, Lady Arabella, mentioned to me that there are some preparations being made for an outing to Beaufort Abbey in a day or two, with some of the young people who have come to the party. Won't you—and Sir Rupert—join us? I'm sure that the trip will prove excessively diverting!"

Helen was not so deaf to Miss Trenton's many years of social tutelage as not to see that it was time either to mend the breach she had made with Lady Georgiana, or to deal with the serious consequences of having made an enemy amongst the ton.

Therefore she smiled back at Lady Georgiana, and said, "I think you are very right, and I apologize for my display of temperament. I would very much like to join the party going to the Abbey."

All the young ladies parted in apparent amity; nevertheless, Miss Sterling breathed a sigh of relief when Lady Georgiana and Miss Peterson said their farewells, and moved on.

The younger ladies were soon replaced by their elders, who, having heard the news or read the London paper, made a point of coming by to wish Miss Sterling joy.

Lady Lacon appeared and said she wished her very well, and hoped that she would come by to her estate, Taylor Hall, and pay a visit.

Lady Arabella Gilbough appeared, and told her she was a very good girl, and that Sir Rupert Fellowes would make her an excellent husband. Lady Arabella also promised to invite her to her next rout, that she would hold in London, later on in the year.

Miss Janet Carteret and Mrs. Partridge came by, kissed her on the cheek, and told her they were so very happy for her. Mrs. Partridge seemed just a bit stand-offish, but Miss Carteret seemed genuinely pleased with the news of her engagement.

Lady Farlow and the Duchess of Minster came by, and inspected Miss Sterling from top to toe, surveying her with their quizzing glasses. In the end, they pronounced themselves very satisfied with her, and told her to her face that they did not think Sir Rupert could have done better for himself if he had selected someone to the manor born, which from these august ladies, was an immense—if back-handed—compliment. The Duchess then suggested that the next time Miss Sterling was in London, she might feel free to come by and pay her grace a morning-visit, and that the Duchess would receive her.

It went on for what seemed a perilously long time, so long that Miss Sterling actually felt moved by such a vast display of acceptance and affection. Everyone seemed to feel so happy for her—Helen Sterling only wished she could feel so happy for herself.

It was a relief to Miss Sterling when the signal was given for the gentlemen to rejoin the ladies in the Grand Salon, prior to going in to the ballroom, and assemble for dancing. It was even more of a relief when she saw Miss Trenton's thin tall figure making her way toward her. True to her word, her very correct companion had forced herself to rise to the occasion, and make her first public appearance at Cornell Castle with her charge in tow.

Miss Sterling, by this time very desperate for friendly company, fairly ran to her, grabbed her companion's hand, and squeezed it with an excess of zeal, for Miss Trenton yelped, and cried, "Helen! Unhand me! Whatever can be the matter? You only cling to me when there is something very amiss!"

Miss Sterling drew Miss Trenton over to one side, and poured out her heart in a torrent of words, crying, "Miss Trenton, we have had our first quarrel, Sir Rupert and I! The worst thing is, I can't find it in my heart to forgive him, for I think he was very wrong!"

"Is that all? Do not worry, Helen! These things happen to all couples, so you need not think very much upon it. Unless I am much mistaken, the next time you see Sir Rupert, he will have forgotten all about it."

"But what if *I* have not forgotten? He was very arrogant, and he did not heed my point of view at all. In fact, he utterly dismissed what I said, *and* was angry that I had said it! Father *always* listens to me—how can I be married to a husband who discounts my viewpoint?" said Helen unhappily.

"You must be brave, and wise, and let it pass. These disagreements are mere trifles, and in time they will recede into memory."

"Oh, I do hope so Miss Trenton. It is the very worst of feelings, to quarrel. Speaking of which," she admitted sheepishly, "I have fed a quarrel with Lady Georgiana and her friends. They were beastly to me this morning, and then they came to me tonight with their faces full of false congratulations and I, well, I wasn't very civil to them."

"No! I warned you about such things, Helen! For the most part, you have always been a well-behaved girl, but you must keep that slight tendency toward temper under better control. It always pays to hide one's feelings under the mask of pure diplomacy. It *never* pays to make an enemy amongst the ton—they can strike back at one in so many subtle ways."

"I am sorry," said Helen, chagrined. "I shall try to keep my temper, and do better, and make you proud of me."

"I have always been proud of you, my dear," said Miss Trenton fondly.

Two footmen opened the doors between the drawing room and the ballroom to signal that the evening's entertainments were to begin. Arm in arm, Miss Sterling and Miss Trenton walked into the larger salon, in which a small orchestra was beginning to play, and gentlemen had begun seeking out dancing partners. She smiled when she saw her father, talking animatedly with his friend, the white-haired Lord Winterspoon. They stopped speaking, and smiled broadly at the ladies. Lord Winterspoon, being of an earlier generation, made sweeping legs to them, each one in turn. Mr. Sterling walked over to his daughter and Miss Trenton, and he complimented them both on the fine figures they presented.

At this, Miss Trenton blushed a little, and said, "You mustn't say such things, sir; it's not as though I am a guest."

"Your bloodlines are far better than my own, Miss Trenton," pointed out Mr. Sterling. "Why should I exclude you from my notice merely because you receive a wage? I am a wage-earner myself. In that, we are social equals, wouldn't you say?"

"I suppose so, but don't you think that people will talk if you are seen to be so familiar with me?" said Miss Trenton worriedly.

"I don't care a fig for that!" said Mr. Sterling, laughing aloud. "Why should I care?"

"But, it might not be well for Helen . . ." explained Miss Trenton. "What if it reflected badly upon her?"

"What do you think, Helen? Should I fear the contempt of the ton, and not compliment the woman who has raised my child as she would her own?"

"Certainly not, Father," said Miss Sterling.

"What will Sir Rupert say?" asked Miss Trenton. "He's a very high-stickler for proper conduct, and it is their engagement which now assures Helen of acceptance amongst the ton. If she does not respect their rules, what will he think of her?"

"If Sir Rupert objects to my treating you with the respect and affection you so richly deserve, then he and I will have to have a little talk," said Mr. Sterling, "For that kind of snobbish conduct is something to which I take exception!"

Miss Trenton blushed a little at his defense of her, and by his compliments to her, very deeply pleased, and sensible of the respects he had paid.

Mr. Sterling then changed the subject by bowing over Helen's hand very formally, asking, "If you are not otherwise engaged, may I have this dance, my dear?"

Helen Sterling smiled lovingly, and then curtseyed in reply, and Black Jack Sterling drew his daughter onto the well-polished wooden floor of the ballroom. As the rest of the ton stood around them in groups and in pairs, watching the dancers assemble, Mr. Sterling and Helen took their places directly across from one another, standing in two parallel lines which formed the beginning position for the set.

It was remarked by more than one group of onlookers that, of the several couples that made up the dancing set, no couple looked at one another with more deep devotion than did Black Jack and his only child.

They drew the attention of the entire party toward them in an instant—he, so dark and sturdy, she, so slender and blonde and—what could one say about her? It was obvious to all the guests assembled that it was the tradesman's daughter, Miss Sterling, who looked the aristocrat.

It was even more obvious when they began to move through the figures of the dance—there was something in the combination of Helen's Sterling's grace and beauty and simplicity that naturally attracted one's attention.

Murmurings of appreciation and admiration made their way all around the crowded floor, that the Sterling girl would do very well indeed.

"I hear your good news is all around the room, Helen," said Mr. Sterling. "I am told the notice of your engagement has appeared in the *Gazette*. Are you well satisfied, my dear?"

"I? Yes, of course, Papa," she said. All of Helen's unhappy feelings were eclipsed as she basked in the light of her doting father's admiration.

"I want nothing for you other than your happiness," said he, moved, "You know that, Helen, don't you?"

"Of course I do."

"If this young man of yours can make you happy, and if you are satisfied and well-settled, then the whole work of my life will have been worthwhile. I have spoken at length with your Rupert, and I am pleased to believe that he seems to feel toward you just as he ought. I would never have given my consent to your marriage, otherwise. I am satisfied that he will make you a fitting life partner, and that he was chosen by you of your own free will. Is it not so?

"Yes, Father," said Helen, now close to tears.

"It has been the work and goal of my entire life—as it was of your dear mother's, God rest her soul—to be able to raise up a child from the poverty into which we both were born, into the light of education, respectability, and into prominence, and perhaps even eminence. I am so proud of you, my dear. If only your dear mother might have lived to see this day! Our own daughter, the toast of London town!"

"Yes, Father," she whispered.

"I can't believe it—it really seems more like a dream—my own dear little Helen, in just a few short weeks, is to become Lady Fellowes!" said Mr. Sterling, with tears in his eyes.

What was she to do? Hearing his high expectations and his pride in her having made such an advantageous match, how could she reveal to her father how wretched she had been feeling? Had he ever had any disagreement in his marriage? The pressure upon her was lowering, and she clung to her father's hand ever more tightly as he helped her through the figures.

She had made her pledge to Sir Rupert, her father was pleased with the match, even counting on it, and despite the second thoughts that had begun to invade her consciousness, she would have to throw them all aside, and live with them.

She had given her solemn vow, and she would just have to do as she had promised.

Across the ballroom, Peter Gilbough watched father and daughter dancing, full of admiration for the picture of familial perfection they presented.

It could not have been easy road for Black Jack Sterling, or for his daughter, Mr. Gilbough reflected. *To seek to enter the ton with wealth that everyone knows bears the stain of trade, is a daunting task. One can only imagine the slights that must be endured: it must have been painful.*

And yet, look at their strengths—it is clear that Mr. Sterling loves his child dearly, and only wants the best for her. It is just as clear how deeply she is devoted to him. A rare, admirable and unselfish relationship.

One can see her deep devotion in those wondrous blue eyes of hers. Really, I must count her as a magnificent young woman.

It was at about this juncture that Mr. Peter Gilbough's mind changed, and what was formerly but a vague desire transformed into a definite resolve.

She is magnificent! I don't care what that dry stick of a fiancé of hers says—I must and will paint a portrait of Helen Sterling!

She possesses the ideal classical face—regard the proportions of her nose to chin, of lips and eyes and forehead—they are all as if found in the master's own sketchbook.

Lips ever so softly curved; straight nose, just long enough and the bridge of her nose just high enough to be interesting. Curved, arched brows, perfectly formed. Wide forehead, high cheekbones.

I shall do it—with his permission, or without! She's not Sir Rupert's chattel yet!

9

Even Sir Rupert Fellowes seemed moved at the picture of devotion Mr. Sterling and Miss Sterling presented, for he watched them intently for a long time, with an appreciative smile on his face. Pleased at the good impression his betrothed and her father were obviously making upon the blue-blooded company in attendance at Lady Gilbough's party, his irritation with Miss Sterling diminished, and he decided to make up with her.

When the music had ceased, and the various couples had cleared the floor, Sir Rupert made his way swiftly through the crowd toward his *fiancée*. It was, therefore, in full view of the ton that Sir Rupert reached for Miss Sterling's hand, took her small hand in his own, bowed over it formally, and brushed his lips to it in a most romantic and gentlemanly way, and said in a husky tone, "You have pledged this next dance to me, my dear."

Despite the anger she had been feeling at Sir Rupert's cavalier treatment of her earlier in the evening, everything changed when she felt his lips touch her skin. Helen found herself responding to his closeness, without really understanding why. Suddenly she found herself blushing, just like a schoolgirl.

The orchestra began to strike up the next tune; unresisting, saying not a word, Miss Sterling allowed herself to be led onto the dance floor.

The various couples who were assembling in order to dance lined up such that the man and woman in the pair were across from one another; the gentlemen then formed one line, and the ladies formed another line, parallel to the first.

The partners first turned toward one another, the lady curtsying and the gentleman bowing. When Sir Rupert's eyes met Helen's, she saw that his eyes held within them such a look of sheer passion that it made her cheeks burn, and her breath quicken. She began to feel faint; she felt out of her depth; she did not at all know what to do.

He is making up our quarrel by making love to me! realized Helen.

The music for the dance began in earnest, and the couples began to perform the figures, just as prescribed. Sir Rupert and Helen Sterling moved to and fro, bowing and curtsying, just as they ought. They held out their arms until their fingertips just touched, as the next movement of the dance required.

The dancing couples stepped up, on their toes, and then back, to the left. They passed down the line, from one partner to another, until everyone had gone down the chain, and they were back with their original partners.

Their two right hands meeting, they circled around one another gracefully. As they did so, Sir Rupert leaned over toward his partner, and whispered to her in a most tender, lover-like tone, "Forgive my ill-temper this afternoon! I am yours always to command, my love!"

It took only those words of passionate affection to dispel all misunderstanding between the two, at least in Helen's mind. The air of misery that had beclouded Helen's entire being for some hours was thoroughly dispersed in an instant of intimacy and affection.

How strange! thought Helen, as the figure changed again, she followed the line of women passing down the set. *How quickly a lover's universe can change. Now all is forgiven him, and all is forgiven me, and the world may resume its usual course.*

Sir Rupert and Helen finished the dance in perfect amity. When he led her off the floor, under the flickering candlelight, he neither offered to bring her refreshment, nor returned her to her party, but steered her most directly toward an side alcove that was draped in chestnut velvet.

He brushed aside the heavy tasseled drape, so she might pass within, and, again without a word, he led her out through a side door which gave out onto a verandah.

The verandah looked out onto the formal gardens; she could smell the faint scent of flowers wafting toward her in the slight summer breeze. Although lit with by several tall, ensconced torches, it was filled with dark patches of shadows, and was entirely empty of guests.

"There is no one here," said Helen, suddenly a little alarmed, and she turned back to re-enter the house, but Sir Rupert blocked her way with a hand held across the door. She retreated away from him, her heart beating very fast indeed.

"Do not be frightened, my dear," said Sir Rupert, moving closer to her and running his hand expertly across her cheek, in a soft touch that made her tremble to her depths. "I wished to be private with you for a moment. Will you allow it, Helen?"

She blushed again, a maidenly response that was almost invisible in the shadows toward which Sir Rupert was leading her. Slowly, she nodded her consent to him, but she could not help looking toward her feet rather than at Sir Rupert, for this world of physical affection was so new to her and seemed so very intimidating.

Sir Rupert brought her chin up with his hand, and made her look at him.

Blushing again, feeling as shy and vulnerable as a deer, she tried to look away from him, but Sir Rupert held her firmly. Suddenly, Helen felt his arm encircling her waist, holding it tightly as he pulled her inexorably toward him.

At once, she understood: Sir Rupert intended to kiss her!

She stiffened at once, for she had never been kissed before, not ever. All her physical contact with gentlemen, including the gentleman she had consented to marry, consisted in the polite kissing of hands, and an occasional a handclasp. Other than that, there had been nothing.

But now, she realized, he had begun to make love to her in earnest. That passionate look that made her catch her breath during the dancing was nothing compared to the look of deep longing he gave her now.

Tenderly yet strongly, Sir Rupert pressed Helen against his whole body, and pressed his lips to hers, leaving them there, savoring her taste, until he felt first her shy, maidenly response, and then, after some time, when her breathing had deepened, and the trembling had begun, he suddenly drew back and let her go.

"I think that will suffice for now, my dear," said he, patting her hand solicitously. "As an introduction. One mustn't rush into these things too hastily, after all. There will be plenty of time to explore these, shall we say, intimate aspects of marriage once we're wed."

'Intimate aspects of marriage?' Helen thought to herself, as she blushed furiously, and turned away from her betrothed to hide her face from Rupert, and from everyone. *He must*

be referring to—oh dear! I cannot even think it! What am I to do?

Helen's mind and body were both in complete turmoil. Suddenly, she could not bear to have Rupert's eyes upon her—she felt desperately shy, and desperately embarrassed. More than ever before, she became aware that she was out of her depth, and that she had entered into an engagement about whose physical consequences she knew all too little.

"It is really too cold out here, Rupert," she managed to say, "I should very much like to go inside, please."

Rupert bowed, and complied with her request at once.

As Helen and Sir Rupert re-entered the house from the verandah, she felt as if the eyes of everyone in the ballroom were fixed upon her, and felt mortified as she imagined that everyone in the room noticed that she had been outside with Sir Rupert, all alone.

The couple walked arm in arm around the other side of the ballroom, where the orchestra was still playing, and there were still many persons dancing, and many other guests standing at the sides of the room, watching.

"I must find Miss Trenton," said Helen, trying to make some time when she could think things over. "I have a bit of a headache, I'm afraid."

"I'm sorry to hear it, my dear. I am to have a game of cards with Roddy Beames, so I shall leave you for tonight, and be off, shall I? Do you wish me to wait until Miss Trenton is found, or can you make your way to her yourself?" he asked considerately.

"Go ahead, Rupert, I shall be just fine," replied Helen, with a certainty she was far from feeling.

Helen Sterling took another long turn around the ballroom, searching for Miss Trenton just as the *contradanse* set was coming to an end; she had reached the side where the orchestra platform had been placed when, at the opposite side of the ballroom, the ten-foot tall double doors opened admitting a flurry of distinguished persons. The butler called out each of their names, and as the new party entered within, a stir passed from one side of the great candle-lit ballroom to another.

Notable among this group of guests was the raven-haired belle, Miss Janet Carteret, who swept into sight on the arm of the great Sir Charles Stanton, the notorious arbiter of fashion, who was as renowned for his wit as for his waistcoats.

The divine Miss Carteret, who this evening was dressed in an unusual lacy confection of French white silk, had been blessed with all the requisite elements of beauty: a fashionably pale complexion, a long aristocratic nose, a swan-like neck, large striking, blue eyes, and a firm, red well-shaped mouth that told of a lifetime of pleasantries and satisfactions.

Sir Charles was a man of less than medium height, not powerfully built, and not precisely handsome, classically speaking, but who possessed an air of strong intelligence about him that could not be denied. It was this innate intelligence that lent Sir Charles a kind of authority and presence which as naturally attracted the attention of everyone around him.

Rather than ceremoniously make their way around the room to greet their friends and acquaintances, as all entrants before them had done, Sir Charles Stanton escorted Miss Carteret toward a pair of gold brocade-covered chairs which Lady Arabella had just caused to be placed on a dais.

There, they seated themselves, with Miss Carteret's chaperone and companion Mrs. Partridge standing just behind them, at the end of the room that was nearer the musicians.

Once they were in place, their hostess, Lady Arabella, began fawning over them mercilessly.

The Duchess of Minster, naturally, did not leave her own chair to come to greet Sir Charles and Miss Carteret, but she did deign to incline her head in their direction when they took their seats, and even went so far as to pay them the singular compliment of condescending to wave to them, and smile; the pair returned both the smile and the wave and then began to hold their court, just as any couple of the blood royal might just as well have done, becoming the natural center of attention.

The obeisance of all the rest of the ton was not long in coming. Lady Lacon and Lady Arabella Gilbough, Lady Farlow, Lady Belleveau and Mrs. Hicks-Aubrey formed the head of a line which automatically formed to pay tribute to the couple. It was a great mark of distinction that the impeccable Sir Charles Stanton had deigned not merely to appear at Lady Arabella's annual party, but had promised he would stay at Cornell Castle for the entire remainder of the fete!

The younger generation of the ton approached next, including Lady Georgiana Locksley, Lady Agatha Winslow, and Miss Idona Peterson, and these were followed by all the other lesser guests who wished to use this occasion to advance themselves socially, until there was a long train of supplicants wending away from the couple, not unlike the endless queues characteristic of royal receptions.

What had been a crowd quickly grew into an even more impenetrable crush; it was another quarter of an hour before Miss Sterling was finally able to discover her companion, Miss Trenton. She had been standing at a far wall with some other older ladies of limited means. However Helen was quite prevented by the crowd from reaching her. The headache now coming on in earnest, she was forced to push her way doggedly through the ocean of silk, sarcenet, and muslins.

"Oh, there you are, Miss Trenton!" said Helen, out of breath from making her way through the crowd, rather overwhelmed by the splendor of the company, "I have been wishing to have a word with you! Something has happened, and I must have your advice!"

"Can it not wait, dear? I believe that is one of the Royal Dukes that is just arrived," Miss Trenton replied, trying unsuccessfully to peer past a tall lady whose head was topped by a turban and feathers. "You can see Sir Charles Stanton and Miss Carteret over there! Aren't they a sight to behold?"

"Yes, indeed. They are a very admirable pair."

"I do so wish to catch a glimpse of a royal!" said Miss Trenton rather mistily. "Not that I should call myself one of those who are so *smitten* with royalty, but you must admit it is rather interesting and exciting, seeing all these people curtseying and behaving in such a deferential manner. It is quite a contagious atmosphere, if you see what I mean."

"I don't, quite, Miss Trenton," admitted Helen. "I mean, yes, I also find it a bit exciting to be in such exalted company, but on the other hand, when I think more logically on it, I don't see what all the fuss is about. They're people, just as we are, and if they are what is called high-born, it is just an accident of nature, not at all indicating some sort of pre-eminence of character or other good qualities."

"I quite agree with you!" remarked Peter Gilbough, coming up from behind them. "Forgive me, but I could not help but overhear your very reasonable argument, Miss Sterling. How are you this evening?"

"I am very well, thank you. May I present you to my companion, Miss Trenton? This is Mr. Gilbough, of whom I spoke earlier."

Mr. Gilbough bowed to her politely. Mr. Gilbough had been hoping to take this opportunity to seek out Miss Sterling's father, so that he might apply to him for permission to take his daughter's likeness, but he soon saw that the father was not in attendance, and so began to pay his courteous respects to her companion, saying, "How do you do, Miss Trenton? You are both looking very well this evening, if I may say so."

"How do you do, Mr. Gilbough?" said Miss Trenton, pleased at the young man's polite demeanor. "It was very kind of you to show Helen around the Castle. We both find it very fascinating."

"We have hardly begun to explore it, Miss Trenton. I hope you both may find sufficient time during this fortnight for me to show you both all the finest things that the Castle has to offer."

At this point, Miss Trenton began a long and rather repetitive monologue about the enriching effect traveling and sightseeing at great houses can have on one's appreciation of art and architecture. While this not entirely enlightening speech was occurring, Mr. Peter Gilbough was studying with renewed interest the outlines of Miss Sterling's face, and doing so with the deliberate, practiced eye of the artist.

He had, for the first time, the opportunity to study his subject's features with a professional eye.

What a face she had! He marked a plane here, a curve there, and the way the light was reflected off one surface and another. He was only beginning to record these features mentally when, to his surprise and astonishment, he found the eye of the artist being superseded and eclipsed by the eye of the man.

He left off admiring Miss Sterling's beauty from a purely aesthetic perspective, and began fully appreciating it as a male. Helen Sterling was a devilishly captivating woman, he decided.

He felt an unusual pang of jealousy, followed by definite regret.

The devil take it! Why had I not had the luck to come upon her first?

Pity about that damned Fellowes having a prior claim on her affections. Perhaps an insult might be arranged, followed swiftly by a deadly duel?

It might just be very satisfying to run Sir Rupert through with a sword, and then be able call the lovely Miss Sterling mine!

Lady Arabella Gilbough, from her place of honor at Sir Charles Stanton's side, had a glimpse of her son Peter very obviously admiring the beauty of Black Jack's wealthy daughter, and doing so in full view of the ton.

What could he be thinking of? she wondered. Didn't the silly boy realize that the Sterling heiress is engaged to Sir Rupert? Of course he did—she had told him so, just this morning! Really, Peter was mooning around that chit with the most irritating repetitiveness! She simply had to set things straight, or Lady Georgiana would see him, and the whole plan would be ruined!

It was such a shame that she hadn't had time to talk to him earlier in the day, as she had certainly planned to do, but then Cook came to her with that horrid problem about an insufficiency of quail and partridge and duck, and she had had to consent to Cook's re-doing the better part of the evening's menu, and there just hadn't been a *minute* extra to let Peter know that he was going to have to offer for Georgiana Locksley!

Lady Arabella waved her fan back and forth wildly, and finally was able to able to catch her son's eye, and indicate to him that he was to come to her at once. He made his way through the crowd without much enthusiasm.

Like his own father before him, Peter Gilbough had never taken seriously the machinations of the *ton* universe upon which persons such as his mother and Sir Charles depended as their life's blood. Peter could hardly have cared less what person or what apparel, or what combination of colors were in fashion, or had fallen out of fashion.

Insofar as he had a talent for colors, it lay in knowing how to combine them on a palette in order to achieve a particular technical effect. His mother's attempts to have him leave off his study of art and transform himself into a pink of the ton were weary-making at best and annoying at worst.

However, it was something he had to endure for politeness' sake, so as not to upset his mother. He must stay at Cornell Castle for a short while, at least—but just until all the details of his inheritance were put right.

After his twenty-first birthday had passed, he promised himself, the terms of his father's will would have been met, he would have his income secure, and could do precisely as he wished, and what he wished was to leave England, return to Venice and live there for the rest of his days, enjoying the way the matchless light of Italy transforms shapes and colors, and being able to study with his esteemed Maestro di Capoletti.

"Peter, where have you been?" cried his mother when her son made his way to her side. He could tell by the shrillness of her voice that she was going to be full of commands, and so it was. "You must stop making a cake of yourself around that Sterling girl! It is useless, absolutely useless! Now, I wish you to go over and greet Sir Charles Stanton and Miss Carteret, at once!" Lady Arabella Gilbough ordered. "They have only just arrived, and I want you to make yourself known to them. I'm afraid you have

spent far too much time lately wandering around the continent with your paintbrushes and paintings or whatever it
is, to have any real appreciation of the importance of the
approbation of Sir Charles and his ilk.''

"You are absolutely correct, Mother," said Peter unenthusiastically.

"Therefore, have the goodness to heed me, and to introduce yourself to them, and be sure to be all politeness!''

"Very well, Mother, I shall do my best."

"Now, what was the other thing? Lady Georgiana! Lady
Georgiana is here, and you will be pleased to find that she
is in great looks this evening, and none of this will turn
out as it should unless you do as I say! Tonight you must
be seen by all to pay her your very particular attentions!''

"Why must I?" asked Peter, in all innocence.

Lady Lacon, overhearing this, snapped her head around
at once, and said in an astonished tone, "Because your
mother and I mean for you to marry her!''

Peter shot his mother a nonplussed look, and said, "I
beg your pardon?"

Lady Arabella Gilbough, furious with her friend for her
candor, made no direct reply, but only said, firmly, "Do
not regard it! It is no matter! Louisa mis-spoke for a
moment. Do be a good boy, and ask Lady Georgiana to
dance, before her card fills up."

"Certainly, I shall do just as you suggest, Mother," he
said, bowing, and wondering if his ears had deceived him,
and whether his mother and her friend were really up to
something, as they certainly seemed to be.

By twelve o'clock, when the ball-room at Cornell Castle
was still filled with many couples, a certain fast set of twelve
young gentlemen made their disappearance, and retired
up to the card-room to take up much more significant

pursuits: drinking and gambling, playing cards for very high stakes.

This set included Sir Rupert Fellowes and his friend Lord Roderick Beames, the Duke of Bidwell's youngest son, who were both extremely enthusiastic players and who enjoyed being rather reckless in playing their cards, and placing their bets. They had just sat down and dealt out for a game, when Sir Rupert seemed to recall something important, which he had to tell his friend at once.

"I say, Roddy! I quite forgot to tell you! I've done it at last! The notice has now appeared in the *Gazette*, which means that you, dear boy, owe me three hundred pounds!"

"You've done what, you devil?" asked Lord Roderick. "I don't recall taking a three hundred pound wager!"

"I've offered for the Sterling!" said Sir Rupert with some satisfaction, draining a glass of claret, and looking pleased with himself, as he always did.

"What? The pound sterling?" replied Lord Roderick, puzzled.

"Not the pound sterling, but just as good as it, *and* twice as stable: to wit, I've offered for Black Jack Sterling's daughter! And been accepted! And seen the notice appear in the papers, which means neither one of us can back out of it without being branded a jilt!"

"Rupert, you devil! All your own money and all of hers, too! Doesn't seem quite fair, does it?" pronounced Lord Roddy, signaling to the nearest footman to refresh both his glass of wine and Sir Rupert's.

He lifted his glass high up, and said, "To your health—and that of your lady!"

"She's not a lady yet," said Sir Rupert, emitting a discreet hiccup as he laid down an ace of spades with a snap.

"Damn your eyes, Rupert! Where did that black ace come from? You're much too clever by far, and I don't like it a bit," said Lord Roddy, pouting just a little. "Well,

I must say I think your girl's a pretty little thing. Very pretty, really. Damnably pretty, if you take my meaning: well-behaved and well-spoken. You'd never know her father wasn't a proper gentleman, at least not to look at her. I think she'll do well for you. I wish you both joy.''

"What, did you think I'd choose a girl who would make a fool of me, even for the money?" asked Sir Rupert. "Of course she'll do well for me, man! I wouldn't have it any other way.''

"You don't make it sound like much of a love match.''

"Love match? What's a love match, Roddy? What men call a love match is just marriage by mutual deceit!'' yawned Sir Rupert.

"I say, Fellowes! I think you're wrong there. When I marry my Celia, I'll do so for love alone!'' said Lord Roddy.

"You're conveniently forgetting your beloved Celia's beloved thirty thousand pounds, aren't you? Good for you, if you can!'' said Sir Rupert, loudly, signaling the waiter to fill up his glass. "I drink to your idea of love! As for myself, I do not deeply believe in mixing romantic love and marriage. The thing is, the Sterling girl will suit me, and we'll suit each other. Her fortune will suit me as well, and I don't really mind that it came from trade. Why should I? A pound is a pound; it don't matter who made it. Her father's a very honest, business-like man, not terribly presentable, but he's certainly been very generous in his settlements on his child.''

"How much, Rupert?'' asked his friend, curious.

"She'll bring me even more than your lovely, high-born Celia,'' pronounced Sir Rupert with obvious satisfaction.

"Damn! You have all the luck!'' cried Lord Roddy.

"It's not luck, it's foresight. I never allow myself to proceed as if by mere accident of chance. This alliance was perfectly deliberate on my part,'' revealed Sir Rupert. "I don't mind that she's got no family to speak of—a pack of relatives only make for complications. Black Jack Sterling only wants his Helen to be happy in her marriage; I have gone well out of my way to satisfy him that I am the man to do *that* job, and there's an end to it. Nothing more need be said."

"*Can* you make her happy in her marriage?" asked Lord Roderick.

Rupert had a distinct gleam in his eye as he added, laughing, "Oh, just you wait and see, Roddy! I'll make the girl happy soon enough, and from that, I bet you I'll have me an heir before next summer, or I'll give you a monkey!"

"Rupert, you old dog!" said Lord Roddy. "You always could get a girl to fall head over heels for you, and I never could!"

"It is one of my talents, I admit it. Any man *might* do so, if he really puts his mind to it. It is merely a matter of cultivating a certain smoothness toward the fair sex, a certain attentiveness, a certain tenderness, a certain *je ne sais quois*. That is all."

"Will you be giving up Jenny Fairchild? Once you're wed, I mean," said his friend.

"Well now, Roddy, nobody said a married man can't still have a little fun, did they?" replied Sir Rupert.

"Not at all! Not at all," said Lord Roderick. "If you're not giving up your fancy-piece, then I'm not giving up my Sally Dix."

"There you are, then," said Sir Rupert, clearing the cards, stacking them, shuffling them, and preparing them to be cut.

The table at which the newly-engaged baronet and the duke's younger son were sitting happened to be being served and cleared by a man who had hovered about them solicitously throughout their entire conversation.

However, that man was not the same servant who had served them at first, nor was he dressed in Lady Arabella's splendid blue and gray livery, though neither Lord Roddy nor Sir Rupert, being rather heavily in their cups, noticed this. In the rather dim candlelight, they took the man to be Thomas, the second footman at Cornell Castle, for that is who it should have been.

However, this person only resembled Thomas in terms of his height and his general coloring. In point of fact, his name was John Snow, and he just happened to be the valet to Mr. Black Jack Sterling, and he enjoyed with his master a relationship of great mutual trust.

John's hearing was very good, and his memory was even better.

10

Doing precisely as his mother had asked, Peter Gilbough first walked over and greeted Sir Charles Stanton and Miss Carteret. He chatted with them amiably for several minutes, and then sought out Lady Georgiana Locksley, and asked for her hand for the next dance.

Having been forewarned by her godmother that she must accept him, Lady Georgiana granted him the dance, albeit unenthusiastically; however, since the couple was dancing well away from the side of the room where Lady Arabella and Lady Lacon were sitting, neither one of these ladies noticed this.

They merely noticed that Peter and Georgiana were dancing with one another; seeing this, they nodded to one another with approbation.

"They are a handsome-looking pair, are they not, Arabella?" said Lady Lacon.

"Indeed. I think the matter only requires the *slightest*

bit of persistence on our part, and we can then let nature take its course.''

''There is no reason why they should not marry, is there?'' said Lady Lacon.

''None at all,'' pronounced Lady Arabella Gilbough. ''They are a perfect match!''

''You know, Arabella, you need not have snapped at me as you did before. You said you were going to tell Peter, and I thought that you had!''

''Well, so I had intended, except I was distracted by the problem with Cook. It is so weary-making, forever having to do one's servants' jobs oneself. Have you told Georgiana?''

''As it happened, I didn't have the chance, either. One of my flounces was down, and so I had to review my entire wardrobe, trying on one gown after another, and then trying on all of my jewels, necklace after necklace, and tiara after tiara, to find which would go best with which, and the afternoon was spent before I knew it! I was so fatigued, I had to lie down!'' said Lady Lacon, pumping her mother-of-pearl fan prodigiously. ''Look, Arabella! I see Cousin Raymond approaching. I wonder what he can want of you?''

''Beyond my home and my income, I cannot think what he wants!'' said Lady Arabella with asperity. ''I can hardly *wait* for Peter's first child to be born so that Raymond may be cut out of the succession, once and for all!''

When Raymond Dulles approached, the disdain of the two ladies was transformed magically by a pair of wide and seemingly genuine smiles. Mr. Dulles asked after their health, and made polite conversation with them, and in general behaved in a most unexceptionable way. This, however, was insufficient to save him from a flurry of criticism as soon as he had departed, for he was seen to seek out the company of Mr. Sterling, who had been deep in conversation with Miss Trenton. This move did not set well with the widow of the vicar's second cousin.

"You see, Louisa? He goes to speak with Black Jack Sterling, and a *governess,* of all people! Who does he think he is? Why does he not behave as a man who is related to me must do? I must say, I think it very wrong."

"Next thing you know, Dulles will be asking the governess to marry him," said Lady Lacon with disdain. "Persons like that do not know what they owe to their family name."

"Surely he has no plans to marry anyone!" commented Lady Arabella, aghast.

"Oh, I am sure he will not do so. I believe he has but a pittance for a living. He has no money on which he may marry. Not so far as I know."

"That's a blessing, at least. I will feel far, far better once this wedding of ours has taken place!" said Lady Arabella.

"There, now, do you see? Peter has left Georgiana, and she is looking none too pleased! What does it mean? I knew we should have told them at the outset!"

"Oh, Louisa, do not refine too much upon it! Perhaps he is only getting her some refreshment. Peter cannot be so blind to Georgiana's beauty that he can fail to be attracted to her, can he?"

"I don't know. See, he is not getting her any refreshment, for he has now gone over to talk with Mr. Sterling, and that vicar, and that *governess!* What can he be thinking of? I cannot imagine! You must do something, Arabella! He's *your* son, after all! You were saying that he is so dutiful! What duty is he doing now, I ask you?"

"Shame on the boy! I will forbid all such behavior, in future. He should not associate himself with anyone of the lower classes."

"In all fairness, Arabella, Cousin Raymond is not precisely of the *lower* classes, however, is he?" pointed out

Lady Lacon. "Nor, in all probability, is that governess of theirs."

"It is their *income* that is *lower*—lower than ours! Their means are insufficient to allow them to live a life of gentility! *That* is enough to draw an indelible distinction between themselves and ourselves!"

"Quite right!" agreed Lady Lacon.

At approximately the same moment as these two ladies were pronouncing sentence upon Raymond Dulles and Miss Lydia Trenton, Sir Charles Stanton was sitting next to the diamond of the first water, Janet Carteret, as he twirled his quizzing glass, and surveyed the various social scenes playing out before them.

"Is it all not vastly amusing, Miss Carteret?" drawled Sir Charles. "I find it so, at any rate. What is your opinion?"

"I have none, for I do not precisely understand your meaning, Sir Charles," replied Miss Carteret.

Sir Charles let go of the black ribbon that held his quizzing-glass, took hold of the glass itself, and raised it to his eye. Slowly, he inspected the denizens of the ballroom, moving from left to right, taking in the whole scene, in its entirety. At the end of his inspection, he shook his head and laughed out loud.

"Here is the cream of London society spread out before us; it takes only an instant of observation to detect what is occurring. It is as if one were watching the tidal flow of the ocean: the unceasing play of human interaction. Over there, like an eddy in a tide-pool, one can see the small cluster of persons deep in conversation regarding how to suppress the latest scandal involving the Duke of Cumberland before it becomes general knowledge—which it already has, of course. To our left, one sees various persons involved with the ascension into society of Black Jack Ster-

ling's daughter—some who are her friends, some who are
her enemies, and some who are waiting to see how the
drama turns out before they decide whose side they are
on. Intersecting with these, are persons belonging to the
circle that surrounds our esteemed hostess, Lady Arabella
Gilbough, and whose own welfare is intimately connected
to shoring up the wealth and influence of that ancient
family."

"I am sorry to be so stupid, Sir Charles, but I still do
not understand your point."

"My point is that all across the room, similar dramas
are playing themselves out. Each player is consumed by
the play, and unaware of the greater perspective: that in
the long run, by the end of their lives, what consumes
them today will seem like child's play in the end, and in
their old age, they will rue the time and sensibility that they
wasted in holding things dear that are ultimately without
meaning."

Miss Carteret stopped fanning herself for a moment,
and began to look at Sir Charles with new eyes.

"Excuse me, Sir Charles, but those are strangely philosophical words coming from a man who is regarded as the
arbiter of fashion, and one who is said to take very seriously
the smallest details of dress and deportment."

"I never said *I* take such things seriously, my dear. You
must learn to know me better, for things—and men—are
not always what they seem. Simply because I am able to
tell the difference between a teal waistcoat and a hunter-
green one, it does not follow that I regard such an ability
as a sign of a superior nature. It is merely a natural capacity.
I call things as I see them—but, as to final judgments—
who's to say?"

Miss Carteret began to fan herself slowly, and pensively,
and then her mind seemed to change, and she inquired,

"By the by, I heard that Sir Rupert Fellowes lost a bundle to you, late last night, at cards. Is it true?"

"If you consider twenty thousand pounds a bundle of blunt, then, yes, he did indeed!"

"I am sorry to hear it," said Miss Carteret, with a pensive wave of her fan. "I quite like Miss Sterling."

"I was not sorry to win his money, but I did think it profligate of Sir Rupert to wager away a good deal of his betrothed's dowry—and to do so before he had even *wed* her!"

"Quite so," agreed Miss Carteret.

"Speaking of which, would you marry me, Miss Carteret?"

She thought for a moment, and then said, smiling, "I must decline, sir, as I always do—but I do not do so without regret, Sir Charles."

"I am sorry, as always, to hear you decline," said the arbiter of fashion. "May I ask again tomorrow?"

"As you wish, Sir Charles," said the divine Miss Carteret, gently.

"An I did not wish it, you may be sure that I would not have asked, my dear. I never make offers of marriage lightly."

11

The morning after the first night's ball at Cornell Castle, Lily wanted to let her mistress sleep just as late as possible, in order to preserve her good looks, but, as it turned out, Miss Sterling's sleep had to be interrupted when her father tiptoed into the room, needing to speak with her on a matter of some urgency.

"Lily? Is your mistress awake?" he whispered.

"No, Mr. Sterling, and she came to bed in the wee hours of the morning. It's best if you speak with her later, if you can."

"That's not possible, I'm afraid. Would you kindly show me in?"

Lily opened the door to the darkened bedroom, and pulled apart several drapes, just enough that Mr. Sterling could see to walk within.

He came over to his daughter's bed, and sat on it as lightly as he could; he leaned over toward Helen and pulled a stray lock of her gold hair away from her cheek, and touched her lightly, so as to awaken her as gently as possible.

"Helen? Helen?" he whispered. "Listen to me, will you? I must go to London to take care of some business, and I must leave right away, for my business is of the very greatest import. I am very sorry to leave you to do so, but it can't be helped. I trust you and Miss Trenton will be well looked after in my absence, and I will return just as soon as I can."

He planted a kiss on her cheek.

Helen was still very drowsy; she looked at her father quizzically, as if she could not quite make sense of his words.

"London?" she asked at last, yawning. "Why must you go back to London? I thought you had settled all your affairs in a way that would last the whole fortnight. Father: is something wrong?"

Mr. Sterling did not answer this question right away, but waited a moment, thinking. Then he said, "Do not be alarmed, Helen, and tell Miss Trenton not to worry, either, for I know how she can make a mountain out of a molehill. I simply need to find out some information, and it must be done on an urgent basis. If there is anything that you need to know, I will write you directly, express. Otherwise, I will return from town in just a few days."

"Father, I don't want you to go all alone. Let us all leave, together," argued Helen. "If you must go, I must go with you."

"John Snow is coming with me. Everything will be all right, you'll see. It will all be for the best."

"Take me with you, please!" Helen begged him. "I don't want to stay at Cornell Castle all by myself."

"Don't be such a goose, my dear! You're not staying here all by yourself—there is Miss Trenton. There is Lily."

"There is Sir Rupert," said Helen uncertainly.

"Of course, there is Sir Rupert. And you will be meeting more and more persons every day."

"I'm sorry, Father. I thought I might be of help to you."

"No, my dear, your place is here. I will be back as soon as I may. Go back to sleep, now. I'm sure there will be many pleasant things to do today—the weather is once again very fine."

Unable to argue more against his going, Helen acquiesced and returned to her deep dreamless sleep.

Miss Sterling was still fast asleep in her bedchamber when Lady Arabella finally called her son up to the Blue Sitting Room so they two might have a little chat. Mr. Gilbough was a little unhappy to be summoned up there, for he had had the good luck to come across Black Jack Sterling in the front hall, just as he was about to leave for London. After exchanging the requisite pleasantries, he had sought Mr. Sterling's approval for the sketch he had wanted to make of Helen. He had been honest enough to explain that Sir Rupert was dead set against his doing so, but Black Jack Sterling seemed to look at the matter in an entirely different light: he had said he looked forward to having her portrait done, for himself. Peter Gilbough had swiftly received the permission he sought, and was now anxious to seek out his subject and begin to work.

Lady Arabella motioned him to a seat, and then kept silent, wondering how best to approach such a tender topic as marriage in a way that would be best received by Peter. She began speaking with careful deliberation, saying, "In a few days time you will celebrate the attainment of your majority, and the final papers will be signed which will turn over Cornell Castle from my guardianship, and into your hands alone. This is a great gift, as well as a great responsibility, but I know it is one for which you are ready, and certainly which your dear Father wished for you, for he knew you loved the Castle as much as he did.''

At the mention of his father, Peter's face turned solemn.

''Your dear father died so suddenly, and you yourself left for the Continent so quickly that there were many important issues that remain unresolved. You may not be aware that your father had definite desires when it came to the disposal of this property.''

''I shall see that they are carried out, at once!'' said Peter reassuringly. ''What were they, Mother?''

''Well, there is the matter of the annuity for Old Mellon. During my guardianship of the estate, I saw to it that he received it, but that task will now fall to you.''

''Consider it done,'' he said.

''As to the estate itself, he wished it transmitted to you intact, and unentailed, which has been done, but with the provision that, in the next generation, the Castle estate must remain intact and unentailed, and transmitted whole. Otherwise, if this cannot be done, you are to sell off whatever land is needed for debts, and then entail it in favor of your grandchild.''

''I shall do just as he wished, of course.''

''Then there is the matter of the Locksley estate, which marches with ours. For the good of that estate and of ours, to increase their value, he very specifically asked that you should offer for the Locksley daughter, since it is she who will inherit that land.''

''Good God!'' cried Peter.

''This means, naturally enough, that it was your father's dearest wish that you should offer for Lady Georgiana Locksley, in order that the two estates be united, and the earldom, rather than dying out, might perhaps be continued upon the Gilbough line. I had not mentioned this before,'' she said, hiding a sly look, ''Thinking that your affections might, during your time on the Continent, have become otherwise engaged, but I think that is not the case. I have not heard you speak of any female with particular affection, nor have I seen you show any girl any particular distinguishing regard. Am I wrong?''

Mr. Peter Gilbough thought for just a moment of the lovely Miss Sterling; he then thought of the baronet to whom she was betrothed, and glumly confessed, ''No. There is no one.''

Lady Arabella Gilbough, terribly relieved at this admission, brightened at once, and asked, cheerily, ''Well, then! Shall we consider that whole matter settled?''

It was such a very fine English morning, and the country-side was so splendid and green that Lady Lacon was up very early to enjoy it. She took a long walk, taking the route that went all along the outside of the Park, and when she returned she felt much better for having had the exercise.

She felt well enough, in fact, to tackle a task she had been putting off: that of letting her goddaughter, Lady Georgiana Locksley, know just how things stood. However complaisant a personality Peter Gilbough might have, Lady Lacon knew that Georgiana was not so complaisant, and would require entirely different handling in order to make her see quickly where her best interests lay.

When her ladyship reached the formal gardens, she called for a footman, and sent him to find Lady Georgiana, and bring her down to meet her.

This was done, and no more than a half hour later Georgiana appeared, looking very fetching in a new bonnet, and wondering why she had been summoned.

''Sit down, my dear,'' said Lady Lacon, indicating a space on the marble bench just next to her. ''It is time we had a little talk.

''As you know, I loved your mother dearly, and when

she became so ill, it was my pleasure to assure her that, after her death, I would always look after you, and, when the time came, to see you suitably settled, just as she would have."

"And you have," said Lady Georgiana, much moved, "And I am forever grateful."

"When you were eighteen I had the great pleasure of sponsoring your come-out and your presentation at Court, and of watching you become a captivating beauty, one of the most admired girls in London.

"You are now nearing twenty, and have been out for two whole Seasons. It is really time for you to be settled down for good. Tell me truthfully, Georgiana—in the time you have been out, have you received any offers of marriage, whatsoever?"

"No," she admitted ruefully.

"There were no offers made to you that you turned down out of hand, without my knowledge?"

"No," she said again. "Not one."

"All right. Is there any gentleman for whom you feel a particular affection, attachment, or affinity?"

She hesitated, finally answering, "There was Sir Rupert, but . . ."

"But in the end, he offered for another."

Mortified, Lady Georgiana nodded.

"It happens. Do not refine too much upon it. Sir Rupert is a practical man, and had to make a practical judgment. I would not take his decision in a personal way."

"Whatever do you mean, Aunt Louisa? I am not a penniless girl! Why should he not have been able to offer for me rather than that Sterling girl?"

"Yes, I thought perhaps you were not informed as to how things stood. Here it is, Georgiana: although, since no other heirs than you remain, you are the sole heiress of Locksley Park, the estate is completely tied up for your issue. There is enough rent coming in to run the place, but there is nothing extra, nor can any land be sold off, even if needed. So, while you appear to be a great heiress, and indeed are widely regarded as such, you in fact will bring no real money, no cash, to your marriage whatsoever.''

"What about Mother? I thought she brought some money of her own when she married Father? Isn't that mine? Isn't that safely tied up in funds?''

"It would have been yours, and should have been, but—you see, when your father died, your mother was sent into such low spirits that began to behave in sad, imprudent ways. The money that had been at her disposal was hers entirely, and she no longer had your father around to advise her or to raise her spirits. She ran through that money in a matter of months.''

"But how?''

"Cards. She was completely besotted with gambling on cards, and for very high stakes, indeed. No one could stop her, and many people tried.''

"I had no idea!'' cried Lady Georgiana.

"By the time she realized all the harm that she had done, and in particular, what she had done to what would have been your marital portion, it was too late. It was all gone. In order to prevent an utter scandal, some gentlemen friends of hers got together and found a legal way for her to release the funds so she could pay the debts she owed, but then there was nothing left to pass on to you. I think it was at that time that her health began to deteriorate, from the shock of it all, and that was why it was so very important to her that I promised her I would take charge of you when you came of marriageable age, and see to your come-out, and make sure that you found a suitable husband, when the time came.''

"You are nearly twenty, and it is time for you to settle

down, once and for all. I first gave you your head, and let you try to find a husband for yourself, but now it is time for me to fulfill my pledge to your mother. I have found a husband for you."

"You have? Who?"

"I have it all worked out with Lady Arabella Gilbough that her son Peter is to offer for you. Upon his majority, he becomes, as you must know, extremely well off, and I can tell you, it is always a great advantage to have married a man of substance. He inherits the whole of Cornell Castle, unencumbered by debt, filled with valuable treasures, an estate whose lands and cottages have been excellently well cared-for.

"You would bring to a marriage with Peter Gilbough benefits of which only he can take advantage. There are so many benefits to joining the Locksley land with that of Cornell Castle—indeed, I cannot think of another gentleman who is in a similar position to regard Gordon Park as an advantage, rather than as a disadvantage. Only a near neighbor could regard them in that light, and besides, he has the funds and the knowledge to be able to make whatever repairs are needed and return the property to a profitable basis.

"Peter Gilbough will enjoy sufficient income that you will be able to make a career as a hostess, much as I have done, for I am sure he will be liberal in his allowances, for that is his nature. He is kind, he is charming, he is polite. He will make you an absolutely unexceptionable husband, for he has no vices—or, at least, none that I know of. If I were you, I would be thrilled at my good fortune."

"And what does Peter Gilbough think of this?"

Lady Lacon walked over to the mantelpiece, and consulted the French clock. She said, "I assume his mother is informing Mr. Gilbough even as we speak. Arabella expects he will go along with it, if only for his father's sake."

"An arranged marriage! I had not thought it would come down to that!"

"You mustn't regard it in the light of a failing, you know. Arabella's marriage was arranged by the two families involved, as was my own, and, I would assume, that of your own parents. It is very much the usual thing among great families—you are surely aware of this! In fact, it is the most common way for two persons to unite. This romantical way of conducting weddings often makes for fickle and unstable unions, and is of very recent fashion."

"It is a bit of a shock, Aunt Louisa."

"Of course it is," said Lady Lacon consolingly, "But you will get used to it."

There was a gazebo near the west pond, quaintly covered in English ivy, where Lady Arabella often had a nuncheon served, and today, because the weather was so very fine, she had invited her dear friend Lady Lacon to partake of the nuncheon with her. They had just finished eating, and the servants had just cleared the dishes and silver away, and the two ladies took some time to relax together, and enjoy the serenity of the countryside.

"Isn't that the Captain Prendergast and Miss Peterson, walking arm in arm down the lane? My eyes are become short-sighted now, but I think it is! I wonder if her parents know?" said Lady Lacon. "They won't like it!"

"Oh, young love! I should so like to be young again!" sighed Lady Arabella. "Wouldn't that be wonderful?"

"I don't know that it would," replied her friend. "I feel happy to be well settled, and to have so comparatively few burdens."

"That's not what I mean, Louisa! I mean it would be

Isobel Linton

lovely to be once again in the summer of one's life, with all the possibilities spread out before one, before all one's choices have been made, and before what may happen, has happened," Lady Arabella said wistfully. "I would like to do it all over again—my Season in London, dancing all night, trying to attract the attention of a gentleman I found compatible. You know, I never really got on that well with Edward, but my parents thought it really a very good match, and promoted it strongly, so what could I do? In all the outward ways, it was a good match: even though I was the daughter of an earl, and Edward Gilbough only a commoner, he had inherited such extensive estates, and had such an excellent income, free and clear, and he came from such a very old family, it seemed very suitable.

"After all, the estate is still very superior. The Castle is a wonderful place, and I was certainly always happy to live here. It has made me the hostess I am today. I have always had the money to do just as I wished, which is always very pleasant.

"But my marriage was not what one could call happy. Edward was so different from me, and so different from any of my friends: he was always sitting with his nose in a book, or up in that horrid room of his, fooling around with his paints and canvases, and smelling of that horrid turpentine. I don't like going about town without a man, and he wasn't the man to do it—he was always so reticent and so bookish! Not a shadow of *panache* about him! He never wanted to go anywhere!"

"In short, your husband was very like your son Peter," pointed out Lady Lacon.

"True! When his father died, I urged him to spend much time abroad so it would get all this nonsense out of his system, once and for all. I thought if I humored him, he would grow out of it. I didn't see him for three years, and I hoped that by now, he might have changed.

"Peter seems to have little or no taste for assuming his rightful position in society, and I am very disappointed by that."

"Do you think that Georgiana will be able to change his ways?" asked Lady Lacon.

"No, I do not. I think they will enjoy precisely the same marriage as his father and I did. A civilized marriage, one which offers the benefits of wealth and privilege, a legal union, but one which unites neither their hearts nor their souls," replied Lady Arabella pensively. "A great pity, but such is the way of the world."

"Too true, too true," sighed Lady Lacon.

12

The omnipresent summer buzz of crickets at dawn had prophesied that the day was to be very warm and very fair. The morning weather proved this to be true, and the afternoon heat would add to the day a compelling lushness.

It was a day that cried out for some kind of pleasant outdoor social recreation, and this was speedily accomplished by the consummate ton hostess, Lady Arabella Gilbough. It must have been soon after her nuncheon that she had the notion to declare that the afternoon should be devoted to a contest involving the art of landscape painting and sketching—solely on an amateur level, of course, as befitted the high stations of her various guests.

In a great bustle and commotion, she sent the Castle servants scurrying around to find all the necessary equipment, the chairs and the sketching paper and the paints and so forth. There were also blankets to be located, and willow hampers packed with silver and china and glasses and foods and napery, all in order to make this event occur in the sumptuous manner characteristic of Cornell Castle house parties.

Several personal servants had volunteered to help the Castle servants: among them, Lily Beeton and Jeffers Pym. Sir Charles Stanton had abruptly announced that he had no need of Pym that afternoon, and could probably tie his tie better by himself. Though stung by this insult, Pym had been enthusiastic about having been given leave to go, for his eye had been well and truly taken in by Miss Sterling's lovely Lily, and his master was always sympathetic in matters of the heart.

All the gentlemen and ladies who had been invited to the house-party were invited to join in the fun of painting-party: virtually all the ladies accepted, but many gentlemen, such as Sir Rupert Fellowes, demurred, preferring to go out to ride, or to remain inside waiting for the newspapers to arrive from London.

Peter Gilbough, of course, eagerly consented to go, as did Raymond Dulles, the vicar, who liked to work in water-colors, although he did not pretend that his work possessed any merit whatsoever. Others, like young Captain Prendergast, came along to enjoy the hopeful chance of contact with a certain desirable young lady.

Sir Charles had declared that the summer heat would likely wilt his cravat, so cried off and remained in seclusion at the Castle, although Miss Carteret, who was known for her fine work in water-colors, accepted with great enthusiasm. There were a number of young ladies who had agreed to join the party; these included Miss Peterson, Lady Georgiana Locksley, and Lady Agatha Winslow, who were not noted for their skill with brush, pen, or charcoal, and who accepted the invitation to the gathering, but declined to paint or sketch. They wore their very best new bonnets and walking-dresses, and put up their parasols, and went out seeking to partake of both the fresh, clean summer air and enjoy an excellent opportunity to attract admiration for their faces and figures.

Lady Arabella and Lady Lacon, and their good friends the Duchess of Minister and Mrs. Hicks-Aubrey, all went along, mainly in order to have an occasion which would serve to allow them to discuss the various burning issues of the day: whether the Duke of Cumberland's scandal was getting better or getting worse, whether Sir Charles Stanton would forever remain a bachelor, whether keeping a large staff was really worth the trouble and tribulation it universally entailed, and to decide upon which was the best home remedy for gout.

Miss Trenton accompanied Miss Helen Sterling on the outing: she had said that in Sir Rupert's absence, and with the presence of so many other guests, her companionship was an absolute necessity. Both ladies had chosen to work their sketches in the challenging medium of charcoal on paper. Of the two, Miss Trenton was the more technically accomplished, while Miss Sterling's work showed a kind of natural vivacity that was most pleasing to the eye; they were looking forward very much to this opportunity to exercise their skills.

Lady Arabella had chosen for the event a spot that was highly picturesque: it was not more than twenty minutes' walk from the Castle itself, and was reached by a winding path that traversed first the formal gardens, then the wide front lawns that gave out onto a more naturalized landscape.

The party settled on the side of a grass-covered hill lightly shaded by a willow tree; the hill sloped gently down to the wide blue lake that had tall rushes on one side of the shore, and wildflowers growing in tall grass toward the other side. There was a pair of swans in the lake, and the lake's color, due to the calmness of the wind, perfectly reflected the wonderful blue of the sky.

The walk to their destination being an excuse for both exercise and conversation; the ladies strolled along happily, arm in arm, chatting about this and that. Some few couples of ladies and gentleman were walking along, among them Captain Prendergast and Miss Peterson, and Mr. and Mrs. Hicks-Aubrey. The vicar had actually offered his arm to Miss Trenton, but, thinking it would be putting herself forward unsuitably, she had politely declined his offer.

Peter Gilbough, albeit reluctantly, had given his arm to Lady Georgiana, and those two, each one now having been informed as to what was expected of them, were trying to go about the awkward business of coming to know one another.

Mr. Gilbough came straightaway to the main point, admitting to the young lady that his mother and Lady Lacon had put the two of them in a very difficult position indeed. Lady Georgiana had received this admission with relief, for it was quite impossible for her to pretend an affection for Peter Gilbough which did not exist: how could it? They had hardly said more than a sentence to one another in their lives.

"Really, Lady Georgiana," he said, "I hardly know where to begin or how to proceed. I had entertained no real thought of marriage, I must admit, until my mother told me it was expected of me, and that my father had expected me to marry you! It came as a bit of a shock, as I'm sure it did to you. *That* is the unvarnished truth!"

"Thank you for your candor," said Lady Georgiana, her heart sinking. "I believe the best we can do is to try to spend some time in each other's company, and in that way we may determine if we—if we should suit."

Mr. Gilbough nodded his agreement, and then grew silent.

He then decided that a discussion of the weather would

be in order, and he attempted to introduce this topic; however, it turned out that Lady Georgiana held no very strong opinions on this subject, so it had to be discarded. Mr. Gilbough tried another idea, that of traveling on the Continent, but Lady Georgiana seemed to be entirely uninterested in this subject as well, only asking questions of him which had to do with what fabrics might be obtained in which European cities, and at what prices, with regard to which Mr. Gilbough knew absolutely nothing and cared less.

In this manner, six or seven subjects were introduced, and then abandoned. By the time the couple reached the spot where everyone was to draw, both parties to the conversation had given up hope of holding one, and had lapsed into an awkward silence.

Mr. Gilbough said a polite farewell to Lady Georgiana, chose the spot where he would begin painting, and obtained from a footman his easel, seat, paint-box and paint-brushes, and began putting everything in order, thinking to himself, *Mother has placed me in the most damnable position! I have nothing in common with Georgiana Locksley, whatsoever! I cannot even contrive to hold a conversation with her! If Father really intended for me to wed this girl, why did he not mention it while he was alive?*

There was, however, no way to answer this question, and so Mr. Gilbough tried to leave off thinking about it, and instead set about putting his mind to work on painting.

The servants who had gone on ahead earlier had spread out over the grass many blankets and cushions, making it more for those guests who wished merely to observe and to chat to one another. Lady Georgiana, having given up, for the moment, trying to maintain polite conversation with the man her godmother had selected as her husband, found a place near Lady Lacon, and sat herself down next to her.

She said, "Aunt Louisa, I can't marry Peter Gilbough!"

"Whyever not?" replied her ladyship.

"We walked together all the way from the Castle, and neither one of us could sustain a conversation for more than a minute!" cried Lady Georgiana.

"What has that to say to anything? I'm sure I never even *tried* to do such a thing with Lord Lacon! You two don't have to become bosom-bows, you know; all you have to do is live in the same house! Well, at least, for *part* of the year, it is expected. You can live in town, if you like, and he can remain in the country," pointed out her godmother. "Or, you can live on one side of the Castle, and he on the other. You need never see him at all, save for the very occasional— um, nocturnal—visitation? If you see what I mean. A few minutes, here and there. Not often. Easy to put up with. Done it myself, after all. Don't look so glum, my dear! After all, you're going to be extremely rich! *That's* what a girl like you should be thinking of!"

Lady Georgiana Locksley, who had a practiced taste for extravagance, tried to console herself with this thought.

After all the artists had been hard at work for more than an hour, a committee of observers spontaneously formed, having the intention of going round from person to person, admiring their works. Lady Georgiana, Miss Peterson and Captain Prendergast, Lady Agatha Winslow, Mrs. Hicks-Aubrey, and Mrs. Partridge, Miss Carteret's companion, formed the core of this group.

The first to be visited was Miss Janet Carteret: her water-color of the swans on the lake was universally pronounced to be of the finest possible quality. Captain Prendergast said he had never seen any woman so fluent with a brush; Mrs. Hicks-Aubrey said that even her own granddaughter could not have captured the place so well; Lady Georgiana

was absolutely effusive in her compliments, saying it was
by far the best picture she had ever seen, that it was a truly
accomplished piece of work, and that she was sure it was
better than anything that was on display at the Royal Exhibition in London, if she had ever seen the Royal Exhibition,
which unfortunately she had *not*. Mrs. Partridge, who
could not have been said to be objective, merely tittered.

Mr. Raymond Dulles was the next, and his watercolor
of the lake was, alas, not so very well received. Mrs. Hicks
Aubrey thought it lacked artistry; Lady Agatha damned it
with faint praise saying that it was well enough, all things
considered. The rest of the party merely nodded. Mr. Dulles was a bit taken aback, but if his feelings were hurt, he
hid them well. He put down his brushes at once, and
decided to join the artistic committee.

Miss Trenton's charcoal sketch suffered a similar fate,
upon group inspection. It was said by one onlooker to be
too timid; another called into question the composition.
Miss Peterson said it was really quite nice, but not to her
taste, and Captain Prendergast agreed with her, as, indeed,
he always did. Mr. Dulles, however, told her after the others
had gone on, in a private whisper that he thought she had
done excellently well.

Miss Sterling had chosen a spot that was well away from
the generality of the group, so she was spared the pain of
any inspection, but Mr. Gilbough was not: the small throng
gathered around him and watched him work for some
time, in silence.

Peter Gilbough had previously begun an oil sketch of
the scene, and it was this preliminary sketch which he had
brought out, in order to add to it. He had used an old
Italian technique for achieving the coloration characteristic of natural light, and it gave his work a depth that was
unparalleled.

Although he was working quite quickly, he was also able

to achieve some very subtle effects: the picturesque scene was at once natural-looking, and yet its effect on the observer had somehow been heightened by the way he composed the picture. He was beginning to capture very well the way the land sloped into the curve of the water, and the shimmering summer light on the lake.

He was making a portrait of the landscape, using the varying greens of the grasses and trees, and the white of the graceful swans to reproduce a summer day filled with peace and serenity.

The vicar was the first to break the silence: he pronounced it a masterful work, truly masterful!

Everyone else hung back a bit, but it was Mrs. Hicks-Aubrey who put words to what the group was feeling. Peter Gilbough's work was not only good—it was *too* good!

"We are not trying to imitate the works of professionals, Mr. Gilbough. We are attempting to work as *amateurs,* in the literal sense; we are wanting to be lovers of art! While the quality of your work is of course excellent, I think it is *because* of that, rather excessive!"

Lady Georgiana, who at first had admired the work of Mr. Gilbough, changed her opinion entirely when she heard this. Mr. Gilbough's work was too, well, too professional, just as Mrs. Hicks-Aubrey had said. It was not a suitable thing for a gentleman to do: in fact, it was an embarrassment. *That* was the gentleman they had picked out for her—an embarrassment!

In this way began a slow, smoldering resentment, one which would soon burst into flame.

Miss Sterling's easel had been set up at a slight distance from the rest, down a gentle slope. Cornell Castle could just barely be spied in the background, towering over the landscape. In the foreground was a weeping willow tree whose trunk leaned out over the lake: it was the willow's gently curved branches that she had particularly wished to try to capture in a sketch.

Lady Georgiana did not herself know what possessed her to seek out Miss Sterling; in some part of herself she might actually have thought that, by paying her attention, she was trying to be polite to her and make amends for their earlier meetings.

But Lady Georgiana's mood was not polite; inwardly, she was seething at the unfairness of life. She was angry at being married off to a man who, she was beginning to learn, was nothing but a rich bore; she was angry that the only man for whom she had conceived a tendre during the season, Sir Rupert Fellowes, had passed her over, and offered for a cit's daughter, who had the audacity to be not only a very substantial heiress—but more of one than herself! Worse than that, was that the Sterling chit was arguably prettier than she!

In such a mood as Lady Georgiana's these last two were crimes, indeed—crimes requiring swift and merciless punishment.

However, Lady Georgiana could hardly admit these unladylike motives to herself, and so, with her mind bent only on virtue, and with the conscious intention of wanting to be helpful, she made her way down the slope, and stood behind Miss Sterling, watching her intently as she sketched.

It must have been the fact that Lady Georgiana was standing much too close to her that began to make Miss Sterling feel uneasy, and then, when she continued to hover over her for a full five minutes, Helen became actually nervous, so much so that she went so far as to ask Lady

Georgiana if she would move back just a little, please, and out of her light.

"Oh, *don't* be like that, Miss Sterling! You must be acquiring that sensitive, artistic nature which makes everything so very difficult! Why, I'm not at all in your way! Do go on!" said Lady Georgiana lightly. "I insist upon it!"

Miss Sterling disagreed heartily, but she said nothing. She was soon aware that her hands were becoming tense, and that they were on the point of beginning to shake with cramping. She tried to ignore Lady Georgiana's critical presence, but her feeling of oppression was becoming worse and worse. Unfortunately, the slight trembling in her hands resulted in a fatal smudge to the sketch, and since she had been using an actual stick of artists' charcoal, her attempt to correct the smudge only spread it around farther, making the picture look very dark indeed.

"Oh, look, Miss Sterling! You have spoiled it entirely!" said Lady Georgiana, in a voice loud enough that the others could clearly hear what she was saying. "What a shame! Yes, the whole thing is ruined: your hand must have slipped. You really must begin again."

Helen Sterling flushed red at this, but made no comment, and made no attempt to put the picture aside and change her paper. She doggedly continued working at her sketch and it was perhaps that persistence that her ladyship found so annoying that it quite pushed her over the edge of civility.

"Excuse me," said Lady Georgiana, seeming to be all sympathy, "But that picture of yours is quite spoilt, don't you think? I really think you must begin again. Oh, dear— don't you *have* another sheet? Surely, of *all* people, *your* father must give you enough pin-money that you can afford to buy another sheet of paper!"

The arrogance of that girl! Helen thought to herself, fuming. *Just who does she think she is? She is just trying to bait me again, but I vow I won't give her the satisfaction of answering back.*

Lady Georgiana continued her loud appraisal at full tilt, undeterred by the look of rancor on Miss Sterling's face.

"Oh, Miss Sterling, do start over again, I beg you; you mustn't be shy about starting over. Admitting one's defects requires the admirable virtue of honesty—just ask the vicar, for he will certainly agree! Besides, I'm sure that Sir Rupert doesn't care a whit about your little accomplishments, one way or another. In fact, I am sure he does not even expect that you *have* any. Why *should* he have expected such things of you? After all," said Lady Georgiana in a confidential tone, "It is *not* as if you have had a very selective upbringing. On the other hand, *I* have had the benefit of very finest tutors, for my family, the Locksleys, being of the peerage, for many generations have been particular about the education of their young ladies. Consequently, I have studied extensively—on a purely *amateur* level, of course!—*both* drawing and painting, of course, and I assure you I am familiar with all the styles. So, don't feel daunted by the task of starting over, for I am very willing to help you to begin again!"

At this, Helen could not help but reply, defending herself as best she could, saying in a clipped voice, "In point of fact, Lady Georgiana, I do not require your kind offer of help, for I am tolerably familiar with the various styles myself. My companion, Miss Trenton, was used to be my governess, and she made me perfectly familiar with the basics of the art."

"Are you familiar with the basic styles, then? Oh, I suppose you *must* be! I do apologize! How silly of me! Of course, Miss Sterling! I'm sure your father bought you *all* the education and accomplishments that money can buy!"

"Education *is* a decided advantage," said Helen with some asperity, her patience at an end.

"Yes, it is," said Lady Georgiana loudly and triumphantly, "And so is money an advantage. *Particularly* when one lacks good breeding!"

13

It was the outside of enough! Everyone on the hillside must have heard Lady Georgiana's set-down, loud and clear! Tears stinging her checks, which were red with anger, Miss Sterling rose to her feet at once, and left the horrid Lady Georgiana behind her. She wanted nothing more to do with these people! She wished to run away from them all, to leave their stupid sphere of influence, and once and for all to get away, become free again, and get out of their wretched sight!

She ran past the gazebo, and past a stand of evergreens, into a shaded copse, where none of the party could see her, and she wept with mortification and anger. After some minutes, Miss Sterling composed herself again, and was about to decide what route she would take in order to return to the Castle, for she had no desire to see any of the persons who had come on the painting outing ever again!

* * *

At about the time of Lady Georgiana's attack, Mr. Gilbough had been very involved in his painting, so much so that he almost failed to see the white figure that dashed down the hill, and took a path leading past the gazebo.

It took a few moments before it registered on his consciousness that the figure had been fleeing in some kind of distress, that the figure was that of a young lady, and finally that the form of the young lady belonged to someone he knew and was fond of: Miss Helen Sterling.

Mr. Gilbough put down his brushes. He deliberately chose not to run away after her, for he knew that to be seen by that group to be rushing off after Miss Sterling could only cause more talk, and would be even the worse for the young lady's reputation.

So he allowed the minutes to run slowly by, and accomplished all the necessary tasks very slowly and deliberately. He wished to make it seem that he had merely tired of painting the lake, and that, having put away his easel and his paints, he was wandering off in search of another view of the landscape.

Taking a different route than the one that Miss Sterling had taken, he set out on the south lawn. He carried his folding chair and easel in one hand, and his paint box in another, and strolled away whistling jauntily, showing none of the deep concern he actually felt.

The roundabout path he had chosen meant it took him some minutes to reach Miss Sterling, who was sitting at the edge of the copse, quite out of the sight of the painting party. Her eyes were red-rimmed; she was wiping away tears with a handkerchief.

"Hullo Mr. Gilbough," she managed to say, with a wry smile. "You must have heard all of that, I suppose. How could one not hear it? She was speaking so loud, as if addressing all of England! I'm afraid you find me not in the best of spirits, as a result."

"I did not hear what she said to you, precisely," said Peter. "What has upset you so?"

"Nothing but the truth, I'm afraid, although she certainly did mean to be unkind to me. I don't know why she dislikes me so. Lady Georgiana seems to go out of her way to insult me at every opportunity."

"I should say that she is jealous of you," said Mr. Gilbough, sitting down next to her.

"Why should she be?" replied Miss Sterling, dabbing at her nose with a handkerchief. "Lady Georgiana has beauty, and wealth as well, and she is an earl's daughter. What have I done that she must deride me?"

"You have done nothing except become engaged to a gentleman who failed to offer for Georgiana, preferring you to her."

"I did not know!" cried Miss Sterling. "No wonder she dislikes me! I never meant to be her rival!"

"My mother told me the story only lately."

"That would explain a great deal," said Helen, trying to be kind.

"But it does not excuse her behavior."

"No, of course not. However, if she has feelings toward him . . ."

"I don't know that she does. I don't know that she has feelings toward anybody, save herself," he declared. "Oh, and by the by, did you know that my mother expects me to wed Lady Georgiana?"

Miss Sterling looked up at Mr. Gilbough with wide blue eyes, taken aback by this revelation. She had no call to feel disappointed by the news, but she was disappointed, in fact, terribly so. She tried her best to conceal her feeling of shock at this unpleasant surprise, for it was no business of hers, after all, who Mr. Gilbough married, was it?

"Oh, dear! I am sorry if I have spoken with disrespect of anyone you hold in esteem! It was very wrong of me to criticize her behavior! I am extremely sorry to have done so, and I beg your forgiveness!"

Mr. Gilbough began to laugh, which Miss Sterling found rather disconcerting.

"Have I said something wrong again?" she asked, not quite sure of what was going on.

"No, not at all! It would be quite sad, if it weren't so funny! My mother informed me just a few hours ago I am expected to offer for Lady Georgiana, toward whom I have no more tender feelings than I do toward that fir tree!" He hesitated a moment before adding, "And quite possibly less!"

Miss Sterling gave Mr. Gilbough a serious and sympathetic look, saying, "It must be some family arrangement, then, is it?"

"So it is. Mother said it was my father's doing, though I find that rather hard to believe. I don't think I ever heard my father say it was his dearest wish that the Locksley lands be joined with ours, but my mother insists that it is so, and was his dying wish! Which, as you may imagine, puts me in rather a difficult position," he said ruefully. "To put it mildly."

"Oh, dear! I don't know what to say!"

"Nor do I. The fact remains that if this marriage was my father's dearest wish, by my love for him, which is very great, I must consent, no matter what my own feelings."

"That seems like excessive filial piety."

"I'm sure, in my position, you would do the same."

Helen Sterling looked at him with a start, and then admitted, "Yes, you are right. Of course I would."

"But that is neither here nor there. What one cannot change, one must endure."

He thought for a moment, and then said in a brighter

tone, "Miss Sterling, let us turn this predicament to our advantage, shall we? Since I am happily provided with the tools I need, may I take this opportunity to sketch your portrait? I have wanted to do so for ever so long, and I have received your father's permission. I ran into him the day he left for London, and he said he would be pleased to have a portrait of you."

"Did he say so?" she asked, clapping her hands with childish delight. "Then, yes, please do so! But first, show me what you have been painting. I would so much like to see more of your work."

Very gratified, Mr. Gilbough brought out the still-wet painting very carefully from his paint box.

"I must be careful, for it takes such a long time to dry out thoroughly," he said, unveiling it. "My man will have my hide if I get oil paint on this coat."

Miss Sterling looked at the painting for a very long time. She recognized at once the view of the lake and the Castle he had chosen to portray: the lake's sky-blue, still waters, the summer clouds scudding overhead, a general feeling of serenity and summer ease.

She pronounced, "You are a very gifted painter, Mr. Gilbough, and you should not be hiding your genius."

"Some talent I may possess, but genius I do not," he sighed. "I only wish I did."

"I think genius is more a matter of application than inspiration," she said. "As long as you take your painting seriously, which I am persuaded that you do, your work will develop of its own accord."

"I may take it seriously, Miss Sterling, but my family does not, as you must be aware. As for the ton, perhaps you heard the harsh judgment Mrs. Hicks-Aubrey placed upon my work just this afternoon."

"Why let that deter you? She is just an ignorant woman, however high-born she may be. You have independent means, as I am given to understand, and therefore, you should be able to do just as you like with your time and occupations. In that, you must count yourself fortunate."

"I do, of course. With that in mind, since we are, at present, alone and unobserved, would you be kind enough to sit still, and let me sketch you?"

"If you like, Mr. Gilbough," said Miss Sterling. "I will do so, certainly."

Lady Georgiana returned to the group slightly flushed from the exertion of insult, but looking otherwise perfectly composed. She said nothing, but smiled in a very self-satisfied way, and chose a spot next to her godmother to sit down.

Miss Janet Carteret stopped her watercolor painting long enough to ask Lady Georgiana what had happened between herself and Miss Sterling. Miss Carteret told Lady Georgiana that she had heard voices raised, but had been unable to make out precisely what had been said.

"It seemed as if Miss Sterling was extremely perturbed by something," remarked Miss Carteret. "What was it precisely that you said to her, may I ask?"

Lady Georgiana just tossed it off with another of her smiles, saying, "Oh, that? It was the merest nothing! I'm afraid I simply gave Miss Sterling a criticism of her painting with which she did not agree."

Miss Carteret looked skeptical at this account, exchanged a knowing glance with Miss Trenton, and dropped the subject.

Miss Trenton, on the other hand, knew that something untoward had occurred, but was not really in a position to act upon it. She tried to make light of it, by saying, "Helen is a very good girl. I'm sure she wouldn't take anything you said amiss."

Lady Lacon was not moved by this account, and made Lady Georgiana come to her side, so she could speak to her in private. She snapped, "What was that all about, Georgiana?"

"I gave the little Sterling girl a little set-down!" replied her goddaughter with a self-satisfied smile. "She richly deserved it."

"What did you say?"

"Oh, I reminded her of her origins," she said with a smile.

"What can you be thinking of, girl?"

Lady Georgiana, for the first time, looked somewhat taken aback, and said, "Do you really think I oughtn't to have done so?"

"Insulting the girl who is as good as Sir Rupert Fellowes's wife can hardly add to your consequence, my dear. In fact, it makes you look like—well, like a spiteful cat!"

Her brow clouded. "Oh. I hadn't thought of it that way. I thought I was merely depressing her pretensions."

"You foolish, heedless, headstrong girl! You will wind up lowering your own reputation, not lowering hers, you know. Did you see just now how Miss Carteret looked at you? She did so with no great approval, I can tell you."

"Oh," she replied blankly. "That's not good."

"And what about Peter Gilbough?"

"What about him?" she asked crossly.

"Have you not noticed that Mr. Gilbough has shown an obvious preference for Miss Sterling, ever since they met? You cannot recommend yourself to your future husband by insulting ladies whom he favors."

"Why should I care what he thinks?"

Lady Lacon's face flushed with exasperation. "Really, Georgiana, you can be quite thick sometimes. You need to care what he thinks, or otherwise he won't marry you. He doesn't have to, after all. You really mustn't treat him as if he were one of your lapdogs, however complaisant he may seem. If he takes you in dislike, you may just wind up on the shelf forever, living in run down Locksley Hall, without means to repair it, or means to live on, as the laughingstock of the neighborhood.''

She rose and took a turn around the room, uncertain as to what to say next, or how to convince this stubborn girl of the importance of following her strictures. Finally, Lady Lacon said, ''I have explained your situation very precisely. Your dowry is so small as to be nonexistent; you have no other suitors hanging round you. The marriage to Peter Gilbough is good graces, so he won't *mind* marrying you, you silly goose! You should be trying to make yourself attractive to him, not insulting his friends!''

''Yes, Aunt Louisa,'' she said, chastened. ''I got carried away. I do see what you mean.''

Sketching Miss Sterling turned out to be rather an interesting artistic process, for Mr. Gilbough discovered to his surprise that the more he sketched the girl's countenance, the more he found to admire in her, and that appreciation did not merely extend toward admiration of her physical attributes, but to the beauty posed by her moral attributes as well.

In her eyes he perceived not only their brilliant blue, but their innate kindness; in her cheeks he seemed to see the rosy blush of modesty; in her lips he found good nature and ready wit.

The qualities of her character were apparent to him in her visage and her comportment, and, as he worked, he became increasingly aware of their magnetic effect upon him; he began to feel a powerful protective tenderness toward her, and a strong wish to be able to act so as to spare her all pain.

At length, he said, "Miss Sterling, I feel I must let you know how very jealous I am of Sir Rupert."

"Why, sir?" she inquired, her cheeks coloring even more deeply.

"I am jealous of him because he met you before I did," he explained, as he continued his work. "I am jealous of him because he came to know you before I did. I am jealous of him because he offered for your hand, and was accepted by you. I am jealous of him because you are one of those rare women who combine outer beauty with inner beauty; fortunate is the man who can count such an exceptional woman as his own."

"Shameless flatterer!" declared Miss Sterling, who disguised her embarrassment by adopting a light, bantering tone. "I vow, you have been flattering me almost since the moment you met me, Mr. Gilbough!"

"Do try to sit still there, Miss Sterling, won't you?" said Peter, continuing to draw her likeness in bold, swift strokes. "On the contrary, almost since the very moment I met you, I have held you in extremely conspicuous esteem! To say the least . . ."

Miss Sterling became very self-conscious, and stared down at the ground, saying softly, "You really mustn't say such things to me, you know, Mr. Gilbough."

Mr. Peter Gilbough stopped for a moment, allowed himself the luxury of a long sigh, and then admitted in a serious tone, "Yes, Miss Sterling, I know perfectly well that I mustn't say such things to you. That's the most hellish part of this whole business!"

He took her hand for a moment, held it close, and then released it.

"Now, out of a sense of mutual honor, and propriety, Miss Sterling, upon that subject, I shall say no more."

14

By late afternoon, the painting party had quite broken up, and all the various ladies and gentlemen who had participated in it had severally or individually returned to the Castle, for it was close on five o'clock when the last of the party finally broke up, and all the guests at Cornell Castle returned to their respective rooms to rest for some time before they began the arduous task of dressing for dinner.

With a few obvious exceptions, the painting expedition was almost universally pronounced to have been a great success, for it had provided both an excess of entertainment and a decent amount of food for gossip—what more than that could one ask of any social outing?

In the eyes of those guests who had remained behind at the Castle, the expedition had also produced a number of pieces of very creditable art: Miss Trenton's charcoal sketch of a field flower, Miss Carteret's watercolor of the lake and its graceful white swans, Mr. Gilbough's remarkable oil painting of the landscape, including the lake and the sloping hill, and the pictures done by Miss Peterson and Raymond Dulles were all acknowledged to have been very well done, indeed. As some of these judgments were in sharp contrast to those made by the self-appointed committee that had critiqued the amateur artists earlier in the afternoon, diplomacy won the day when approbation was won by all.

Mr. Gilbough meanwhile, had escorted Miss Sterling back to the Castle, unobserved by anyone save for Lily, Jeffers Pym, and the ever-observant Miss Janet Carteret, none of whom thought it necessary to inform Sir Rupert Fellowes of this circumstance.

Dinner on that evening was, as always, a lengthy affair, but provided no particular difficulties for those persons with whom we are concerned. This was in part because our couples were separated due to the long orders of precedence which obtained at the Castle, as at most formal affairs. Even Lady Arabella Gilbough was unable to converse with her bosom-bow, Lady Lacon, for Lady Arabella had to attend to the Duke of Minster, her highest ranking guest on that day, who had acceded to his wife's request that he come into Buckinghamshire and bear her company for a while.

It was that sort of party, where every day, a few new guests arrived, and a few guests left, but the core of celebrants remained in general, very much the same. The guests in this way having become comfortable with one another, that very night after dinner, when music was called for, it was the divine Sir Charles Stanton who, though previously unknown to her, called on Helen Sterling to sing at the pianoforte while Miss Janet Carteret played.

Miss Carteret had noticed that some persons had been behaving with little civility toward Miss Sterling, due to her origins, and she had mentioned this privately to Sir Charles Stanton. Sir Charles, himself of good breeding but of modest means, was no snob, and felt disposed toward lending some of his countenance to Black Jack Sterling's daughter.

When Miss Carteret had explained the situation, Sir Charles was ready to help, saying, "If it will please you, my dear, I shall bring the girl into fashion!"

That is how Miss Sterling came to be invited to sing while accompanied by Miss Carteret, and in point of fact, Miss Sterling acquitted herself well. She sang "A Scots Country Air" in a sweet tremulous voice, one that wrung sympathy even from such a dragon as Lady Lacon, who tearfully admitted to Lady Arabella Gilbough that, in all her years, she had never heard such an affecting performance of that tune.

Lady Georgiana, naturally enough, remained unmoved by Miss Sterling's performance, while Mr. Gilbough's admiration for Miss Sterling merely increased in an even more poignant fashion. Peter watched Sir Rupert most carefully as Sir Rupert listened to his fiancée's singing, and Mr. Gilbough was unhappy to note no special fondness in Sir Rupert's eye nor any demeanor that could match his own feeling of pleasurable attachment.

It was at this very moment he began to suspect that the engagement between Sir Rupert and Helen must have been mainly a matter of business, rather than an engagement of the heart, and he began heartily to resent both Sir Rupert and Black Jack Sterling, whom he blamed for the whole affair.

As her gentle soprano tones wafted through the music room, he thought to himself with regret, *If only I had the good fortune to meet Helen earlier! If only I had had the chance to try for her, surely I would have made a better partner than Fellowes!*

* * *

Polite applause greeted the performers once again, but Miss Carteret and Miss Sterling declined to continue, offering their places at the instrument to other young ladies of talent, such as Miss Idona Peterson.

Sir Charles Stanton came over to the pianoforte, and complimented Miss Carteret on her deft playing, and complimented Miss Sterling on the easy sweetness of her voice.

"You both sounded charmingly," he said with enthusiasm, "I wish we had known more of your talents earlier on, Miss Sterling. You must not keep your light under a bushel, in future."

It was a fact of London society that merely to be spoken to by the arbiter of fashion was enough to grant one high social success, whereas to receive from him an accolade or a personal compliment assured one of entrance to heaven itself. In fact, the great Beau Brummell used to try to repay his huge gaming debts merely by giving public attention to his creditors.

To be singled out for approbation, in a setting as select as that at Cornell Castle as Sir Charles was doing on behalf of Miss Sterling, was to cause questions about her lineage and the source of her father's wealth to be consigned forever to oblivion.

From that night, Miss Sterling's social success was assured, and sealed. From that moment on, barring major scandal, not a word of censure would be permitted. Even Lady Georgiana, much as she disliked it, would have to hold her tongue, for to go against the strictures that had been laid down would be as detrimental to her own social standing as if she had insulted one of the patronesses of Almack's to her face.

After she finished enjoying a lengthy, animated conversation with Miss Carteret and Sir Charles Stanton, Helen returned to her companion Miss Trenton, whose excitement at this development of events could not be denied.

"My dear, it is greater than all things! You are made, at last! I need worry for you no longer!" cried out Miss Trenton.

"Sir Charles only complimented me on my singing, Miss Trenton. Surely it cannot signify so much."

"But it does, my dear, it does! You are fully accepted now! Between this, and your marriage, nothing shall ever harm you, my dear!"

"I had not supposed that it would," said Miss Sterling, warily. "I am not at all sure that I like so much attention. I have done nothing to warrant it, I know."

This subject might have been debated further, but at that moment, Sir Rupert Fellowes came up to them, greeting them warmly, and pressing his fiancee's hand to his lips.

"You look lovely as ever tonight, my dear. May I congratulate you on your conquest of Sir Charles Stanton? It seems quite complete. I cannot tell you how very proud of you I am at this moment. You have exceeded all my expectations!" he said, beaming.

Unaccountably, this shower of compliments made Helen Sterling really a little annoyed, rather than gratified. As a person, she found Sir Charles genuinely charming, and was certainly pleased to have made a friend of him and Miss Carteret; however, there was a distinct toad-eating quality that characterized his vast retinue and which she found nauseating. Just as bad was the reflected glory, in which Sir Rupert and the retinue were apparently happy to bask, which seemed to Miss Sterling to be a worthless thing.

Artifice or not, toad-eating or not, once the ton saw that Sir Charles had not merely accepted her, but seemed to approve of her, it was as if in a fairy tale: she had turned from Cinderella into a princess.

In merely the half hour after her warm conversation with Sir Charles, following her performance *a deux* with Miss Carteret, a veritable receiving line formed in front of Miss Helen Sterling, as the various members of the ton who had not already acknowledged her or been introduced to her, queued up to do so.

One by one the high-born came by to pay Miss Sterling their respects.

It was even worse, she thought, than it had been the night after her engagement had been announced in the *Gazette,* for while becoming betrothed to Sir Rupert Fellowes was an important achievement, becoming an intimate of Sir Charles Stanton meant that she was now top of the trees.

Lady Arabella Gilbough and Lady Lacon came by and kissed her warmly on each cheek, pronouncing her to be very charming, and having a most pleasing natural talent at singing; they said they hoped they would be able to enjoy her voice for many seasons to come.

Lady Farlow sought her out, and tried to engage her in a long, rambling conversation about her own study of singing when she was in the schoolroom, and reminiscences of her performances, and which Miss Sterling tried to shorten as civilly as possible.

The Duchess of Minster signaled Helen to come to her, and her grace kissed her on both cheeks, and told her she and dear Rupert really *must* come by Hallet House at Christmas-time, and that she might even bring that father of hers. She also said, with a sly look, that she looked forward to introducing Miss Sterling to Sally Jersey at Almack's next season.

Lady Georgiana and Lady Agatha did not come by, and were notorious by their absence, for they were furious that

Miss Sterling's star was on the ascendant, and had no notion of adding to her consequence.

Mrs. Partridge did not come by to chat with Miss Sterling, but sought out Miss Trenton, and spoke with her just as kindly as one might wish. Raymond Dulles first came by to speak with Miss Sterling, and then to speak with Miss Trenton, giving them both effusive congratulations.

Mrs. Hicks-Aubrey, after completing the circuit of kisses and congratulations returned to where the Duchess of Minster was sitting to say to her grace, "To marry a baronet is very good; to charm the life out of Sir Charles Stanton is even better. Now, it will require a great scandal indeed to injure Miss Sterling's ranking amongst the Upper Ten Thousand!"

Peter Gilbough made his way through her crowd of admirers, and attracted Miss Sterling's attention at once.

"How nice to see you! I feel quite overwhelmed—there is such a crush of persons around me. All of a sudden I seem to have become the very soul of popularity," said Helen.

"That is because you have received the divine *imprimatur* of the arbiter of fashion," he pointed out. "Would you care to dance? There must be more space on the dance floor than off. I think you will find it a relief."

"Yes, I'd love to," said Miss Sterling.

They went through the completion of the various figures of the dance, and both were aware of their mutual pleasure in each other's presence.

Just as the dance was coming to an end, Mr. Gilbough remarked that, based on the sketch he made of her during the painting outing, he had begun to paint a portrait in oil of her, for her father, at his wish.

"Perhaps some time, when it is convenient to you, you might sit for me again, so that I may improve the piece?" he asked. "I should like to make sure that I have gotten the colors of your complexion just right. For, although I now know your face from memory, memory alone can sometimes be misleading.''

"Yes, that would be fine. I am glad that Father asked for it, for perhaps Sir Rupert will not be so disapproving," she said. "I do wish Father were here. I miss him more than I can say. I feel quite alone.''

"You need not feel you are alone," said Mr. Gilbough solemnly. "Please know that, although we have not known each other very long, I hope I can count myself your true friend, always.''

Miss Sterling blushed and thanked him most deeply for his sentiments.

Sir Rupert Fellowes, watching the pair from across the ball-room, devoutly wished that his hostess' son would leave his heiress alone.

15

It was near on two in the morning before Helen Sterling was able to leave the dance floor, so besieged had she been with desirable dancing partners; even Sir Rupert had stood up with his fiancée twice. Knowing that Sir Rupert found dancing barely tolerable, Helen credited her recent ascension to her fiancé's change of heart.

All in all, the experience had been gratifying, but hardly satisfying. It was nice enough to know she had been accepted, but she did not really enjoy being idolized. It was pleasant enough to enjoy society's approbation, but the fickleness with which it was imposed made her uneasy, if not suspicious.

Lily, who had, as always, stayed up until her mistress came home, was busy undoing the tapes and ties of Helen's ball-gown, and all the while Miss Trenton was regaling Lily with long descriptive accounts of her mistress' social triumph.

"But, Miss Trenton! You need say nothing more! The

house is all abuzz with the news already. I met Jeffers Pym in the hallway, and—"

"And he stole a kiss from you, did he?" asked Helen with a laugh.

Lily blushed, and said, "You mustn't say such things, I'm sure. Jeffers told me that he himself heard Sir Charles Stanton pronounce you 'an excellent girl.' Jeffers said that the whole of the Castle is quite at your feet."

" 'Jeffers said this, Jeffers said that,' " said Helen, laughing. "Your dependence upon him is quite remarkable!"

"Do not tease me, Miss Helen," she pleaded, adding in a whisper, "We two, Jeffers and I, are deep in love!"

"Good luck, then," she replied. "Just don't let it generally known. I shouldn't like it if they sent you home, you know!"

"Nor would I, miss. I'll be careful."

When Lily had finished brushing her mistress's long blond hair for the requisite thirty minutes, then braided her hair for the night, and helped her into her night dress, and tucked her into bed, Helen did not drop off to sleep at once, even though she was tired and it was so very late.

She could not help but review the events of the day, and the thing that her mind kept mulling over, the thing that bothered her most, was Sir Rupert.

She could not quite decide how she felt about her *fiancé*.

She kept running hot and cold about him, and thought this very odd indeed.

One minute he would seem the perfect romantic, and the next minute he seemed was cold, and then overbearing. Sometimes he seemed so charming, and sometimes it seemed as if he were just treating her with no more care than he would his quill pen.

Is this the way everyone's fiancé behaves? Is this the

usual thing? Should I be worried, or not? Are my feelings
a concern, or not?

I wish my mother were alive, for she would guide me.

Miss Trenton is doing the best she can.

*Miss Trenton said that my father will be so pleased when he
learns I am doing so well in society. She said he is so very pleased
about my marriage. She said I should be over the moon about it,
but I told her tonight that I am not over the moon. I don't know
what I am.*

*Then she said, oh well, it's usual for a bride-to-be to have the
jitters.*

At any event, Father likes him. That's what's important.

"Stanton, how can you have such luck?" cried Sir
Rupert, throwing down his cards in disgust. "Is it sorcery,
for I swear, it must be! I have never seen a man whose
luck never seems to turn against him."

"Ah, my dear Fellowes, that is because I have severed
my emotions from my game. Once I was down a tidy
amount, say twenty thousand pounds or so, I would never
try to recoup my losses by playing against the same gentleman, the same game of cards, for the same amount of
money, as you have. The whole event cries out for the tide
of fortune once again to turn against one."

"Don't talk such gibberish, Stanton," said Sir Rupert
crossly. "Spare me your philosophizing, at least. I only owe
you money, not attention."

"Just so," he replied politely, signaling to the nearest
footman. "Would you care for claret?"

Sir Rupert Fellowes nodded, brooding, and scribbled
on a piece of paper, and passed it over to the arbiter of
fashion, saying, "My vowels, Stanton."

Sir Charles Stanton read over the paper very carefully,
then folded the paper and put it into his waistcoat pocket.

"When may I expect you to make them good?" he inquired very gently.

Sir Rupert glowered, and gave him an angry glance, saying, "I shall need a bit of time, I'm afraid. I shall have to make some . . . financial . . . arrangements."

"Of course," Sir Charles replied, draining his glass. He stacked the deck on the green baize table, and neatly pushed his chair in. He made his salutation to each of the gentlemen in the room, and left.

"Damn his luck!" said Sir Rupert. "How am I to pay him forty thousand pounds?"

Commencing in the early morning hours, a terrible thunderstorm raged on and on for what seemed like days; Helen Sterling lay in her bed, transfixed, listening to the ominous noise, and waiting for the rain to abate, but it never did.

By the time that Lily had rung down for some chocolate, the thunder and lightning had ceased, but the rain was pouring down incessantly; it would obviously be impossible to do anything other than remain safely inside until the weather cleared.

Helen had not yet dressed when there came a sharp knock on the door; her father's valet, Jack Snow, had just arrived from London, and had brought an urgent missive for Miss Sterling from her father.

Having exchanged a few hasty words with John Snow, ones which caused her color to change completely, Lily brought the letter in to her mistress on a silver salver, and then she hastily left the room, obviously discomposed. Miss Trenton was there in attendance as well, wrapped in a dressing-gown, and she waited impatiently as Helen tore apart the wafer, unfolded the letter, and scanned its contents.

She read the letter out loud.

> My dear Helen:
> I do not know quite how to tell you this, but I shall try my best to be brief and honest. Some events have occurred in Nottingham and abroad which have resulted in serious financial reverses for my firm. The simple fact is that these events have been of a disastrous nature, one from which I cannot think I will quickly—if ever—recover.
> I am more sorry for this than I can say.
> Please believe I remain your most affectionate
> Papa
>
> P.S. Share this sad news with Sir Rupert: you may show him this letter, as we cannot keep our situation secret for very long. Do not lose heart. I will come for you just as soon as I may."

"What does it mean?" cried Miss Trenton.

Helen Sterling replied, "I cannot say precisely. Something is terribly wrong."

"If I may say so, miss," interjected Lily, wringing her hands, "John Snow says it means your father's money is all gone. He says your father is ruined."

"Ruined?" said Miss Trenton, "Oh, no! How can that be?"

"John Snow spoke of Luddite rioters having burned down the cotton mills and factories in Nottingham, leaving not one stone standing. He said there was also the problem of some investments having come in badly—apparently your father had invested heavily in a ship, more heavily than anyone knew, and word has just come from abroad that the ship was lost in a storm and sunk. He said that, upon hearing of all these reverses, your father's other investors called in their debts suddenly, your father was forced to pay them off at once, and as a consequence has lost his fortune."

"I cannot credit it. It is so sudden," said Helen, "Surely there must be some mistake!"

"It was just the same with my family," said Miss Trenton, who appeared to be in a great state of shock. "One day I was an heiress with a tidy fortune and a bright future, and the next thing I knew my father had lost everything, and I became a poor relation, having to beg a place to stay, or to go into service. I am so very sorry, Helen."

"I am sorry, too, miss," said Lily. "Whatever will you do?"

"I cannot say until Father comes. I hope it cannot be as bad as all that. I should like to go at once back to London, but since Father specifically asked that I remain here, and said that he would come for me, here I shall stay."

"Will you be wanting to dress and go down to breakfast, then, Miss Helen?"

"Oh, no!" said Miss Trenton. "That would be fatal! It cannot be long before this news is widely known; you must see to it that the letter is read by Sir Rupert at once, and we must all think together about how to present you, once the truth about your fortune is known."

"What is there to think about, Miss Trenton? If it's gone, it's gone, and that's all there is to it."

"But what about Sir Rupert?"

"What about him?" asked Helen, puzzled.

Miss Trenton gave her a meaningful look, and said, "Do you intend to hold him to his engagement to you, now that the terms of the financial settlement cannot be met?"

"There's no call to do that, is there?" asked Lily.

Helen Sterling colored, and looked grave for the first time, saying, "Of course there is. Miss Trenton is quite right. I must release Sir Rupert from our engagement."

"Or you could offer to release him, if that is his wish," suggested Miss Trenton.

"I shall do whatever is necessary and honest. There is no reason the man should marry me under false pretenses."

John Snow's breakneck arrival in the thick of the rainstorm, and the tragic drama of the news he carried, was such that it swept through the servants' hall like wildfire, whispered valet to maid to scullery maid downstairs, and was swiftly carried upstairs to the quality, brought in by servants carrying the morning tea.

By the time the ladies of the ton had dressed and come down to the Lesser Gold Dining Room to take their breakfast, everyone who was anyone knew all the sordid details of Black Jack Sterling's sudden downfall; some of the quality, such as Miss Carteret and Sir Charles Stanton, deplored the news, but an uncomfortable number of persons took in the bad news with satisfaction, if not delight. Miss Helen Sterling's position in society, which only yesterday seemed unassailable, was once again in doubt, for, to be low-born *and* impoverished as well, was to be severed from high society.

"Poor Sir Rupert!" cried Lady Arabella Gilbough. "What a scandal! What is he going to do if the girl don't release him?"

"She can't very well afford to release him now, can she?" said Lady Lacon philosophically. "I wouldn't, if I were her. He offered for her hand, fair and square, and now he's stuck with her. Think what a boor he would look if he tried to wriggle out of it. Besides, she must of all things be practical. Where are they going to live now, if not at Sir Rupert's estate?''

"I suppose you're right, but I cannot like it. I think now that she is ruined that I really must move their rooms. I gave them the very best chambers in that wing, and it seems an excessive accommodation, under the circumstances. They can both squeeze into a single chamber, one in back of the old west wing, and be very comfy there. Her father isn't here, at any rate, which saves us all a lot of embarrassment. He will just send for her, one supposes, and then she will just go away.''

"I certainly don't expect her down to breakfast, that is certain,'' said Lady Lacon, as she buttered her toast, broke it off, and dipped the piece daintily in a soft-boiled egg. "It must be disconcerting indeed to go to bed a great heiress, and wake up as a pauper!''

"Isn't it the most astonishing thing, Agatha?'' asked Lady Georgiana. "I cannot say I am at all surprised by the news about the Sterling fortune, for although such a complete loss of money and social status is nothing one likes to see happen to *anybody,* I cannot think that it is surprising that it did happen in that way! I think that money made from trade is . . . well, it's just not *like* other money. It's not like having a *proper* fortune, having one's own lands, and one's own tenants. It's just so—changeable. A fortune of cash money is just so—well, vulgar!''

"Isn't it, though?'' agreed Lady Agatha.

"One does not absolutely *have* to have a fortune and lands in order to be presentable in polite society,'' remarked Miss Peterson uneasily. "Or does one?''

"Oh, Idona, you're thinking about your Captain Prendergast! *He* comes from a good family," said Lady Georgiana. "The Prendergasts are received everywhere, so the whole matter is completely different!"

"Of course it is. Miss Sterling was a nobody—but a very rich nobody! Now she's a nobody without a penny to her name! She may just as well be a milliner!"

"Which is probably precisely where she'll end up!" crowed Lady Georgiana. "As a bonnet-maker on Bond Street—and why not?"

"What, do you think Sir Rupert will refuse to marry her?" asked Miss Peterson, wide-eyed.

"I don't see why he has to marry her, now that she's poor!" said Lady Georgiana. "What would be the point?"

"Surely it is matter of honor. Of keeping one's word. He couldn't just drop her like a hot coal, could he?" asked Miss Peterson.

"He dropped me like a hot coal, and for no good reason except that Sterling chit had more money than I. My godmother told me so! Now, however, things are different, and who knows what might happen?"

"But he hadn't actually offered for you, had he, when he changed his affections from you toward Miss Sterling?" inquired Lady Agatha.

'No," she admitted.

"There's a big difference. I think he must go through with it, unless *she* cries off," declared Miss Idona Peterson.

"Maybe we should give the girl a little encouragement, then, so she does the right thing, and lets him off the hook!" suggested Lady Georgiana.

"She probably thinks she *must* marry him now—after all, who else does the family have to depend upon. Why ever would she call it off?" asked Idona.

"I'm not sure, but if I think about it just a little, I'm sure I can come up with a suitable approach. I have a very sensitive and creative spirit!'' said Lady Georgiana brightly. ''Everyone says so!''

Downstairs, backstairs, in the servants' halls, even in Pug's Parlor, among the poorer ranks of society, there was at least the appearance of more sympathy for the young guest whose fortunes had fallen so quickly and catastrophically. Now that the servants and the Sterlings were on more equal footing, so to speak, most the remarks the menservants made about that evil turn of fate were of a philosophical nature, rather than a critical nature.

''Shouldn't invest in ships in the first place, that's what I say,'' commented Berwyn, the august elderly butler. ''Not that I have a chance of doin' it, but I don't think it's a sound place to put yer cash.''

''That wasn't the only thing. Them toffs'll say ye shouldn't pay people a decent wage, as Black Jack did, that's what I say,'' said John, the footman. ''High wages just make men lax, and then they show their gratitude by burning your mill down!''

''It wasn't his own workers that burned the mills down, was it?'' asked Jeffers Pym, Sir Charles' man. ''That would be biting the hand that feeds you, wouldn't it? I heard it was Luddites.''

''Dunno. I haven't seen the papers,'' said Thomas, the second footman.

''I thought Higgins was to bring them down yesterday,'' averred Berwyn. ''Didn't he do it? He generally don't miss a trick, no matter what the weather. Her ladyship won't be pleased if she don't get her London newspapers.''

''Oh, I met Higgins on the road,'' said John Snow, smoothly. ''He said they'd all be a day or two late, for the carriage from London had overturned in the mud, and the first load of them was spoilt.''

"Who's going to tell the mistress so, then, for I won't!" cried the butler, enjoying a joke at Lady Arabella's expense. "She'll have Higgins' hide, and well he knows it! Her ladyship don't like to get her London gossip cold!"

16

It must have been close on two o'clock when Lady Arabella, depressed by the weather, which continued its dreary downpour hour after hour, sent round word to her guests that a session of charades was being organized in the Gold Salon. Miss Trenton, Lily, and Miss Sterling debated for some time whether they ought to come down to join in, but in the end they agreed that it appeared craven for Helen to hide up in their chambers, and that since, sooner or later, she would have to face everyone, it might as well be over and done with.

Lily was so upset she was ready to lay out half-mourning for her mistress, but they decided upon a day dress of dusky blue, with a white fichu and a simple gold locket that held a single diamond.

"Will you now have to sell all your jewels, Miss Helen?" asked Lily anxiously.

Miss Sterling looked surprised, and then answered, "Well, yes, I suppose I might have to—if Father needs the money, which he well might. I hadn't thought of the implications of my situation, but I suppose I must."

"You needn't worry about having to turn me off, Miss" said Lily reassuringly. "I'll stay by you to the end, wages or no."

"I don't believe that will be necessary, Lily. You have yourself to think of, after all."

"Well, *I'm* not leaving you!" declared Miss Trenton. "I know what it is to be rich, and I know what it is to be poor, and rich is preferable, but I am very willing to join you under any circumstances!"

"Wait! I think we're getting a bit ahead of ourselves. We're talking as if Father and I were walking straight from Cornell Castle into the poorhouse. After all, there can be no doubt that Sir Rupert will stand by us. We can safely assume that we shall all be welcome in his house."

"The ignominy of it! She'll probably expect me to welcome that father of hers to Pease Hall!" said Sir Rupert Fellowes. "Not only must I welcome a wife who brings me nothing with which to relieve my increasingly precarious finances, but who comes complete with a passel of hangers-on in tow! I won't have it, and so I'll make her know. I'll take her, and I suppose that father of hers can visit once and a while, but that's an end to it!"

The baronet's face was filled with ire and gloom, as he asked his man, "There couldn't have been some sort of mistake, now, could there, Jeffries? You don't suppose that Black Jack's man might have exaggerated the situation just a bit? Perhaps it was just *one* of the mills that burnt down, rather than *all* of them? Perhaps some money was lost, but not every damn ha'penny?"

Jeffries shook his head sadly, saying, "I'm afraid his man

was very clear in that respect. It is gone, all gone, like candle snuffed out in a windstorm."

"Well, I'm sure I don't know how I'm going to settle my debts to Sir Charles Stanton. I had counted on Helen's money, and why should I not have? It was as good as in my hands already!" he declared loudly. "I wouldn't have tried to erase my debt to him by repeating the wager, save that I thought I could get Black Jack to cover the bet, just in case I lost!"

"If I might be so bold as to intrude, sir, mightn't you suggest to the young woman that since the terms of the agreement now cannot be met, that she should, in all honor, how shall I say, withdraw her affections from you?"

"Shabby! Shabby! It is out of the question!" raged Sir Rupert. "I should *like* to do so, of course, but then it should seem like such a low, ungentlemanly gesture that I could not bear the censure the polite world would heap upon me. Which is not to say that I don't think that is precisely what *ought* to happen! She *should* break it off, of course! But if *she* don't, *I* cannot!"

He took a restless turn around the room, and poured himself a glass of brandy, and tossed it down in one gulp.

"Oh, when I think that I might have offered for that red-headed Locksley wench! If I were going to marry a chit without much dowry, I'd have gone after her, for I'll vow to you that *she'd* be a rare armful on a winter's night! D'ye know I might have been an earl if I'd kept up with her?"

"No, sir, I did not."

"Her family's line has died out, and there was some talk of finding a husband for her who would agree to take on the name and succession in a second foundation! I'd have liked to have been Earl of Locksley! Would rather be dead rich, of course, but I wouldn't mind having a title, not a bit! Now I have to look after Helen, who likely has been reduced to a poor sniveling miss, while Lady Georgiana, a real female, is busy batting her eyes at Lady Arabella's paint-spattered, bird-witted son!''

"Alas, sir," said Jeffries Pym lugubriously, "It does not seem quite fair."

When Miss Sterling entered the Gold Salon, she knew all eyes would be upon her, and it was so. Very neatly dressed, looking proper and pretty, she filed in with her companion, Miss Trenton, and they seated themselves upon two chairs toward the back of the room.

The Duchess of Minster, who was very fond of theatricals, had taken it upon herself to organize the group of about sixteen persons into two teams: she had Lady Georgiana Locksley and Lady Agatha Winslow as her assistants, and those two young ladies were busily filling out slips of paper at the Duchess' command containing the words which must be acted out: names of historical characters, famous plays, famous poems, famous books and phrases.

Sir Charles Stanton and Miss Carteret, who were very fond of the game, were kind enough to pull Miss Sterling from her shy seat at the back, and bring her forward, and insist that she play with their team, which, with great help from Mr. Peter Gilbough, was handily defeating the opposite team, led by Mrs. Hicks-Aubrey, who was an enthusiastic player, but somewhat uninventive.

Miss Sterling proved a valuable asset, for she was very good at guessing the answers: it was she who identified Raymond Dulles' attempt to portray "Napoleon," and Miss Carteret's rendition of "Romeo and Juliet."

Then Captain Prendergast sallied forth, acting out "Troilus and Cressida," which was guessed by Miss Idona Peterson, and the scores became more nearly matched.

The excitement mounted, until the two teams were running neck-and-neck; at that point it was Miss Sterling's turn to act out the phrase, and she opened her white slip of paper with much enthusiasm, for the gaiety of the game had quite eclipsed her personal troubles.

As she perused the slip of paper, a look of chagrin clouded her face, and she cast a desperate glance toward Miss Trenton, as if to ask for advice. Miss Trenton, however, turned out to be deep in conversation with Mrs. Hicks-Aubrey, of all people, debating certain subtle details of the rules of the game.

Miss Sterling paled and took a deep breath, and decided she would act as if nothing were amiss. Because she knew who had prepared the slips of paper, she knew that the hand of Lady Georgiana Locksley had to have been in this, but she decided she must not let Lady Georgiana get the best of her, and proceeded merely to act out the phrase that had been given to her.

The first word in the three word phrase was "the" and was easily guessed through the appropriate conventional signs.

The second word had three syllables, Miss Sterling indicated. She then proceeded to act out a person counting money, for "count," drew the word out for "her." After the team had guessed "counter", and she pointed down toward her shoes.

Miss Carteret at once called out, "Feet!"

Sir Charles Stanton cried, "Count! Her! Feet! I've got it! 'Counterfeit'!"

Miss Sterling nodded her head to show she was correct, and began to act out the second word in the phrase. She pointed toward her head, and picked up a ringlet.

Sir Charles guessed, "Tendril!"

"Gold!" cried Mr. Gilbough.

Miss Carteret shouted, "Counterfeit gold! That must be it!"

Miss Sterling shook her head no, and indicated her team must try again.

"Not gold ... not ringlet ... then, hair!" cried Sir Charles, and Miss Sterling nodded that this was right.

She indicated a letter, and made a sort of serpentine in the air.

"Snake?" asked Mr. Gilbough.

"Curve?" cried Miss Carteret.

"Ess? Hair-ess!! Heiress!" guessed Sir Charles Stanton. "Counterfeit heiress! The Counterfeit Heiress!"

"Yes, that's it!" acknowledged Miss Sterling, showing the white slip of paper around for proof. "Did I do it in under two minutes, I hope?"

"Yes, you did. Good show!"

" 'The Counterfeit Heiress'?" asked Mrs. Hicks-Aubrey, looking puzzled. "Sounds like a race-horse, or a ship. Never heard of it. Is it some kind of new book?"

"No, it's some kind of new *guest* at Cornell Castle! It's Miss Sterling! *She's* the counterfeit heiress!" cried Lady Georgiana Locksley, who along with Lady Agatha Winslow, had dissolved into helpless whoops of laughter. "Isn't that too, too funny? How amusing that, of all people, she should draw that particular phrase! It's so very apt!"

Helen Sterling merely stared at the two girls without speaking, rather more amazed than mortified.

Lady Agatha asked, sniggering, "Your team guessed that so quickly! Why, you have *such* talent for charades—you should be on the stage, Miss Sterling! Whatever will you be going to act out next for us, Miss Sterling? Oh, I have an idea! How about acting out the phrase 'poor relation?' "

"Yes, do! Or how about acting out 'all to pieces?' That would be fun to do, why don't you do *that* one?" suggested Lady Georgiana contemptuously. "Or how about 'pockets all to let'? Why not do 'not a feather to fly with?' "

"No, Miss Sterling, do 'mushroom!' " cried Lady Agatha,

giggling hysterically. " 'Pretentious mushroom' would be even better!"

"Better yet, Miss Sterling, show us how you play 'dished up!' " cried Lady Georgiana. "Don't you think your fiancé would find it amusing? I think he would! After all, he must have a *wonderful* sense of humor, Sir Rupert, or he would find your recent financial reverses quite intolerable, don't you think? One can only assume that he finds it funny!"

"*We* certainly do!" said Lady Agatha.

The elder ladies present, from the Duchess of Minster to the prim Mrs. Hicks-Aubrey had begun to whisper amongst themselves, thinking that those girls had really gone too far this time. It was Lady Lacon who was chosen to tell the young ladies that they had said quite enough, and send them brusquely from the room, still giggling.

Lady Lacon actually apologized to Miss Sterling for their behavior, saying, "I am more sorry than I can say, Miss Sterling. They behaved very badly indeed, and they know better. I will insist that they make you an apology."

"Don't bother. They were just having a bit of fun at my expense."

"If that was fun, it was of the most malicious kind," said Mr. Gilbough, coming over to offer his arm to her. "You are perhaps weary of company, Miss Sterling. May I escort you somewhere? Back to your rooms, or perhaps you would like that tour of the dungeon I once promised you? It is still raining, though I think the thunder has ceased, so although the weather is not all that you said you wished, the dungeons might be pleasurably sort of damp, and evil-looking in the rain. What do you say?"

This brought a welcome smile to Miss Sterling's face, and she replied, happily, "Why, Mr. Gilbough! You are always so very kind to me, and are always ready to rescue me from the effects of one scrape or another. To continue our tour of the Castle would be very good—"

Miss Sterling stopped speaking in mid-sentence, for just as she was putting her hand on Mr. Gilbough's arm in a friendly fashion, Sir Rupert Fellowes strode into the Gold Salon.

Instantly her hand dropped to her side as he swiftly made his way over to his fiancée, took her hand up to his lips, and bowed.

"How do you do, my dear?" he asked. "I was happily informed by Jeffries that you were here, and if you are not otherwise engaged with Mr. Gilbough, perhaps it might be convenient for me to have a word with you, if I may?"

A little reluctantly, Miss Sterling curtseyed to Mr. Gilbough, and explained to him that she would love to take up his offer of a tour at another time, and added that she would as well like to see how the portrait was coming along, whenever it might be convenient for him.

At this, Sir Rupert stiffened.

"Portrait? What portrait?"

"Of me," admitted Miss Sterling.

"I thought I had specifically forbidden you to sit for this man. Are you telling me you acted precisely as I had asked you *not* to do?"

"Do lower your voice, Sir Rupert," begged Miss Sterling, embarrassed. "My father gave his permission."

Sir Rupert looked around and saw that everyone was staring at him. He took Miss Sterling's arm a bit roughly, and steered so as to remove her from the room. He said not another word to her until he had brought her to the library, made sure that no one else was there, and closed the thick doors behind them.

"This is really the outside of enough! How dare you behave toward me in such a way, Helen? I will not tolerate it, and so you must learn! You asked your father's permission since I had refused you mine! It will not do! Since you are to be my wife, you must learn the kind of behavior that is expected of Lady Fellowes, and not continue to defy me in this care-for-nothing way!''

"I am so very sorry, Sir Rupert," she said, hanging her head.

"So you should be. I am more scandalized than I can say about this business with your father, and beyond the shame of having one's financial affairs bruited all about town, is the dishonor of having your name on everyone's lips. It is extremely unsuitable, and I hope to heaven that once this scandal dies down—which it must do—you will seek to conduct yourself with modesty and propriety at all times. I dislike above all things having my family mentioned as the subject of gossip.''

Miss Sterling gave him a dark look, and inquired, "Perhaps, Sir Rupert, you wish at this time to be relieved of the scandalous burden of our engagement?''

"Break our engagement? Oh, no! By no means! I will not allow it!'' he thundered, frightening her a little. "I will not appear in the light of high society as a dishonorable lout! Besides, who are you to say such things to me? Have you no sense of gratitude to me? Don't you realize that if I were to cast you off now, no one at all would receive you? Where would you live? Where would your father live? What would become of you? I think it best that you take some time to consider the fate that has, unfortunately, befallen you, and to realize that I am now your only hope of maintaining your good reputation and station in life. When seen in that prudent light, I hope you will quickly learn to render me the obedient respect that is due to me as your husband and protector. Good day, my dear.''

17

Miss Helen Sterling, former heiress to a vast fortune made in trade, had fully intended to remain isolated in her chambers for the remainder of the afternoon while she contemplated her present and her future, but this was interrupted when she received a brief note from her hostess, Lady Arabella, to the effect that since her party had grown so small with her father's departure, would she very much mind occupying a smaller set of rooms in the Long Corridor?

It didn't take very long for the change to be accomplished, and her new rooms were just as small and dreary as her new life had become. The windows looked out onto the stable courtyard; the drapes were sad, old, and dusty beige. Miss Sterling, however, found she did not mind.

Lily Beeton, however, was outraged by such shabby treatment, and cried, "Who does she think she is? No one else has come that has a prior claim on the other rooms, what can she mean by treating you this way? You're still Sir

Rupert's fiancée, aren't you? You must tell him, for this move is an insult!''

Miss Trenton tried to suggest that perhaps Lady Arabella expected a family who would require a larger suite, but Lily thought the whole thing unforgivable, and, as she left to go downstairs, said that she was looking forward to speaking her mind about it at the servants' afternoon meal.

When they were alone, Helen said, ''Miss Trenton, I am so upset at what has happened. Not just about the loss of the money, but about all these people—or most of them at any rate. I want to go home—wherever that is to be, now. Do you know something else, Miss Trenton? I don't think I want to marry Sir Rupert Fellowes. I don't want to be Lady Fellowes. I just want to live quietly with you and Father.''

Miss Trenton paled, and replied in a serious tone, saying, ''You mustn't do that, Helen! I will have your father forbid it!''

''Why should I marry him? Before this party, I had warm feelings for him. Since I have been here, I have found him overbearing and unsympathetic, and I have quite begun to take him in dislike,'' she said with asperity. ''Whyever should I marry someone who I have taken in dislike? It would be madness!''

Speaking with great feeling, Miss Trenton said, ''Poverty is madness, my dear Helen! I can advise you very well, as one who knows. When my family's fortune was lost, I, too had a single chance to marry so as to be comfortable, and for reasons like yours, I turned the offer down. I had no feelings toward the gentleman, and he was much older than I was, so, against the wishes of my family, I turned him down. I, of course, never received another offer, and I soon went into service as a governess.''

''It was the most fatal mistake I ever made. I should rather have done anything, and married anyone, rather than have to live hand to mouth as I have done. Before I had the good fortune to come into your father's employ, my life was a constant misery of deprivation and humiliation, some at the hands of women with whom I had once been equal," she said with great emotion.

"Don't be a fool, Helen. Marry Sir Rupert, and give all your love to the children you will have."

Helen Sterling thought about this for some time, and then she said, "Miss Trenton, the truth is that I have begun to have feelings for another man."

Miss Trenton, astonished, asked, "For whom?"

"F-for Peter Gilbough," she admitted.

Miss Trenton shook her head ominously.

"A very polished, charming young gentleman, is Mr. Gilbough, but you can put that possibility quite out of your head, for the handsome Mr. Gilbough is pledged to another—you must know that, do you not? Mrs. Hicks-Aubrey told me all about it this afternoon. His family has arranged for him to marry a girl who inherits lands that march with Cornell Castle—Lady Georgiana Locksley, the one who has been so unkind to you ever since we came."

Miss Sterling was listening very intently, and her face betrayed her unhappy state of mind.

Miss Trenton continued, saying, "So, if the idea of marrying the rich and charming Mr. Gilbough is what's turning you away from Sir Rupert, you may as well forget all about it. In your present situation, you have nothing to bring to such a marriage, and Lady Arabella would never allow it. Look at how you have fallen in her esteem merely as a guest—she has treated you very shabbily, making us leave our old accommodations."

"I don't think that Mr. Gilbough has any warm feelings toward Lady Georgiana. He needn't marry her just to please his family, does he?" asked Helen.

"Likely he has no warm feelings toward her, but when

it comes to joining lands, and advancing estates, no one cares what the young people think. For those who are wealthy and noble, marriage is not a personal pursuit."

"This is all very lowering, Miss Trenton," said Helen in a small voice.

"Yes, it is, rather. You must not let yourself be romantic, Helen. There is too much for you to lose. Don't throw away your last chance for happiness: marry Sir Rupert, and make him a good wife."

"You are right," said Helen, very chastened. "I must of course go through with it. This marriage means the very world to Father."

Dinner at Cornell Castle that evening was uneventful; Helen Sterling and Miss Trenton remained in their room, and chose not to go down at all for the rest of the evening, thus depriving the company of the sight of the scandal-clouded young lady. Out of sight being out of mind, the various ladies and gentlemen turned toward other important *on-dits* involving the naughty Duke of Cumberland, the rich Miss Petrie's proper parentage, and debates on whether or not the summer weather in Buckinghamshire would ever again turn fine.

After dinner there was music to be had in the music room, provided very sweetly by Miss Idona Peterson, a rapt Captain Prendergast standing by her side, turning the pages of the music for her, while Miss Peterson's mother looked on, fuming, trying to figure out how she was to extricate her daughter from this unsuitable attachment for a poverty-stricken younger son.

Lady Arabella Gilbough and Lady Lacon listened with great pleasure to Miss Peterson's rendition of several country tunes, while they discussed the progress of their plan to marry Lady Georgiana Locksley to Peter Gilbough.

It was clear to both ladies that things were not proceeding with the easy dispatch they had hoped for and fully expected. Neither party had shown the slightest bit of enthusiasm for the match, and the behavior of Lady Georgiana in particular had been execrable.

"She is being only barely civil to Peter, you know," pointed out Lady Arabella. "She keeps trying to insult Miss Sterling, a favorite of Peter's, in hopes that if she can make Miss Sterling appear a fool, Sir Rupert will suddenly come to love her and offer for her. Sadly, it is Georgiana who appears the fool."

"I don't know what to do with her! I explained her situation very precisely, and I was sure she understood her position very well. She says one thing to me, and then does another! In some sense she understands that her marrying Peter would be terribly advantageous to her, but I think she is tangled in some kind of romantic expectations, and I suppose the truth is, she just don't like Peter above half."

"I find that insulting, Louisa. Peter is a prince," said Lady Arabella crossly.

"You always say that! I don't want to hear about princes! At any rate, I did not mean to suggest any insult toward him. But, what can one do with these young people, filled with wild ideas bred in novels? Look, there she is now! Let us talk to her, and try to put some sense into her head, before she ruins all her chances and Peter begins to take her in dislike."

"I am afraid he may already have done so. She was very wicked-behaved this afternoon: it was the worst thing she's done yet. I was not at all amused."

Lady Lacon waved the girl over, and when Lady Georgiana dutifully came, she had at least the good grace to appear once again chastened and repentant, which was due in large part to her godmother's having rung a peal over her, letting her know in no uncertain terms that she had done wrong.

"Georgiana, I have asked you over here, in the presence of Lady Arabella, so you may give us your word that you will stop your foolish scheming, and do just as you have been told. If you do not wish for us to act on your behalf, say so right now! This match is of benefit to you, and you alone. If you do not wish it, say so now, and save all our time!"

"I do wish it," she said, looking at the ground, wishing she were otherwhere.

"Georgiana, it is true that I wish my son Peter to marry you, but above all I wish him simply to marry, and if he don't marry you, why, then, there are other fish in the sea! My thought of marrying him to you was to enlarge the family holdings, and to help Lady Lacon, a dear friend, who feels responsible toward you. If you continue to act in a heedless way, I will simply find another suitable girl who appreciates the match with Peter for the excellent advantages it brings. Is that quite clear?"

"Yes, ma'am."

"Good. However, for the nonce, kindly don't tell Peter that I would countenance his marriage to anyone else, for I do prefer you to all others, and would have him believe I would approve only of you."

"Thank you, ma'am," said Lady Georgiana, showing rare gratitude.

"I arrange for Peter to accompany you on tomorrow's outing to Beaufort Abbey, do you solemnly promise that you will do your very best to be a charming, pleasing companion to him?"

"With none of your tricks, girl!" interrupted Lady Lacon. "You know what I'm talking about."

"No, ma'am. No tricks. I'll mind my manners, I promise."

"Well, then. Let's try to get on with it, shall we?"

When, somewhat later, the two ladies met with Peter Gilbough to try to bring him into line, they met with even more resistance.

"She's a virago, Mother, and there's an end to it!" said Peter.

"Lady Georgiana is my goddaughter, I will have you recall!" said Lady Lacon. "You must not speak of her in that way."

"Forgive my bluntness, Lady Lacon. You yourself heard how she behaved this afternoon toward Miss Sterling. It was intolerable!"

"That was very wrong of her, I grant you. However, I feel that under your guidance she will grow to be a fine woman and make you a fine wife."

"I don't want her as a wife, Mother. I tried to bear with her, for the love I have for you, and in my father's memory, but the fact is, we two simply do not suit, and I do not at all want to marry her."

Something in Lady Arabella seemed to snap suddenly, and she said, "See here, Peter! If you don't marry Georgiana, everything will go to Cousin Raymond! Don't you know that?"

"What do you mean?" said Peter.

"I meant just what I said. Your father left all his affairs in a very queer fashion, indeed, and I particularly did not want to have to tell you this, but under the terms of his will, if you do not marry according to his wishes, then we lose the Castle, and it, and all the money goes to your second cousin Raymond Dulles, the do-good vicar."

"Oh, Mother, you can't be serious! Old Mellon would have told me. Father, for that matter, would have told me. I came home from the continent precisely to work out the settlement of the estate. I have done so; I have seen Father's will. There is nothing left that remains to be done, and there are no provisions such as you suggest."

His mother waited for just a moment, and then went on the attack, saying sharply, "I'm afraid you are wrong, Peter. There are special provisions in the will. Why, I thought Mellon had explained everything to you! It was all worked out years ago, by your father and Lady Georgiana's father, and it was assumed that you would go along with it. The legal papers were left in my control, and only to be used if you balked at the marriage.

You see, I think your Father did not want to force you into this marriage, or even to apply pressure, *unless* you refused to follow his wishes through love for him alone. In fact, I think he thought the idea most distasteful, which is why he kept the coercive provisions so secret. He thought you would do as he wished, just because he wished it, and I must say that I thought you would, too. Why must you try to resist doing as he wanted? I can't think why you're being so stubborn, Peter. It's not like you."

"Not like me? With all due respect, Mama, not having seen me over the past three years at all, and hardly having seen me during the whole of my childhood, how could you possibly be expected to know what I am like?" said Peter, with a scowl.

"These three years you've been traveling I grant you, we of course have seen little of you—how could it be otherwise? As to not having paid proper attention to you when you were a child, you wrong me, Peter. You misremember! I was the very tenderest of mamas!"

"I never saw you but for five minutes a day, Mother! A whirl of silk, a quick kiss on the cheek, the smell of powder and paint, and you were gone!"

"Well!" said his mother, flustered. "You could hardly expect me not to go about in society, could you?"

"Oh, certainly not! Never mind. It is of no importance. The thing I must determine is, whatever familial understanding might have been wished, or anticipated, surely I am not legally *required* to marry her."

A guilty gleam stole into Lady Arabella Gilbough's eyes. "You cannot have been attending me! I just explained that you *are* required to do so, or we lose the Castle to the vicar. How can you be such a slow-top? There was a settlement worked out and agreed to long ago. It was not my doing, after all!"

She shrugged, and added, "Your fortune comes to you, as it comes to many young men, not without encumbrances—your receiving your full due depends upon your marrying in accordance with your family's wishes. *Your father's wishes.* Having said so, I trust you will regard this matter in a different light."

"Mellon never said a thing to me about this."

"Why should he have? There was nothing to be done until you reached your majority, and were ready to marry. Ask Mellon now, if you like," said his mother, indicating a cottage that could be seen through the window.

"Poor old Mellon is not in his wits longer, as everyone knows," said Peter unhappily.

"A sad thing, old age," she agreed.

"It must be written down somewhere. I really must see it put down in writing. Father surely would not have left things so precariously."

"It most certainly exists, and I'm sure I can put my hands on it, though I would have to make some inquiries; it's not the sort of thing one keeps in one's dresser drawer, after all. However, I really don't see *why* you won't accept your own mother's assurances, for heaven's sake, Peter!'' she said, beginning to weep openly. ''It is very lowering that you won't take my word for it!''

''Oh, Mother, do stop crying!'' he shouted.

''How can I stop, when your selfishness will result in everything we have being settled on that silly vicar!'' she said, dissolving into tears.

Peter Gilbough threw up his hands, walked to the window, and stared out at the formal gardens of Cornell Castle, which were blooming with the colorful lushness of summer.

I love the Castle, and I always have, but must I really sacrifice my life for the good of my estate? Must I force myself into a false marriage? Is this really what my father wished for me?

Mr. Gilbough weighed things in his mind, and then made his decision.

''Very well. I will try to like her, Mother,'' he declared. ''I will try my best to do as you and Father wished.''

After Peter had gone, Lady Arabella and Lady Lacon reviewed his demeanor and his performance for clues as to what his future behavior would be.

''I thought he sounded very complaisant, did not you?'' asked Lady Lacon.

''At the end, he was, but he fought it off with such stubbornness I hardly recognized my own flesh and blood. Oh, Louisa! The trials and tribulations of a mother! Who could have known that my little prince would grow up to be so opinionated and so obstinate? It was only when I turned into a watering-pot that I got anywhere with him!'' explained Lady Arabella. ''I'm sure I did not expect it of him—his obstinacy came as a complete and vast surprise. That is the thing about leaving one's children to be brought up by servants. In the end, one is presented with a version of them one does not really recognize.''

"Well, one would not really want to bring them up one-self, of course," opined Lady Lacon. "Although I believe I have heard that the Duchess of Devon was a very doting mother."

"My point precisely! Look at that family, and see where all that doting got them! Too shocking for words!" said Lady Arabella. "Really, with children, one cannot be *too* severe! I feel that I have failed, somehow. I was too lax with Peter, giving him too many kisses, and too few blows. Still, at the end, he seemed resigned to do as we ask, though resentful."

"What do you think it means?"

"I think it means I'm lucky I thought up that bouncer about his fortune!" exclaimed Lady Arabella.

"That whole scheme about the will and his fortune was a lie? Why, if so, it was well done, Arabella, very well done. What a quick thinker you are!"

"It was an inspiration of the moment, but how am I to keep it up?" sighed Lady Arabella "I must find someone or something to back up my claim, for Peter is not such a nodcock that he wouldn't try to discover in writing the precise terms of Edward's will."

A sly look passed over Lady Lacon's face, and she said, "I have a third cousin who is an attorney."

"Do you really?" said Lady Arabella Gilbough, rather shocked. "I'm so very sorry to hear it!"

"That's not what I meant! Everyone must have lowly connexions somewhere in one's lineage. It is only a matter of how far away they are, and in any case, at times like these just such a low connexion can prove useful. I think Mr. Robert Dearden might prove useful to you, by being able to recreate a secret written codicil to your late husband's will. All I need are the names of the parties in involved. Shall I do it?''

"Oh, Louisa, would you? A secret codicil, something all nicely written down, something that I could *show* to Peter to prove my point! It would be just the thing!''

"Easily done. I will send for my cousin directly.''

18

As many had predicted, the next day turned out as fine a summer's day as ever had been seen in Buckinghamshire. The sky was clear blue, there was the very slightest of breezes, and the heat of the day was soothing rather than oppressing.

Under this strong inspiration, Lady Arabella completed the arrangements, for whoever of her guests wished to join in, for an outing to an especially lovely neighboring estate, Beaufort Abbey. The Abbey was famed across all England for its elaborate, beautifully maintained formal gardens, and for its surrounding parklands, including wide swathes of grassland parks laid out in the naturalistic, picturesque style that had become the latest fashion.

As it was a good two hours' drive away, making sure that sufficient carriages were made available to convey the entire party *en masse* required extra work by her ladyship's stable boys, to make sure that all her guests' carriages would be ready at one time. First, permission had had to be obtained from the Beaufort family—though the family was not in residence, word had been sent to their steward, who gave his permission quickly.

Next, provisions for an elaborate outdoor luncheon had had to be obtained, baskets, linen and silver counted out and packed well ahead of time, and a large group of servants sent on ahead. There would be fresh fruit offered in the afternoon, local cheese, and excellent wines brought down from London at great expense. However, when it came to entertaining her guests in style, as well as furthering her match-making schemes, Lady Arabella Gilbough was not known to indulge in economies. Everything about the event was to be of the very first stare, as usual.

The day being just as glorious as anyone could hope for, the ladies outdid themselves vying to catch the eyes of the gentlemen. Each one wore her finest walking dress and matching bonnet, and some ladies carried parasols to protect their pale complexions.

Bowing to his mother's wishes just as he had promised, Peter Gilbough was escorting Lady Georgiana, who was on her best behavior. Even Mr. Gilbough had to admit that Lady Georgiana looked fetching in her Pomona green gown from Madame Fanchon, which was both elaborate and elegant, very much suited to her ladyship's personal style.

Riding in Mr. Gilbough's carriage, acting as chaperones and critics, were Lady Arabella herself and Lady Lacon. This combination made for a very stiff performance by both the young persons, who spent the entire time of the journey from Cornell Castle to Beaufort Abbey discussing the finer points of the summer weather, to the delight and enlightenment of no one.

Mr. Raymond Dulles rode in an elderly landau, and escorted Miss Peterson and her cousin, Lady Agatha Winslow, and Lady Agatha's mother, Lady Winslow. Lady Winslow felt almost annoyed at being conveyed in rather a shabby carriage by a man whose eligibility as a suitor entirely depended upon the early death of or failure to produce issue by Mr. Peter Gilbough, but decided that it was as well to keep on good terms with the man, just in case fortune were to smile upon him. Besides, Lady Winslow thought, even the secondary heir to a fortune was better than to permit Idona to spend any more time with that poor Captain Prendergast, who was making such a cake of himself over the girl!

Sir Rupert Fellowes took up Miss Sterling in his spanking perch-phaeton, which was so very high-sprung that Helen thought she might actually become ill from the rocking motion of the vehicle: suddenly she felt a great sympathy with Miss Trenton, and wished she'd brought one of Lily's home remedies along.

Miss Janet Carteret, dressed in a lovely walking dress of lemon muslin, which she wore with a deceptively simple chip-straw hat, a rakish bow tied at the side of her head, was handed up into Sir Charles Stanton's barouche, which also conveyed her chaperone, the ever-tittering Mrs. Partridge. During the drive, as Mrs. Partridge was occupied in admiring the landscape, Sir Charles availed himself of the opportunity to propose marriage to Miss Carteret once again. The belle of London declined politely, and scolded him for having asked her again prematurely. She tried to make him promise he would wait at least another month before he asked again, but this time, to her consternation, Sir Charles firmly, though most politely, refused, leaving Miss Carteret to puzzle out his change in behavior.

Everyone being quite tired after the journey, some light refreshments were first provided for the guests, to be partaken in a particularly pretty spot where blankets and cushions had been set out, so that everyone might enjoy an hour of country quiet and rest.

At the hour's end, Lady Arabella said it was time to be off, or nothing could be seen. First, there was a strolling tour of the Abbey itself, accompanied by the Beaufort housekeeper, who, at the head of the group, kept up a constant monologue detailing the various famous possessions, works of art, and the dates of the various architectural improvements, which were many.

After this, the group split up, and the various couples formed into smaller groups in order to stroll through and explore the vast gardens and park surrounding Beaufort Abbey.

Sir Charles and Miss Carteret chose to enter the Great Maze of Beaufort, an immense maze made from a ten foot tall yew hedge that had to be trimmed and shaped on almost a daily basis. It had been so treacherously designed that, whenever any guests entered it, they had to be watched by a gardener who sat on a high chair to the side of the maze, so he might see and direct out any guests who found themselves hopelessly lost. Sir Charles, however, claimed he knew the secret of the maze, and so was permitted to enter with Miss Carteret, without any watcher being present in the chair.

Mr. Gilbough and Lady Georgiana decided they would explore the walled Northern Garden of Beaufort, which had been opened especially for Lady Arabella's party by one of the legion of gardeners and groundskeepers. Their conversation continued to be strained and uneasy, as both tried as hard as they could to pretend interest in topics which they respectively found of minimal interest.

Both Mr. Gilbough and Lady Georgiana were trying to be on their very best behavior, and to this end, tried to stick to neutral topics, such as expressing their opinions on the selection of colorful plants, and on their patterns, and on the probable expense of their upkeep. Their conversation, though stilted, was at least now taking place.

Having thought carefully on the subject, and having an innate fear of poverty and social oblivion, she realized that by marrying the man who had inherited Cornell Castle, she would be in a very enviable position, indeed. Peter Gilbough seemed to Lady Georgiana to be just the sort of man who could be cozened into anything she wished; she needed only to put her mind to it.

Certainly, she might have a cicisbeo—it was quite the thing, and he might well serve to fill any empty places in her heart. After she had borne the man an heir, he might even allow her the freedom to take up other, more intimate acquaintances—who knew? All in all, to marry Mr. Gilbough was hardly a fate worse than death, was it? Lady Georgiana now felt nothing but gratitude toward Lady Lacon, who had known all along of the seriousness of Lady Georgiana's position, and had tried to take the best steps she could to assure her goddaughter of a comfortable life.

She apologized as prettily as possible for her behavior toward Miss Sterling, saying that it was just a prank, and not a very funny one.

"I think I acted out of an excess of high spirits," she explained, "But I certainly regret my actions, and am ready to be guided by you in all things."

At this juncture, Lady Georgiana deftly turned the conversation to the present outing, saying, "It is really very gratifying to see that, over the generations, each successor to Beaufort Abbey undertook an addition to the whole—making some sort of addition either externally or internally or both. Do you think to do the same with Cornell Castle?"

"Oh, no, not at all. I shall leave everything just as it is, maintaining it well, of course. I do not intend to reside at the Castle, in fact. I think I shall leave its running to my mother, who enjoys that sort of thing. I intend to spend as much time as I can living abroad."

"You can't be serious!" said Lady Georgiana, with horror. "What would one do outside of England?"

"I am perfectly serious, Lady Georgiana. I have other interests, and they do not include becoming a country gentleman."

"But what about—?" Lady Georgiana stopped, not sure how to proceed.

"Why beat about the bush, Lady Georgiana? We both know what is expected of us, do we not?"

"Yes," admitted Lady Georgiana, trying to make the best of a difficult situation.

Mr. Gilbough chose his words carefully, adding, *"If you and I were to do as certain persons close of us have suggested, I should have no difficulty in installing my wife either at the Castle or at a house in town. I, for my part, would consider myself free to do as I wished. This would include my spending a large part of the year in Europe, or wherever I pleased."*

"Certainly. That would be very fair."

Good heavens, she thought to herself, *is this really the way my life will turn out? Conveniently married off to a friend of the family, a rich man who has no feelings for me, and for whom I have no feelings?*

I'm not sure if I can go through with it. Aunt Louisa will be furious with me if I don't, however, and who can blame her?

I said I would do it, though . . . and what if this is my last chance at a wealthy marriage?

What am I to do?

"Excuse me just a moment, Mr. Gilbough," said Lady Georgiana, disconsolately. "I seem to have suddenly acquired the headache, and I really must sit down for just a moment."

"Certainly," he said, guiding her to a bench near a fountain.

"Oh, no, Mr. Gilbough, you need not wait for me. Please do go on and see the gardens, by yourself. It would not do to come all this way and not see the sights. Besides, my headaches resolve more quickly in solitude. When I am better, I shall return to the carriages by myself."

"Just as you wish," said Peter, bowing to her and slipping away, happy to have some time to put his own agitated thoughts in order.

Perhaps half an hour after Mr. Gilbough and Lady Georgiana entered the Northern Gardens, Sir Rupert Fellowes and Miss Sterling, having finished touring the formal gardens, entered within as well.

Like their counterparts, Sir Rupert and his fiancée had been struggling all day to make conversation. They had exhausted the conventional topics such as the weather, the beauty of the countryside, the cleverness with which the garden had been planted, the immense expenses that such a large household must necessarily incur, and were searching for another similarly insipid topic.

At length, Sir Rupert asked, "Have you heard from your father?"

"No, not a word. I am really rather worried," said Helen in an agitated way. "I had thought surely to have heard from him by now. What if he is unwell? What if he should harm himself?"

"I'm sure you should not be worried," he said, trying to be gentle. "You must put your mind on the future, not on the past. Speaking of which, you will be very happy to learn that I have finally found a suitable position for your Miss Trenton! My cousin Regina is in need of a governess for her five children, and I have arranged for Miss Trenton to go to them as soon as you leave the Cornell Castle. I told Regina that Miss Trenton is a treasure, and because of that, she was willing to offer her a very nice wage. I informed Miss Trenton of this just before we left this morning, and she was, of course, extremely grateful to me, as one might expect, for she had been, she told me, very worried about finding a new position.''

Miss Sterling looked at him in such a state of unhappiness that Sir Rupert was taken aback for a moment.

She cried, ''But I don't want Miss Trenton to leave me! Surely she does not have to! She is my friend!''

Sir Rupert looked a bit alarmed, and replied, as carefully and politely as he could, ''My dear, she is not your friend. You are her employer. It would not be suitable for her to stay on as your paid companion after your marriage. Surely, you were aware of this. Miss Trenton certainly was. It's just not done.''

''I want her to live with us, Sir Rupert. I had always intended that she should. She is like a mother to me!'' said Helen with desperation.

''I wish you will stop staying that, and do lower your voice! I am persuaded you must be guided by me in these matters, as your husband, since you do not seem to quite understand just how things are. She is *not* to live with us,'' he said, beginning to lose his patience. ''I remind you that it is you who are coming to live in my house, not the reverse. If your father's pockets were not to let, perhaps he might give her an annuity so she might retire, but as things are, one must be practical, and find her a good position. This I have done. Now, as long as we are on the subject of suitable employees, once we are wed, I or my cousin Regina will be selecting for you a more suitable lady's maid. That girl Lily of yours is quite impossible— my man Jeffries told me all about her. She is a hopeless gossip, spends far too much time in male company, and draws all too much attention to herself and to you!"

"Oh! Rupert! You are trying to take from me both Lily and Miss Trenton? This is the outside of enough!" Miss Sterling cried, very unhappy. "Be kind enough to leave me at once, or I shall say something we shall both regret!"

"As you wish, madam," said Sir Rupert with some asperity. "But be assured that I *will* be master of my own house!

"Furthermore, Helen, you may rest assured that I shall lose no time in mentioning these recent and oft-repeated lapses of your conduct to your esteemed father, upon his return to Cornell Castle. I feel certain that your father can and will convince you, as I apparently cannot, of the duty that a wife owes her husband!"

Shocked, Helen turned pale, and replied, shaking all the while, "Indeed, I do apologize! I shall try my best to become a conformable wife!"

"I should hope so!"

With these words, Sir Rupert and Miss Sterling parted company, Sir Rupert heading for the entrance door, and Miss Sterling heading for the southeast gardens, nearly running, and tears beginning to spill over onto her cheeks.

She came upon a marble bench near a sundial; she seated herself, and tried to calm herself, but it was no easy thing to do.

Lady Georgiana Locksley, whose headache had resolved with surprising speed, had just reached the entrance door to the walled garden, and was reaching for the latch when she was surprised by the sudden appearance of Sir Rupert Fellowes, whose face was still red and whose demeanor appeared discomfited.

"Sir Rupert!" she said, blushing a bit. "You startled me!

How do you do? It has been a long time since we have met."

"It has been some time," replied Sir Rupert, who automatically cast a surveying gaze over her and noted that her figure was just as excellent as he remembered, and her face even more handsome. "You are looking very well, Lady Georgiana."

"Thank you, Sir Rupert," said Lady Georgiana, blushing prettily once more. "I believe I have not yet wished you joy, have I?"

This reminder of his recent unpleasant discussion with his fiancée was enough to send a scowl to his face, a scowl that did not go unnoticed.

Aha, she thought to herself, *they must have just quarreled! If Lady Lacon knew, she would kill me, but is it really too much to hope that I might still displace Miss Sterling in Sir Rupert's affections?*

With this thought firmly in her mind, she shrieked loudly, and then stumbled to the ground, landing in a small heap.

"What is the matter, Lady Georgiana? Have you hurt yourself?" asked the baronet.

"It is the silliest thing, Sir Rupert! I have acquired a stone in my shoe, and I had thought I had got it out, and then I stepped upon it, and the most dreadful pain ran through my foot, and I collapsed from the hurt, and I am most seriously afraid that I shall not be able to return to the Abbey without some assistance!"

She turned upon him her most endearing smile, and held out her little hand.

"Will you be kind enough to assist me?" she asked.

"Of course," he said enthusiastically, offering her his arm.

She took it in both of hers and leaned on him heavily,

so close to him that he could feel her warmth and the faint, fruity scent of her perfume.

An attractive girl, Lady Georgiana Locksley, he thought to himself. *A damned attractive female!*

Why did we break off? Of course, it was that Black Jack Sterling was prepared to make a better settlement!

What a pity that I was blinded by greed.

The elderly senior groundskeeper at Beaufort Abbey was called Old Piggott, and he was so very old that, nowadays, few demands were ever placed upon him. He lived in a tiny cottage on the grounds more in the capacity of a pensioner than a worker. Today, when the Abbey staff was put in the unenviable position of hosting large party from Cornell Castle, Old Piggott had been called up for duty, and his duty was merely to see to it that the walled garden was opened for the guests, and then, once whoever wished to view the garden had done so, to carefully shut the garden up once again.

Old Piggott saw a lady emerge, leaning very heavily upon the arm of a gentleman, and chatting away with him in an animated fashion. The old man waited for some minutes more, to see if any others were to come. He waited a good five minutes, but no one else appeared. Assuming that no one else had visited the garden, Old Piggott locked the garden door with his rusty key, tested it, and left to enjoy his customary afternoon treat, made daily for him by his fond daughter-in-law, a pot of hot tea with a very great deal of sugar.

Helen Sterling had composed herself entirely by the time that Peter Gilbough came upon her, as she sat in the ivy-covered garden, and thus the two friends greeted one another with a kind of bittersweet happiness, each one very obviously trying to behave with the greatest propriety and circumspectness.

"Miss Sterling! How do you do?" asked Peter.

"Very well, thank you."

"Where is Sir Rupert?" Mr. Gilbough inquired, looking around in vain.

"He—uh, he has gone on ahead," replied Helen, trying as best she could to betray no emotion. "Where is Lady Georgiana?"

"She—she has developed the headache, and has gone on ahead also. May I accompany you back to Beaufort Abbey? It is getting late, and I believe it is time for our party to return to the Castle."

"Thank you, yes," she replied, accepting his arm, and walking slowly and silently with him all the way back to the entrance-door.

Mr. Gilbough tried to open the old wooden door, but was unable to do so. Thinking the door must be stuck, he tried again, using both hands, but could not. He kicked the door with his foot, and then tried to ram it open using his broad shoulder, but it was of no avail.

"I think we've been locked in."

"Locked in? Oh, no—how can that be?"

"When I shake the door, I can hear a padlock rattling on the other side."

"Who could have done such a thing?" cried Miss Sterling, alarmed. "If we aren't back when the others are, it will cause a great deal of talk."

"It can't be any of our people who have done it, for how would they have come upon a key? It must have been one of the servants; perhaps one is still around."

Mr. Gilbough commenced to call out loudly for assistance, but no one came.

"This is useless; I can't break down the door, and there is obviously no person within hearing. I'll see if I can somehow get over it."

He decided to look for a spot at which he might scale the stone wall, and presently he found it: about fifty feet from the door there was an old section that had partially collapsed.

"Miss Sterling, if you will accept my assistance, I believe there is a way we can climb over the wall just down here."

"Oh, thank you, Mr. Gilbough! I am afraid that if I am discovered here alone with you by Sir Rupert, I will be in great trouble."

"Why should you be?" said Peter with some asperity, as he stepped up onto a portion of the half-fallen wall, extended his hand toward Miss Sterling, and deftly guided her to follow him.

Miss Sterling did not immediately reply, as she was intent upon not placing her foot on an insecure stone; she found a purchase, shifted her weight to it, and allowed Mr. Gilbough to pull her further up. Then she said, "I will be in trouble if we are late, because Sir Rupert is very conscious of how people will talk and gossip. He always says he wants his wife to behave with the strictest propriety, and I seem to be a little weak in that area, for he is always telling me that I am."

Mr. Gilbough flushed red for a moment. "Our being locked in the garden was entirely an accident. It is not as if we had come out here to escape notice and to enjoy a private moment together, is it?"

"Certainly not," said Miss Sterling firmly, now reaching up to climb further up onto the pile of rocks. "You are right: Sir Rupert cannot object! After all, it is not as if we had purposely been trying to arrange a clandestine meeting!"

"Of course not!" said Mr. Gilbough. "What a ridiculous notion!"

"What reason would we have to do such a thing, after all?" she pointed out. "We are friends."

"Fast friends," Peter agreed. "Very good friends indeed."

At this juncture, a piece of cracked stone shifted on the high pile, and gave way, causing Miss Sterling to lose her footing, and tumble dangerously until Mr. Gilbough swiftly stopped her fall by scooping her up into his arms in a single, deft motion.

"Thank you!" she gasped, frightened. "I should have broken my ankle, had you not caught me!"

He carried her over the wall, and set her down again on some rocks on the far side. Peter's hand was still on her small waist, steadying her, when she turned and looked up at him. In just that moment, when he looked into those incalculably deep blue eyes of hers, he felt as if the world had shifted on its axis; it was as if her being had reached inside him, and touched him in the most intimate way.

It seemed to him that what was occurring between them was somehow inevitable, and that it was predestined. Helen felt, when their eyes met, as if she had known him since the beginning of time.

Almost against his will, he murmured, "I love you, Helen. God help me, I love you so very much."

She was aware that her breathing had become faster and more urgent, but the entire sensation was different from the pale, purely physical responses she had felt with Sir Rupert. It was she who felt utterly open and utterly vulnerable, but gained such strength because she trusted him above all things, and loved him above all things; she felt as if she would wish to entwine her body with his until the end of time; she would be willing forever to intermingle their bodies, their minds, their very souls.

Helen began to cry, but her small, stifled sobs were tears of joy, as she confessed in reply, "As I love you."

They clung to one another, they pressed themselves against one another so strongly it seemed for a moment they would meld into one.

Peter swept her back into a deep passionate kiss that was returned with a profound inner hunger that Helen had never before felt, and never before known existed. There was between them an inexplicable quality of sheerest enchantment.

He took her hands, each one, and kissed it over and over again, telling her by his touch alone how much he treasured her, wanted her, loved her and desired her.

"Oh, Peter, Peter . . ." she whispered, feeling for this timeless moment as if nothing in the world was real save herself and the man she loved, who loved her in return.

At last Miss Sterling began to weep in earnest, holding onto Peter's strong arms as if her life itself depended upon it.

"Why must it be like this? Why could I have not met you a few weeks ago, and not Rupert?" she cried. "It's so unfair!"

"I have had the same thought myself, a thousand times, since I met you. I have wanted to murder Sir Rupert; I have dreamed of calling him out to a duel; I have thought to carry you off in secret to Gretna Green, and marry you myself, before he could."

"C-could we not do so?" Miss Sterling asked shyly.

"Yes, we could," he admitted. "It would cause a scandal, but we could."

"We would be going against my father's dearest wish," said Miss Sterling.

"And against my father's dearest wish, as well," said Mr. Gilbough, keeping her still safe within his embrace.

She sighed deeply, and let another tear slide down her

face, which Peter wiped off with his hand. Helen shook her head, and said, "Oh, Peter, I do wish to leave everything behind, and go away with you, but I haven't got the strength. I am afraid you will think me a poor, craven creature, but I think I cannot act against my father. I haven't the will to cry off from my engagement—after all, I know nothing against him, and he behaved very well throughout all of this. It is not as if he has mistreated me— how can I break my word and make a fool of him? When I see clearly, I think that all his criticisms of me are perfectly reasonable, even more than reasonable.

"I am the one who is at fault. I am the one who, though betrothed to him, fell in love with you. It was my doing, none of his. How can I then run away to Scotland, or in fact to do anything except continue down this hard path fate has laid out for me?" she asked, tears running in streams down her cheeks.

"Don't cry, my love," he said, brushing them away with his fingers.

"It was only that I was so young. I didn't know—about love. How could I have known about it?" she explained, much moved. "If I had only known that *this* feeling that I have now, with you, toward you, is what love is, then, of course, I would never have accepted him! I mistook mere attraction, mere infatuation for real love, but I vow, I did not mean to! I did not mean to serve him ill, it is just that I had no experience of love! How could I know? He was the first man ever to hold my hand, or to make love to me! I was a foolish child, and I made a very foolish and costly mistake, but at least it was an innocent error. It was innocent, and yet—I did give him my word of honor!"

"I know, my dear," said Peter, running his hands softly along the length of her cheeks.

"Then there is Father to be thought of," she continued, glad at least to have someone to talk to about all the things that had been running through her mind. "And that is the hardest thing of all. You have no idea how many men flung themselves at the Sterling heiress when I came to town. I felt like a flower covered in honeybees, and one by one, my father discovered their weak points, and got rid of them. He is very careful with me, and his approval of my marriage is as necessary to me as my own breath. When Sir Rupert offered for me, I could see how pleased he was: he wants me to become the wife of a baronet. He wants to be able to call his daughter, Lady Fellowes and he also thinks my mother would have liked it. How can I let him down?"

"You do not think that plain Mrs. Gilbough might have been enough?" asked Peter fondly.

"Very likely, if it had happened first, it would, but now that I have given it, how can I break my word? Father gave his word to Sir Rupert as well. Now that he has lost his fortune, I think my welfare is of even more concern to him. It would be different if Father knew you first, or if all these plans had not already been made."

"Then we must be honorable, and honor our promises, I suppose. But, Helen, at least you must allow me tell you how desperately I have come to love you! I know that every word, every glance, every touch is forbidden to me—and yet I cannot get you out of my mind. From the first minute I saw you, I wanted nothing so much as to touch you, and to be allowed to come to know you and to love you. The realization that this can never come to pass, and will never come to pass, is inexpressibly painful to me—I am desolate. Please forgive me. I know that making such a declaration at this time is the worst thing I could do, and I hate myself for it.

"If you must marry Sir Rupert to keep faith with your father, then that is what must be done. If I must marry Georgiana to keep faith with my father, then I must face that, as well. But only know, for good and for always, that I truly love you, Helen Sterling, to the depths of my heart, and I swear by my life, that no one shall ever supplant you in my affections."

"Dearest Peter," said Helen, deeply moved, "You know that we must swear never to see one another again."

"I know it," said he, simply.

"Listen to me, Peter. We must promise never again to speak, never again to lay eyes upon one another again, certainly never again to be alone in each other's company. If we do not, we will never have the strength to lay our love aside. Will you promise me?"

"I promise," whispered Peter. "I will go and stay at my father's cottage, at least until you leave the Castle. When you are gone, I will marry Georgiana, and we will go far away to live."

"Yes, my dear. It is the right thing, the wise thing, the honorable to do," she admitted.

The two lovers embraced once more, embracing for a long lingering time, cherishing every second, and knowing that it was an embrace that would be their very last, before they would be parted from one another, for ever.

It was nearly four in the afternoon by the time that Lady Arabella Gilbough gave all the carriage drivers the order to hitch up all the horses to their carriages to convey the party back to Cornell Castle. Word soon spread from guest to guest, and all the ladies and gentlemen began to assemble on the cobblestone walk in front of Beaufort Abbey.

"Have you ever seen anything so divine as the view from the West Park? I would have died to get a piece of my property done over by that Capability Brown!" Mrs. Hicks-Aubrey was saying.

"Someone else would have to die, and leave me his

fortune, before I could indulge myself in such a pricey pastime. Have you any idea what those trees cost? And all the ones that had been there before were felled, or moved! It is a pretty enough place, but I have better use for money, I can tell you!" declared the Duchess of Minster.

Amid all the hubbub and commotion of guests gathering, and comparing the events of the day, Lady Arabella tried to count her guests, to make sure everyone had returned, so that the trip back could begin and everyone arrive in time enough to dress for dinner.

"Twenty! I only count twenty," she said to Stubbs, her head groom.

"I believe we are missing four persons, your ladyship," he explained. "I have not yet seen Miss Carteret nor Sir Charles Stanton, nor Miss Sterling, nor Master Peter. Shall I have the rest set off for home, or do you wish for everyone to wait, and go together?"

"We shall wait a little," ordered Lady Arabella scowling. She made her way through the company, asking the crowd if the two missing couples had been seen, and in her wake, some eyebrows were raised when the identities of the missing were learned.

"I saw Sir Charles and Miss Carteret enter the Grand Maze!" volunteered Captain Prendergast, trying to be helpful. "Perhaps they have become lost within it? Send a servant for them! Or else, I could go myself?"

Captain Prendergast was just on the point of going, when Sir Charles Stanton, with Miss Janet Carteret leaning heavily on his arm, rounded the corner of the Abbey that was nearest to the Maze.

Sir Charles looked his usual impeccable self—tall, dark, and handsome, and dressed to perfection in biscuit breeches, buffed top-boots, a teal green coat, and an immaculate white shirt and cravat, tied in the D'Amboise manner. Miss Carteret, though looking very lovely indeed, seemed to have adopted a very deep, almost permanent blush. Further, both of them were smiling a smile no one had ever seen on their faces before, the provenance of which one could only speculate.

The couple, however, acted as if nothing of note had happened, and their credit with society was such that no further inquiry was made. Sir Charles handed up Miss Carteret and Mrs. Partridge into his carriage without a word; there he awaited the signal to return to Cornell Castle.

Group by group, most of the rest of the guests did the same; even so, however, there was still no sign of Miss Sterling or of Mr. Gilbough.

Lady Arabella approached Sir Rupert Fellowes, who had been standing next to the carriage that conveyed Lady Georgiana Locksley, chatting away happily with her, and inquired of him if he knew where Miss Sterling might be found.

"She has not come yet?" he said in an annoyed tone. "I really hadn't noticed; I had thought she would be back long since. We were all in the walled garden together."

"With your son," Lady Georgiana supplied helpfully.

"Oh! They must be together, then," said Lady Arabella, somewhat annoyed. "What was he doing with her, and not with you? I'll send someone to fetch them back."

"There is no need for that, Lady Arabella," said Sir Rupert unhappily. "I shall have to go myself."

"They do seem to seek out each other's company with boring regularity, do they not, Sir Rupert?" said Lady Georgiana, trying to stir up trouble. "I wonder that you allow it!"

"I wonder that that girl cannot regulate her own behavior!" said Sir Rupert, not even trying to hide his irritation.

"I cannot seem to get it through her head that she must behave as I see fit! When we are married, I promise you that she will *not* behave in such a care for nothing way, or else I will see to it that she remains safely locked up back home at Pease Hall!"

Sir Rupert was on the verge of setting out for the garden when someone spotted Mr. Gilbough and Miss Sterling walking up the path from the northwest quadrant.

Miss Sterling's hair was really quite disheveled, and her dress had mud and rock dust on it; there was a slight tear in her once-lovely walking dress. Mr. Gilbough's coat appeared dusty and torn, also. All in all, they presented a very odd appearance.

Lady Lacon whispered to Lady Arabella in a snide tone, "What have we here, Arabella? You really must ring a peal over him, I think. He is like to upset all our plans!"

As soon as the couple came amongst the carriages, it was clear to all the guests that the couple was very embarrassed to be seen together, and singled out together, and to have arrived so late, and to have arrived in such a disorganized state.

Taking the bull by the horns, Peter approached Sir Rupert at once, and presented Miss Sterling to him, saying, "Here she is. She is perfectly well. I am sorry we were late. We had some difficulty in exiting the garden. Good day."

Mr. Gilbough thought the less said the better, so he then merely bowed himself away.

Sir Rupert took her hand, led her over to his carriage, and helped her up into it. He then followed her up onto his seat next to her, while Miss Sterling explained nervously, "We were locked in the garden by mistake."

"How very inconvenient for you," Sir Rupert said mildly, inwardly raging, as he took up the reins.

"We had to get out by climbing over a wall," she said, in a tone filled with guilt.

"I see," he replied dryly. "How very tiresome, I'm sure."

"But it is the truth!" she blurted out, more loudly than she had wanted to. "Someone locked us in! We weren't having a clandestine meeting, if that's what everyone thinks!"

Overhearing this, someone in the party gasped out loud.

Helen Sterling felt that this entire interchange was intolerable. Every word she uttered seemed to make things worse for her! She felt at once guilty, and angry at feeling so guilty, and angry at having to explain herself, and angry at feeling blamed for what was, after all, just an innocent accident. More than this, she felt dangerously confused about her feelings.

"That will do, Helen!" Sir Rupert hissed. "Say no more, I beg you, and have the goodness to sit here and, and be still!"

Humiliated, blushing, Miss Sterling did as she was told. She felt the hot sting of tears on her cheeks, which she attempted to wipe away with her small, gloved hands. Somehow, once again she was sure that everyone in the whole party was talking about her.

She was quite correct. It was very odd, really: Sir Charles Stanton's *tête à tête* with Miss Carteret in the Maze passed by almost without notice, while Miss Sterling's *tête à tête* with Mr. Gilbough had become the talk of the party.

"Isn't that the outside of enough!" whispered Lady Agatha Winslow to Miss Peterson.

"How can she behave that way to Sir Rupert?" cried Mrs. Hicks-Aubrey. "After all, he *is* still willing to marry her!"

"She don't know which side her bread is buttered on!" averred Mrs. Partridge.

"Very careless, I say. Really very vulgar," said Lady Winslow. "Scandalous!"

One of the elder ladies, after bemoaning her behavior in no uncertain terms, said, "Of course, after all, what more can you expect? Miss Sterling is a common tradesman's daughter. Not even that, any longer. She's the daughter of a bankrupt!"

19

Mr. Peter Gilbough, the sole heir to Cornell Castle, returned there in the very blackest of moods. He had ridden back with Lady Georgiana Locksley and his mother and Lady Lacon, but no one spoke for the whole of the journey, lost in separate worlds of thought.

Lady Georgiana was thinking of how kind and considerate Sir Rupert had been to her; she was thinking how warm was the touch of his hand on hers when she leaned on him for assistance. She was wondering how she would somehow be able to trade Mr. Gilbough for Sir Rupert.

Lady Lacon was wondering how she would ever find another suitor for Georgiana, who clearly was not trying to make herself attractive to Mr. Gilbough, but had been fighting the whole thing since the very beginning. She was so irked by the unfilial behavior of Georgiana that she was thinking of throwing up her hands entirely, and letting the girl work out her marital plans all by herself.

Lady Arabella was wondering why, of all people, her son

would be making a cake of himself over that Sterling chit—especially now, when she's not worth a brass farthing! Despite the series of increasing pressures (admittedly, largely invented) she had been putting on her son to marry Georgiana, the girl of her choice, he seemed to be disregarding them with increasing energy.

Had he found out that his father had had no intentions at all as to his son's marriage? Had he found out there was no secret codicil? How could he? Was he simply flying in the face of reality? That seemed to be the case—and it was that heedlessness that made Lady Arabella shudder, frightened that he might do something odd and headstrong, fleeing back to the Continent to paint, and leaving the Castle in the hands of—horrors!—Raymond Dulles, the vicar of Hadleytown, the man who was just as dull as his name implied.

As to Peter, his thoughts were filled by nothing more than Miss Helen Sterling. In the days since she had come to the Castle, he had moved from admiring her, and flirting with her, to appreciating her beauty, wit and intelligence. From there, things had moved forward with lightning speed, and quite against his will, and certainly against his sense of honor, he now found himself deeply immersed in love with a woman who rightfully belonged to another gentleman.

The carriages reached Cornell Castle; the various occupants emerged and went their various ways. Most returned to their chambers in order to rest and then begin to dress for dinner; Mr. Gilbough retired first to his personal chambers, and then to his painting studio; from there, with the help of a few servants and a cart, he moved his paints, and brushes, and the sketches of Miss Sterling out to the White Cottage.

After making sure he had everything he needed by way of fresh food and drink, candles and bedclothes, he gave orders that he was not to be disturbed. He intended to remain at his father's White Cottage, working and painting in his solitary style, until he had come to terms with things.

The White Cottage that had been his father's refuge and workplace was made in the old style, with thick white-painted mud walls, wood-beam reinforcements, and a thick, sloping thatched roof. Everything was covered in dark green ivy, which grew so densely that it was difficult to perceive what was beneath, except when it peeped out near windows, or in places the ivy had not grown.

Before his long tour, Peter had made sure to give orders to the Cornell Castle staff that the White Cottage be perfectly well maintained; it would have been easy to let it fall into ruin after his father's death, and his own long travels on the Continent. But he had made a special fund to cover its expenses, and left it with specially trusted servants, so that when Peter visited it that evening, it looked just as he had seen it last.

Every time that Peter went within the little cottage, it made his heart ache, for it reminded him of his dear father.

The cottage interior was dark and quaint. There was beautiful old burnished wooden furniture that had been in the family perhaps since Tudor times. As he looked into the large fireplace, where meals were sometimes cooked, he could almost remember the many times he had sat there as a child, perfectly content, playing in the warmth of the fire as his father painted in the next room.

His father's room was unusual, and the only part of the house that veered from tradition, for his father had caused a whole section to be redesigned so that a large window could be installed on the north facing side of the cottage. That was where his father was used to work, to his mother's despair, hour after hour and day after day.

To that room, Peter Gilbough had directed that his paints and his paintings be brought; when he arrived, since it had begun to get dark, he had some wax candles lit, and then began to arrange things just as he liked. On the main easel he placed the preliminary oil sketch of Miss Helen Sterling. To the left, on another easel, he placed the detailed sketch he'd done of her in charcoal, on the day that everyone went out sketching by the lake.

As he looked at her picture, the mere memory of her was enough to evoke a deep sense of attachment. Then, considering the actual situation that faced them, he felt a profound sense of loss.

The honorable course was perfectly clear to him: he must see things as they are, he must love her enough to let her go. She was promised to another, a man of whom her father approved. Though he loved her, and now knew he loved her, he also knew it was time to keep away from Helen Sterling, at all costs, before this brief interlude cost her her engagement.

Peter Gilbough knew nothing bad enough of Sir Rupert Fellowes that could justify trying to take Helen away from him. True, he had of late made a few imprudent bets, but those could be covered one way or another through refinancing the man's holdings.

It was not as if the man had been marrying her for her money; now she had none, and Sir Rupert was still holding true.

Sir Rupert had asked for her hand in an honorable way, and had won her hand and her love in an honorable way; what call had he to thrust himself between them? It was true that the man seemed perhaps too fond of seeing things his own way, but that was a failing many a gentleman might have, and still remain a gentleman.

No, Sir Rupert had a prior claim; he himself had none, save that of the heart.

* * *

Miss Sterling and Sir Rupert drove home in his high-perch phaeton, each saying little, and each thinking a great deal. Sir Rupert Fellowes was wondering how in heaven's name he was going to pay off forty thousand pounds worth of vowels to Sir Charles Stanton. He was most of all worried that he might have to sell off some land, and he was rather inclined to think that a particular piece of desirable property his aunt had left him, land that just happened to be next to Sir Charles Stanton's hunting-box in Leicestershire, might have been the whole reason behind Stanton's having accepted such high stakes in the first instance.

Sir Rupert despised the very idea of selling family property. That was the damnable thing about gaming debts—unlike the butcher, or the grocer, or one's tailor, who might be strung along indefinitely, gaming debts were debts of honor, and had to be settled with dispatch. When the debts were as large as the ones Sir Rupert had foolishly incurred, settlement could mean ruin —or could mean breaking up an estate meant to be passed on to one's heirs unbroken.

The devil take it! Here he was, with this pretty little blond girl sitting next to him, sullen and mute, an heiress to whom he had become betrothed with the full and explicit expectation that she would provide him the means with which to continue his favorite pastime—gambling at cards for very high stakes. Now she was no longer an heiress, but merely an albatross around his neck, and one who was growing increasingly unmanageable.

It seemed to Sir Rupert that, since her father had lost his money, all Helen's vulgar habits and inclinations were coming to the fore, unchecked. Time after time, it seemed to him, he had explained to her, in a precise and gentleman-like fashion, the reasons why this action or that action was unsuitable behavior for a lady of quality—and yet, time and again, Black Jack's daughter would defy him.

It was becoming more than a nightmare. Worse than a nightmare, it was an embarrassment.

Which, in the universe of the London ton, was worse than death.

Miss Helen Sterling, on her part, was conscious of little else but exquisite pain. She felt rather like a sleepwalker, going through the motions of living, but without those motions having any real feeling, or any real life. She felt as if she had been neatly split into two persons—one was the Miss Sterling who had survived the excursion to Beaufort and was able to answer her fiancé's questions in neat, polite monosyllables; the other was the real Helen, who inhabited Miss Sterling's deepest heart, and who was the keeper of all true emotion and all love, who had to be hidden away, never to be shown in the light again.

It had to have been the wraith of the real Helen Sterling who dressed and went down to dinner at Cornell Castle that night, and who was able to smile, and to chat, and to ignore all the little darts and jibes and insults and setdowns that were aimed at her by the various members of society—some of whom had, only a day previously, gone out of their way to acknowledge her as the toast of the ton.

Tonight, however, she wore her best mask of manners.

Miss Trenton joined Helen and the rest of the company in the music room after dinner, but even having an ally present was not enough to change Helen's mood.

"Tell me what is the matter, my dear," said Miss Trenton. "You haven't been yourself since you came back from

Beaufort Abbey. Have you and Sir Rupert quarreled again?''

She shook her head no, and said no more. Miss Trenton, unaccustomed to such silence, began to worry in earnest about her charge, and devoutly wished that Mr. Sterling might come back from town at once.

Peter Gilbough had no thought of returning to Cornell Castle so long as Helen Sterling was still there. He thought it would be better this way, better for both of them to endure a clean break now, and then go on about their separate lives.

To continue to see her again, at the table for dinner, or to listening to her singing, or to dance with her, or to have to watch her dancing with another—to watch her dancing with the man she had promised to wed—would be unendurable.

So, he had retired to the White Cottage, and he fully intended to throw himself into his work. He would work on his oil portrait of her, the one that Sir Rupert had forbidden him to paint, the one that her father had requested, and into that portrait he intended to put all of his heart and his soul, and the great dimensions of love that he felt for Helen Sterling.

He began in the early evening, when he first moved his belongings over there, and he began painting like a man obsessed, stopping for nothing save a glass of claret. Hour after hour, as the daylight faded, he lit candle after candle, till his work room was filled with a host of candles, with their flickering light cast upon Helen's portrait, and the workroom had begun to take on almost the appearance of an altar or a shrine.

He *must* have something to remember her by.

*   *   *

Lily and Jeffers Pym were spying on the company through a crack in the door that led to the backstairs.

"Look at my mistress, standing with Sir Rupert. She looks so unhappy, doesn't she?" said Lily. "Something must have happened at Beaufort Abbey—she came back in a rare mood, and she wouldn't even tell me or Miss Trenton what was wrong, which is quite unlike her. And where is Mr. Gilbough? Why is he not here? He always comes in after dinner."

Jeffers Pym replied, "As to what happened at the Abbey, I heard that Miss Sterling and Mr. Gilbough created quite a stir, coming back late, and in each other's sole company."

"They're in love! I knew it! I've been watching it grow from the start!" said Lily, excited. "How romantic!"

Jeffers added, "I also heard that Mr. Gilbough, after their return from the Abbey, suddenly had all his belongings taken out to the White Cottage, and is planning to take up residence there, and will not be returning to society for some time."

"No! She's all set to marry the wrong man, and poor Mr. Gilbough the wrong woman! We must do something!"

"Very well, my dear Lily, but what must we do?" Jeffers asked sensibly.

Lily thought for a moment, and then whispered into Jeffers Pym's ear for some time. The valet smiled, and nodded first to indicate his understanding, then to indicate his agreement. Pym stole a brief but sweet kiss, and then departed.

Miss Helen Sterling was on her very best behavior. She had spent the entire evening, so far, with her companion, Miss Trenton, on one side of her, and her *fiancé*, Sir Rupert

Fellowes, on the other side. She smiled when smiled at, she spoke only when she was spoken to, and otherwise merely existed, as the shell of her former self.

She knew Sir Rupert was very angry with her, but she was not angry with Sir Rupert. She had quite ceased to feel anything at all, and in this new state of numbness, she was fully prepared to marry him. Why should she not?

Miss Sterling was quite surprised when Jeffries suddenly appeared in the music room, for he was, as a rule, not expected to appear among company. However, he appeared to be bearing an urgent message for Sir Rupert, for he apologized to her and to Sir Rupert, repeatedly in his usual pretentious manner, until Sir Rupert lost his temper, and told him to just get on with it.

It appeared that Sir Rupert was wanted in the library on urgent business.

He took his leave of his fiancée, and said he would return right away.

"Are you afraid I'll cause more comment while you're gone, Sir Rupert?" said Miss Sterling with acerbity. "Are you sure you don't want me to come with you, just to be sure I don't embarrass you?"

Sir Rupert's face showed his anger and frustration, but he tried to keep a civil tone, as he said, "I'm sure you won't do any such thing, my dear, not with Miss Trenton here to advise you."

"Oh! Then it's lucky you haven't sent her off to your sister Regina's just yet."

"Very lucky."

As soon as Sir Rupert left to go to the library, the valet turned to Helen Sterling and whispered in her ear.

As she heard the message, the expression on Miss Sterling's face changed entirely; it took her a little time to realize who had been the bearer of the message, and what he had asked her to do, but when she had, she nodded her head to indicate her willing agreement.

A new look of hope suffused her face; she looked around the room, and wondered how best to make an exit.

Then, all at once, Miss Helen Sterling disappeared.

There was no one at all in the library.

Sir Rupert Fellowes waited there amongst the dusty volumes for several minutes before he realized that he had been tricked and taken in; clearly, the message had been nothing but a ruse to get him to leave the music room. He swore to himself that he would turn off Jeffries the minute he saw him next: he could hardly believe that his own man would plot against him!

He was, therefore, unsurprised when he returned to the music room and saw Miss Trenton standing just where she had been, but now she was all alone. Miss Sterling was nowhere to be seen.

"Where has she gone?" he demanded of her companion.

"I'm sure I don't know," replied Miss Trenton with as much dignity as she could muster.

"Don't play the fool with me," snarled Sir Rupert. "You know as well as I do that I am this girl's last hope. Nothing good can be expected for her from this dalliance with Lady Arabella's son, for his mother will cut him off without a penny, and so she has told me. If Miss Sterling is so imprudent as to run off with Mr. Gilbough, you may be sure I will not run after them. I will cry off from the engagement—and they will find themselves together but destitute. I feel sure you know enough of living in straitened circumstances that you would not want that to happen to Helen.

"For all the love you bear your young charge, you must tell me at once what has become of her."

"I don't know what has become of her, Sir Rupert."

"Is this your notion of being a good chaperone? You are not serving her well, believe me."

Miss Trenton turned red with embarrassment. "She was here only moments ago. Jeffries, the valet who bore a message for you, had a message for her as well. After she heard what he said, she left. She said nothing to me about where she was going, or when she would return."

To the displeasure of both Miss Trenton and Sir Rupert, the vicar of Hadleytown, Raymond Dulles, chose that moment to suddenly appear.

"Hullo, Miss Trenton. Hullo, Sir Rupert. Are you enjoying the evening? The music is particularly pleasant tonight, don't you think?" he asked, in a jovial mood.

"Excuse me, Mr. Dulles; I cannot speak right now. I have urgent business to attend to. Miss Trenton, I am sure I can trust you to keep this matter private until it can be satisfactorily resolved," he said, bowing. "I must bid you both good evening."

"Well, Miss Trenton, what was that all about?" he asked. "Sir Rupert was showing none of his customary good manners. I wonder what was wrong?"

"He has some business to attend to," she said, showing none of the anxiety she felt. "Just as he said."

"Oh. I see. Well, you're looking very nice, tonight, Miss Trenton. Would you do me the honor of granting me a dance?"

"A dance? I? Good heavens, Mr. Dulles, I'm just Miss Sterling's companion. It is not at all the thing for you to keep pressing me to appear in company with you."

"But, Miss Trenton, I-I greatly esteem you. I-I should I-like to make my—"

"Pray, say nothing more, Mr. Dulles! I am very happy

to have made your acquaintance, but indeed, I had no thought of forming any ... of having any ... of making a-a-a—

"Any attachments?" Mr. Dulles asked hopefully.

"No, sir, certainly not, and I beg you will be kind enough to change this subject at once."

"Of c-course, Miss Trenton. J-just as you wish. S-so tell me, is Mr. Sterling back from L-London yet?" the vicar asked. "I've had some news from my friend Elroy, and I w-wanted to tell him of it."

"No, he's not back yet." said Miss Trenton, wringing her handkerchief. "I wish he will come just as soon as he may!"

The path from Cornell Castle to the White Cottage was very short: it threaded through the park on the east side of the Castle, where a thick stand of trees had been planted, and where the stand merged invisibly into the old forest that had once surrounded the entirety of Cornell Castle. The White Cottage had been built in such a location that it too was hidden among the tall trees; from any main view of the Castle, the Cottage was lost in the trees, hidden away from sight, and yet could be reached by foot in only a matter of minutes. It was thus at once very private and very convenient, another reason that Mr. Edward Gilbough had found it such an excellent hideaway.

After speaking with Pym, Lily ran along the footpath just as fast as she could, and it was not long before she reached the Cottage. From the window outside she could see Mr. Gilbough hard at work; she saw the flickering candles, all around the room, and she saw the canvas that bore the image of her mistress: it was like enough to Helen Sterling to make her gasp in astonishment.

"Lor', he *does* love her, then!" she said to herself,

knocked on the door, and entered without waiting for his answer.

"Excuse me, Mr. Gilbough, sir," she said, out of breath, "But I am Lily, and I'm Miss Sterling's abigail—"

"Yes, Lily, I know you. What is wrong?"

"And I've a message from her, for your ears alone, sir," said Lily, and she motioned for him to lean over so she might whisper the message in his ear.

As he listened to what Lily had to say, Peter's face whitened, and took on a look of extreme gravity. He threw on his coat and cravat at once, saying, "Of course, I will come to her at once!"

A few curt inquiries of a footman had led Sir Rupert to the verandah where he had made love to Miss Sterling only a few short days before. He had fully expected—or feared—to see his fiancée in the arms of another man, kissing him passionately, and he was very relieved to discover her alone. With just a bit of good fortune, there might still be time to avert this scandal.

"Helen!" he cried. "Helen, what do you think you are doing? Who are you waiting for? You must come inside, at once!"

"No, I mustn't," she replied evenly.

"If anyone sees you," he whispered through gritted teeth, "There will be a deal of talk!"

"There already *is* talk," pointed out Miss Sterling sensibly. "There has been talk about me since the very first day I arrived at Cornell Castle! First, no one *really* approved of me. Next, when the official notice of our engagement appeared in the *Gazette*, everyone grudgingly welcomed me into the ton. Then, they all not merely greeted me with open arms, but fairly *courted* me after Sir Charles showed me some kindness, and then, *after* Father lost his fortune, I became the butt of everyone's jokes, all over again. After all of it, and after everything you've said to me, especially in the past day, I can tell you one thing of which I am very certain: I'm sure I do not care a fig about what they say about me now!''

"But, I care what they say!" said Sir Rupert, reddening visibly.

"Ah, yes, but I do not!" she said with certainty.

"You *must* care what they say! They are society!"

"My dear Sir Rupert, in the light of matters involving life and death, society's fickle whims and fashions are easily seen for what they are: vapid, inconsequential, quite without meaning. I will admit, at one time I was anxious to be accepted by high society. Now, suddenly, I see things as they truly are, and I no longer have any interest whatsoever in the judgments of the ton.''

"I am betrothed to you. I care for your reputation, even if you do not!"

"You don't care about my reputation—you care about *your* reputation, because you belong to that world. I don't, not any longer: I have lost my fortune, with it my *entree* into the ton, and now I have lost all interest in it. I need not worry about having to please anyone any more, save myself.''

"Oh, Helen, I cannot believe that you are so lost to propriety that you would behave in such a thoughtless way.''

"Well, perhaps, but of course, after all, I'm *not* a lady, am I? What more could you expect? I was just a rich tradesman's daughter you found convenient to marry. But you know the interesting thing about all of this, Rupert? It's that my manners certainly suited you well enough when I was a rich heiress! You made hardly any complaint about me, then. But once I had lost my fortune, increasingly, everything I said and did you found fault with! Along with becoming poor, I had suddenly become ever more vulgar and common, and you were hard-pressed to keep me in line.

"I know the only reason you refused to cry off from our engagement is that it seemed to you dishonorable to do so. You thought it would cause even *more* scandal, and scandal is the last thing you can bear to live with.

"Here, Rupert," she said, holding out her hand to him. "Take your ring. I was fond of you, and I know you did your best, but I'm afraid we really should not suit."

"What do you mean, Helen? Are you actually trying to jilt me?" he thundered at her. "Me? Sir Rupert Fellowes? How *dare* you treat me in this manner!"

"How dare I?" she asked, contemplatively. "It is an interesting question, isn't it? Yes, I suppose it's really rather vulgar of me, once again, to do you the discourtesy of jilting you, is it not?"

"How can you treat this matter so lightly, Helen? Had you no feelings toward me? Do you think I had no feelings for you?" cried Sir Rupert.

"I think you had some, perhaps, but very little, very few," she said, simply. "I think that when I lost my dowry, you were stuck with me. Take your ring, Rupert, please. Think of the advantages: you will be free to find yourself another heiress. I should try a real lady of quality this time, Rupert. I'm sure you deserve nothing but the best."

"What will your father say?" asked Sir Rupert.

"What *will* Father say, I wonder?" repeated Miss Sterling in a disinterested tone. "Oh, look, here is Mr. Gilbough! Perhaps he knows the answer to your question! Mr. Gilbough, what do you suppose my father will say when I inform him that I have broken off my engagement to Sir Rupert? I would explain to him the reason, which is that we should not suit."

Mr. Gilbough's face lit up with a smile that was glorious in its extent.

He ventured, "Perhaps Mr. Sterling will say that you must do as you think best?"

"No! He won't!" shouted Sir Rupert, feeling very humiliated. "He will say you are going to be a pauper, and that is the truth. He will say you are a fool to go against a marriage he had approved of, and that I had stood by faithfully, even under the most difficult circumstances."

" 'Difficult circumstances?' " asked Mr. Gilbough. "To what do you refer, Sir Rupert? Do you mean your loss of Helen's dowry, or your loss of forty thousand pounds to Sir Charles Stanton, or to both?"

Humiliated, Sir Rupert reddened and made no reply. This aroused some compassion in Miss Sterling's breast, and she replied, almost tenderly, "You *were* faithful, Sir. Rupert, I will say that for you, though I think perhaps it was in spite of yourself. But still, you know, it is best this way, for we really should not have made agreeable partners."

With a look of disgust on his face, Sir Rupert faced each one of them, and threw up his hands, saying, "Very well, suit yourselves, then. I'm sure it's now no business of mine what becomes of you. I wish you great joy—if that can be had in your little hovel, which I doubt, for I know perfectly well how things have been left, Gilbough—you know how talk goes around backstairs. Jeffries told me all about it. You'll have nothing, either one of you. Good luck, Helen. Good luck, Mr. Gilbough. I hope you will enjoy keeping your pigs and cows—if you can even *afford* them!"

Having said his peace, Sir Rupert Fellowes turned on his heel, and stalked off, letting the verandah door slam shut as he left.

"Rather a poor loser, is he not?" inquired Miss Sterling, as she allowed herself to be embraced by Mr. Peter Gilbough.

"Not when playing cards," he replied, "Though, tradi-
tionally, losing at love is thought to be far more painful."

"Pooh! He never was in love with me!" said Miss Sterling,
tossing her head. "He thought I belonged to him, that's
all."

"Forget about him, and kiss me, my dearest," ordered
Mr. Gilbough, in a low voice that brooked no opposition.
"I've come for you. Everything will be alright now, I
promise."

They remained thus together, kissing long and tenderly,
for quite some time, until Miss Sterling said, through tears
of joy, "I'm so glad you're here, so very glad. Whatever
prompted you to send for me?"

"I didn't send for you," he said, surprised. "You sent
for me!"

"I didn't, I swear to you!" cried Helen. "I said no such
thing!"

"Your abigail, Lily, came out to the White Cottage and
gave me an urgent message, from you, saying in it that you
loved me to utter distraction!"

Helen colored at once, and said, "I never used such
words to her to describe my feelings for you!"

"Lily said unless I came to you at once, she could not
answer for the consequences! She made me fear for your
life!"

"Shocking girl! I never said such a thing!" cried Helen,
now laughing through her tears. "On the contrary, I
remember the pledge we made, never to see one another
again! I was perfectly resigned to my fate! You should
have seen me, I was like a lamb walking meekly to slaughter.
I was all ready for my martyrdom, and I would have gone
through with my promise and with the whole charade until
Sir Rupert's man, Jeffries—or Jeffers, as I suppose it *really*
was, came by and sent poor Rupert off to the library on
some wild goose-chase or other!

"When Sir Rupert had gone, Pym told me that *you* had urgently changed your mind about your promise, and that *you* were unable to live without me! He made me fear you might take your own life! He said you begged me to break off at once with Sir Rupert, and that you would marry me, regardless of the consequences, and that if I agreed, I was to come at once to meet you here on the verandah!" she explained.

Peter Gilbough laughed and said, "One begins to understand the intricate machinations behind this auspicious meeting."

"Well, after all, Lily was right! Of course, I love you, Peter," said Helen in a voice warm and lazy with passion, as she brushed her cheek against his broad shoulder. "I do love you—to utter distraction!"

"As I love you," replied Peter, picking up her chin with his hand, and cherishing her mere presence. "I think we must forgive them for their timely interference in our affairs."

"Oh, yes, I think we must. Otherwise, I *never* would have had the courage to leave off following the 'honorable' course," admitted Helen. "Would you have?"

"No, or perhaps I just would not have acted in time. While I was at the Cottage, I had already decided I could not bear to marry Lady Georgiana, no matter whether it cost me the Castle or not. I had not, however, gotten to the point where I would have sought to interfere with your engagement to Sir Rupert, however much I might have wished that *you* would break it off."

"We were fortunate that events occurred to disentangle us. I can tell you, I am very glad I did cry off, for I had thought I never could! But now, I see that Father's wish is for me to be happy, not merely to marry a wealthy man, and have a title. I don't think he feels that way at all— he's not that kind of person. You will see when he comes back, rich or poor, he will be quite the same as ever. In any case, however happy I was to have received his approval, the decision to marry is a decision I now realize I must make by myself, alone."

Peter Gilbough knelt down next to Helen, and enfolded her hand in his large one. He looked up into her brilliant blue eyes, and asked her, with a loving smile, "So, tell me, my dearest Helen, will you marry me? I can offer you little more than myself. I have the Cottage, for Father gave it to me outright—the deed is in my name. I can sell it, and we can live abroad, quite cheaply. We can take your father and Lily and Miss Trenton or whomever you wish. I think I can support us all through my painting. I can offer you a simple life, and I can offer you my undying love and affection. Helen, will you marry me?"

"Yes," she whispered, happier than she had ever been. "Yes, my dear, of course I will marry you."

20

The ubiquitous Lily Beeton and Jeffers Pym were observing with pleasure this tender scene played out in the verandah beneath them, as they leaned out from an open mullion window in a guest-room in the east wing; they were fully satisfied so far with the results of their impromptu scheming.

"It really didn't take much, did it, Jeffers?" pointed out Lily, watching her mistress in the strong embrace of the man she loved.

"Not at all," replied Pym. "A word to one, and a word to the other, and everything fell into place, just as it should have."

"Do you think Sir Rupert should have recognized you at once?" reflected Lily.

"Not really. Why should he have? I took good care to rumple my coat, and do my cravat in the silly, old-fashioned style my brother Jeffries affects, and I took care to speak in just his stentorian tones. Few people have ever seen us together in one room, so they have no idea how alike we are. Even if Sir Rupert realized that his valet's twin was in the employ of Sir Charles, I'm sure he would have no thought I'd have the audacity to try and trick him. It just isn't done, is it, save in operas and in plays?''

"But you did it, Jeffers, my dear," she said, taking his arm, and snuggling against him.

"*We* did it, Lily," said Pym, "And I must say, I think we did very well. I think they will be very happy, indeed, and that's the point of it, and when I tell Sir Charles, he will find it a wonderful story, for he has a great sense of humor! Of course, my dear brother, when he finds out, will surely murder me, but that's neither here nor there.''

"If Jeffries ever tries to harm a hair on your head," said Helen's abigail darkly, "He will have Lily Beeton to deal with and so you may tell him!''

Pym said, with a laugh, "Be merciful to him, my dangerous beloved!''

Jeffers Pym withdrew his head from the window, and pulled Lily back in the room after him. He put his arm around her waist, and leaned her back against the side of the window, and began kissing her intently.

"Do you know, Lily, I had once thought of posing as my brother, and then making an attempt to steal a kiss, and so testing to see if you would be faithful to me?'' said Pym.

"Stupid man. You think I can't tell you apart?'' said Lily, smiling. "Rubbish! I could tell you apart blindfolded. Besides, whyever would I *want* to kiss your brother Jeffries?''

"There *is* that," said Pym, well satisfied.

It might have been the glowering countenance that Sir Rupert Fellowes presented when he came back into the music room that told everyone that something momentous had occurred, but it took very little time for a rumor to sweep the assembly to the effect that Miss Helen Sterling, former heiress to a vast fortune, had had the unspeakable audacity to cry off from her engagement to the handsome baronet.

"When did it happen?" asked Mrs. Hicks-Aubrey. "Just now, did you say, your grace?"

The Duchess of Minster nodded sagely, "That is what I am given to understand. A very dangerous decision, I believe. Whatever will the girl do now? No one will receive her."

"Forgive me, but I shall always be glad to receive her, your grace," interrupted Sir Charles Stanton. "What has she done but cry off from an engagement, after all? It is a lady's prerogative to do so."

"To call the Sterling girl a lady in the first place is coming it a bit too strong, Sir Charles," said Mrs. Hicks-Aubrey. "Is it not?"

"I must respectfully disagree," he said smoothly. "Miss Sterling's manners, her air, her education, her comportment, all speak of gentility and elegance. I shall certainly always be pleased to know her, rich or poor."

"Very well, Charles," said her grace. "We all know what *that* means! We shall have to let her in. I don't mind, really, for she seemed a sweet little thing, even when she had her money. However, do you suppose that, without it, she will be able to keep company? I should think not, after all."

At this point, Lady Arabella Gilbough, a look of shock on her face, fairly flew across the music room in order to question her most eminent guests.

"Is it true?" she cried, out of breath. "Has the Sterling girl jilted Sir Rupert?"

"So it is said," replied Sir Charles. "You may ask Sir Rupert himself, for he is just over there speaking with Lady Georgiana, but I would say, judging from his behavior since he entered the room, that it seems very likely he has been released from his engagement."

"Oh, dear! Oh, my!" cried Lady Arabella. "Where is my Peter? I was told he had gone off in a huff to stay at that silly Cottage of his father's, but what if he has not? If he finds that Sterling girl is free, I'm sure he'll offer for her!"

"How can he offer for her?" the Duchess of Minster asked. "I thought he had no money if he did."

"You don't know Peter! He is so headstrong, I am afraid that under the influence of such a girl as that Sterling chit, he might do anything that took his fancy!" she cried.

"You may well be right, Lady Arabella," said Sir Charles smoothly. "Look who has just entered the room. Isn't that your son, Peter, with Miss Sterling on his arm? They seem very much attached to one another, do they not?"

Mr. Gilbough and Miss Sterling had just entered the music room, arm in arm, and very apparently having eyes for none but one another. They walked at once to Miss Trenton and Mr. Dulles, who had been speaking together since Miss Sterling's departure. Miss Trenton began crying at once, and Mr. Dulles, shook his second cousin's hand strongly, smiling.

"My God! He must have offered for her! A penniless nobody! Oh, my heavens, what am I to do?" cried Lady Arabella.

Lady Lacon joined the company, and pointed out, "I think you and I must both make the best of things. We did what we could, but events have turned out otherwise, and we really must adjust."

"Oh, but to have *such* a girl for a daughter-in-law!" said Lady Arabella.

Sir Charles Stanton turned and gave Lady Arabella a critical glance, adding, "I'm sure that I, for one, will always value Miss Sterling's friendship!"

Lady Arabella caught herself, and reversed herself quickly, saying, "Y-yes, yes, of course, Sir Charles. She's a sweet little thing, and I'm sure Peter is very fond of her. I wish them very happy."

"After all, at least Peter is going to marry!" said Lady Lacon, "That was your first concern, my dear, was it not?"

"You are right, Louisa. At least now I need not worry about moving to the Dower House, for I'm sure Peter won't make me do so, will he? You don't suppose he will be angry at me for having making up that fib about his fortune? If he's angry at me, he could make me move, and then I don't know what I would do!" she sniffed, beginning to cry. "Oh, I have been very wrong, haven't I? I ought not to have schemed so hard to get him to marry Georgiana. He might never forgive me!"

"I'm sure he will. He has a very even temper."

"And what will become of your Georgiana? Who will marry her now, Louisa?"

Lady Lacon fanned herself, smiled, and indicated the opposite side of the music room, where Lady Georgiana and Sir Rupert were sitting next to one another, and talking with great animation.

"I think, Arabella, that nature is taking its own course once again. I always knew that Georgiana had a preference for Sir Rupert—now that he is unattached, I think that my goddaughter will be using all her wiles to see that he attaches himself to her, just as soon as possible."

"But what about his debts? I heard he had lost a small fortune to you, Sir Charles. Is that not the case?"

"He did, in fact, lose a tidy sum, but Sir Rupert has the means to settle it without major loss to his estates," explained Sir Charles. "There is a piece of hunting land I want, and if he will only agree to give it up, his debt to me will be settled. I am persuaded, furthermore, that in future Sir Rupert will never again play for such high stakes.

The last thing a gentleman likes to part with is his land. He has certainly learned his lesson, and I don't think he will make Lady Georgiana an improvident husband."

"Well, if he has learned from his mistakes, and won't be wasting his blunt on cards, then they may have my blessing to marry, and at once!" said Lady Lacon. "I, for one, am sick to death of all this scheming and match-making, and I had much rather return to the ladylike occupation of gathering and passing on gossip. I'm not really well suited to all this intrigue."

Lady Georgiana and Sir Rupert were engrossed in a competition as to which one of them could cast greater blame on the behavior of Miss Sterling and Mr. Gilbough, and it was proving to be a very close contest. Almost as soon as Sir Rupert had re-entered the music room, Lady Georgiana, sensing that something was amiss, had gravitated straight to him; when she discovered how things had turned out, it was only the work of a moment before, for tact's sake, she had stifled the intense joy that had arisen within her at the news that he was free, and replaced it with a look of profound sympathy for the victim, Sir Rupert.

As soon as his sad story was told, Lady Georgiana pronounced Miss Sterling a chit lacking all gratitude, and a care-for-nothing schoolgirl who could not even be trusted to keep her word. Sir Rupert called Mr. Gilbough an interfering weasel, and a headstrong fool who had no care for the honor of his family name.

Once these criticisms had been mutually agreed to, the couple was able to move on to the more enjoyable occupation of each expressing their respective regard for the other's sterling behavior in these times of trouble.

Lady Georgiana said of Sir Rupert that no one, under the circumstances, could have borne recent events with

more honor and gentleman-like conduct than he had. Sir
Rupert said that Mr. Gilbough's waywardness must have
been hard indeed for Lady Georgiana to tolerate, and that
she had handled herself throughout, like a thorough lady.

They moved from these topics directly into expressing
the regard they had always had for one another, ever since
the last London Season. Sir Rupert said he had held Lady
Georgiana in the greatest esteem ever since he had met
her, in fact; she had always been regarded by him as one
of the most handsome young ladies of his acquaintance.

Lady Georgiana shyly accepted this praise, and expressed
her long-time held regard for Sir Rupert.

At this point, Sir Rupert began to look very serious,
indeed. He took Lady Georgiana's hand in his, and said,
"I have felt that I made a great mistake last spring when
I transferred my affections from yourself to Miss Sterling.
Every time I saw you here, I was struck even more deeply
by your beauty, your good character, your good sense, and
your elegance of manner. As a betrothed man, I was of
course unable to express these feelings. Happily, I may
freely do so now. I had come deeply to regret the choice
that I had made.

"Will you permit me to continue?" he asked her.

"Of course, Sir Rupert," said Lady Georgiana, her heart
beating faster than it ever had before. "Do go on."

"I know it may be too late even to try to win your heart,
but will you at least give me leave for the attempt?"

"Rupert, Rupert, you have won my heart a thousand
times over!" cried Lady Georgiana, anxious that he should
know precisely how she felt at once.

"Have I?" he asked, uncertain.

"I was broken-hearted when you shifted your regard
from me, toward another. Oh, I know at that time she was
the more prudent choice, and in matters of marriage, one
must be prudent, so I do not blame you for what you did."

"I blame myself, Georgiana," said Sir Rupert.

"We must rejoice in the simple fact that it has all worked out for the best."

"I do rejoice in it. I could never have been happy with that girl. She didn't listen to me, not in the slightest! Can you credit it?" he asked.

"I would always listen to you, Rupert," she said in a silky voice, moving closer to him. "I would always do whatever it is you wished."

His breath began to quicken.

"Why don't you come out with me to the verandah, my dear, just for a moment?" he said huskily.

"Yes, indeed," she replied, smiling.

When Peter and Helen entered the music room together and Miss Trenton learned of their engagement, she was at first thrilled, then frightened for them. She was very concerned about how they would arrange their financial affairs, which was a significant thing, considering that Mr. Sterling would be unable to help them. At least, thought Miss Trenton, Helen would be married to a man who clearly loved her above all things, and she would not have to face life alone. If they were poor, at least they would be happy in each other.

For it was obvious to anyone who had eyes to see that Miss Sterling and Mr. Gilbough were over the moon with happiness. In the first place, they were in alt with love for one another, and in the second place, they were exhilarated to be able finally to appear in public without having to conceal their intense mutual regard.

"Having shared our joy with Miss Trenton," said Peter, "I think I really ought to present you to my mother as her future daughter-in-law."

"Oh, no! Don't you think it is too soon?" cried Miss

Sterling, nervous. "You know she won't be pleased at your choice. She doesn't want the Castle to go to the vicar, which it will if you don't inherit. She told me so."

"She tells that to everybody. I never met a woman less likely to hold her tongue than my mother. No, Helen, I think we should face the matter directly, and have it over with. Are you game?"

"I am if you are," she said, and allowed herself to be led to the group where her future mother-in-law was standing.

The introduction of Helen to Lady Arabella as her son's intended might have taken quite a different turn save for the felicitous fact that the arbiter of fashion, Sir Charles Stanton, happened to be standing right next to her ladyship. Very conscious indeed of this, Lady Arabella was trying extremely hard to get her conflicting emotions completely calmed down, and to put her real feelings under wraps.

This girl is to be your daughter-in-law, she said to herself. *It is very important to be civil to her. Your plan, though daring and enterprising, did not succeed. You must just give it up, and go on with things.*

Put on your best ton smile, and give the children your blessing.

Lady Arabella Gilbough took a deep breath, and went ahead with it.

"Peter, my dear!" she said, reaching out to him with both hands. "I had heard you were staying in the Cottage for a few days! How nice that you could come! By the by, why did you?"

"Oh, I had urgent business to attend to!" he said, laughing. "Mother, I have the pleasure to inform you that I have just asked Miss Sterling, here, to become my wife, and that she has consented!"

"Oh, really?" said Lady Arabella, trying hard to look pleased. "What a surprise! How nice! Has your father given his consent? I thought Mr. Sterling had gone to London."

At the mention of her father, Miss Sterling blushed, and seemed nervous for a moment, but quickly regained her composure, and said, "Yes, my father, as you may know, has been out of town, but we hope he will approve the match."

Approve the match? thought Lady Arabella. *Hah! Pauper that he has become, he will sink onto his knees and thank God for the match!*

Lady Arabella said, sweetly, "Of course, we all hope he will give the match his blessing. However, did I not understand that you had a previous engagement? Has that, uh, been, shall we say, terminated?"

Miss Sterling blushed again, eager to have this interview end, and replied, "Yes, I was betrothed to Sir Rupert Fellowes, but, over time, I decided we should not suit, and I have returned his ring."

Lady Arabella's heart sank at this news, for with it all her plans were overset. The couple would certainly be able to marry, and there was really nothing that she could do about it. It would be better to be agreeable about his choice: at least, the girl was pretty and pretty-behaved.

"You think that you and Peter and will suit, do you?"

"I know we will, Mother," said Mr. Gilbough.

"All right, very well. What can one do in the face of true love?" said his mother, kissing Miss Sterling on the cheek. "You have my blessing."

Sir Charles stepped forward, took Mr. Gilbough's hand, and shook it in a friendly fashion, saying, "Congratulations. I'm sure we all wish you the very best of luck."

Lady Arabella had just begun to wonder precisely how she was going to explain to her son that she had shamelessly misrepresented the truth about his inheritance, when her train of thought was interrupted by a great stirring amongst the guests.

A tall dark figure was striding through the music room directly toward Miss Sterling.

"Father!" she cried, running toward him, and flinging her arms around him. "You have come back! We've been so worried for you!"

Miss Trenton came over to greet him, saying warmly, "How good it is to have you back, Mr. Sterling! Was it a long journey?"

"Not at all, not at all," he said jovially. Turning to Lady Arabella, he said, "I can't thank you enough for taking such good care of my daughter in my absence. I am sure I could not have left her in better hands."

"Certainly not," said Lady Arabella. "We knew you were called away on business, Mr. Sterling, and I must say we were all very sorry when we, uh, heard of certain business reverses that you have suffered."

"Reverses?" said Mr. Sterling. "Ah, yes, those! Tell me, is everything just as it was before I left for London? Is there any news?"

"Why, yes, Mr. Sterling!" cried Miss Trenton. "How did you guess? Your daughter, I think, should be the one to tell you."

"Tell me what, Helen?"

Helen looked a little shy and nervous, but explained, "You see, Father, while you were gone, Sir Rupert and I . . . well, we decided we shouldn't suit. I have returned his ring. I hope you don't mind very much that I broke off the engagement. I know I did it without seeking your approval, but I . . . I felt it was not the right thing to do."

"I see," he said seriously.

"There is something else," she began.

"What might that be?" Mr. Sterling said.

"I'd like you to meet Lady Arabella's son, Peter Gilbough, a great and dear friend of mine."

"How do you do, sir?" said Peter. "This is perhaps an awkward time and place for such matters, but in your absence, I have asked your daughter if she would do me the honor of becoming my wife, and she has given me her consent. If you had been here, I would surely have applied to you first, and so I hope you will forgive me for not having done so. If you would give us your blessing, I would be much obliged."

"Do you love Helen?" he asked, not the sort of man to beat about the bush.

"I do, sir. Very much indeed," replied Peter, taking hold of Helen's hand.

"You don't mind about her, uh, lack of family background?" Mr. Sterling inquired, looking at Mr. Gilbough very intently.

"To the contrary: Helen is everything a man could ever want in a wife," he declared.

"You don't mind if she brings no dowry?" Mr. Sterling asked, skeptically.

Peter thought for just a moment, before replying, "This marriage is purely a matter of the heart."

Mr. Sterling looked rather pleased at this. "Very good, young man. Very good. Now, tell me, how will you be able to support my daughter?"

Peter Gilbough began to look a little guilty when he heard this question, and had begun a slightly stammering reply when Mr. Sterling interrupted him, to ask, "Your mother is Lady Arabella Gilbough. Does that mean you are the heir to all this estate?"

Wondering how to explain what had happened, he began, "Well, I *w-was* the sole heir, and I was to take f-full possession of the Castle and a substantial inheritance from my father upon reaching the age of twenty-one, which will be tomorrow, but since I am to m-marry against—"

It was unbearable. Lady Arabella had to interrupt, unable to watch her only son portray himself as a pauper in front of Black Jack Sterling, asking lightly, "Marry against what, Peter? You're certainly not marrying against my wishes, if that's what you mean. No, Mr. Sterling, for a while there was a tiny misunderstanding as to just how things had been left, but that is all straightened out now."

"Is it?" asked Peter, perplexed.

"Yes, it is! Didn't I tell you? How remiss of me! It turned out that that so-called secret codicil I was telling you about was nothing but a sham! Isn't that singular? Someone has played a very amusing trick on us, you see, Mr. Sterling, and we all thought that Peter was going to have to marry Georgiana, that red-headed girl over there, and that if he didn't, he would lose all his money! But you see how much Peter and Helen love each other! *He* was willing to marry *her,* even after you lost your fortune, and *she* was willing to marry *him,* even though she thought he didn't have any fortune at all! Isn't that perfection?"

"Yes, it's quite impressive," said Mr. Sterling seriously. "Money should have nothing to do with marriage."

"And as you can see, it hasn't! But I must assure you, Mr. Sterling, that now everything has been all straightened out, and Cornell Castle on the morrow will be in Peter's competent hands, and he will have a wonderful income, and Miss Sterling will be assured of a wonderful, wealthy life. And you *won't* make me move out into the Dower House, now, will you, Miss Sterling?"

"No, certainly not," said Helen, wondering what was going on.

"You are a good, sweet girl, and I will be happy to have you in the family!" said Lady Arabella, satisfied at last. "Even though you're not an heiress!"

"Not an heiress?" asked Mr. Sterling. "Oh, Helen's an heiress, all right and tight! I'll settle on her the same funds as I settled on her the last time, Mr. Gilbough. You can put it aside for her daughter, when she has one."

"Really?" said Lady Arabella, nonplussed. "It was my understanding that . . . that is to say, we were all under the impression that . . . how shall I put it?"

Miss Trenton ventured, "We heard you'd had, er, certain financial reverses . . . of a delicate nature. In fact, you said so yourself! In that letter!"

Sir Charles interrupted to say, "Not to put too fine a point on it, we heard that you hadn't a feather to fly with."

"That your pockets were to let," said Miss Carteret.

"That you were all to pieces," said Lady Lacon.

"Oh, *that!*" said Mr. Sterling jovially. "That was just a rumor!"

"A rumor?" said Lady Arabella, not comprehending.

"Just a rumor," said Black Jack Sterling, shrugging his shoulders in a casual manner.

"So you're *not* done up?" asked Lady Lacon.

"No, it was just a rumor," he replied. "I'm still well-breeched. At high water. Up in the stirrups. Flush in the pocket. Well-inlaid. Same as before."

"I see," said Sir Charles Stanton politely.

"In fact, I started the rumor myself," explained Black Jack Sterling. "My man John Snow helped, of course."

"Father! Whyever would you do such a thing?" cried his daughter. "We were beside ourselves with worry for you!"

"It was done rather in the manner of an experiment," explained Mr. Sterling. "I had heard some rather disconcerting information about your former fiancé, with regard to some recent wagers, and some other things, and I decided I should test the waters just a bit, and see what would happen if things were not just as they seemed."

"I never knew you had a sly side to you, Father," complained Helen. "Of course, there *was* all that business about helping the poor boys in Hadleytown."

"Who told you about that? Raymond Dulles? At any rate, I never really tried to keep *that* a secret. I just never made much of it, that's all."

"You never told me," said Helen. "You never said a word."

"It was just a project I had, my dear," explained Mr. Sterling. "I have many such projects. As to the letter about my loss of fortune, I hope it didn't cause you any great embarrassment. I just thought to create an occasion where you needn't be the Sterling heiress for a little while, just to see if that would affect which way the tides would flow. I hope you will all forgive me if there has been any inconvenience from this misunderstanding."

"So, there were no riots?" asked Miss Trenton.

"No riots."

"There was no shipwreck?" asked Lady Lacon.

"No shipwreck. You can read all about it in the newspapers, if you don't believe me. It was necessary to my plan to cause the London papers to arrive a little bit late, I'm afraid. I hope no one was badly inconvenienced."

"I'm so glad it turned out not to be true!" said Miss Trenton passionately. "I was so worried for you!"

"Were you, Miss Trenton? I think you and I must have a little talk, for now that Helen is to be married to Mr. Gilbough, there is the important matter of your future to be discussed."

Miss Trenton's face fell at once, and she turned away from him, appearing to be on the point of tears.

"I will be able to get a new position, Mr. Sterling, I'm sure I will," she said bravely. "I have been thinking about it since we arrived."

"I have been thinking about a new position for you,

also," said Helen's father. "To that end, may I have the honor of this dance?"

"But I'm a companion! I may not dance!" said Miss Trenton, aghast that he would even think of breaking with convention in such a way. "Sir, I may *not* dance!"

"Oh, yes, you may!" said Mr. Sterling with steely determination, leading his lady out onto the dance floor by the hand. "And, by God, you shall!"

Helen thought she had never seen Miss Trenton looking so radiant, and she said to her betrothed, "It looks as if Father has plans all his own for dear Miss Trenton!"

"I am very happy for her, and for him," remarked Peter. "She is a fine woman."

The muscians began to tune their instruments, and a few more couples were needed for the set. Helen and Peter decided to take their place for the cotillion, standing up next to a beaming Miss Trenton and Mr. Sterling. The music began in earnest, and the couples started to perform the first graceful steps.

At that time, Lady Georgiana and Sir Rupert Fellowes walked into the room from the verandah, blushing and smiling, and whispering to one another.

"All of a sudden *everyone's* smelling of April and May," commented Sir Charles Stanton, who was watching intently while the dancers went through their various motions. "With all of this pressure to form permanent attachments, you don't suppose that you might find it in your heart to change *your* mind, as well, Miss Carteret?"

"I might, Sir Charles," she said with a mysterious smile. "I'm beginning to think I might."

Epilogue

Mr. and Mrs. Peter Gilbough were married in London, and traveled to the Continent for their honeymoon, which lasted nearly a full year, allowing Mr. Gilbough to acquaint his new wife with all the art treasures that he most admired. He was able to study further with Maestro di Capoletti, and she was able to further her knowledge of Italian. When it became clear that Mrs. Gilbough was increasing, the couple came home to Cornell Castle for the joyous event.

The christening of Mr. and Mrs. Gilbough's first-born son and heir, who was named Edward John Gilbough, after his grandfather, proved another occasion for Lady Arabella Gilbough to entertain the ton. The event was blessed by the presence of Sir Charles and Lady Stanton, Mr. and Mrs. John Sterling, and Sir Rupert and Lady Georgiana Fellowes, all of whom had put their past differences behind them, and had become fast friends.

Among the honored guests were Mr. and Mrs. Jeffers Pym, both of whom had retired from domestic service, and were well on the way to making their fortune—in trade.

ROMANCE FROM FERN MICHAELS

DEAR EMILY   (0-8217-4952-8, $5.99)

WISH LIST   (0-8217-5228-6, $6.99)

AND IN HARDCOVER:

VEGAS RICH   (1-57566-057-1, $25.00)

YOU WON'T WANT TO READ
JUST ONE—KATHERINE STONE

ROOMMATES　　　　　　　　(0-8217-5206-5, $6.99/$7.99)
No one could have prepared Carrie for the monumental
changes she would face when she met her new circle of friends
at Stanford University. Once their lives intertwined and became
woven into the tapestry of the times, they would never be the
same.

TWINS　　　　　　　　　　(0-8217-5207-3, $6.99/$7.99)
Brook and Melanie Chandler were so different, it was hard to
believe they were sisters. One was a dark, serious, ambitious
New York attorney; the other, a golden, glamourous, sophisticated supermodel. But they were more than sisters—they were
twins and more alike than even they knew . . .

THE CARLTON CLUB　　　　(0-8217-5204-9, $6.99/$7.99)
It was the place to see and be seen, the only place to be. And
for those who frequented the playground of the very rich, it
was a way of life. Mark, Kathleen, Leslie and Janet—they
worked together, played together, and loved together, all behind
exclusive gates of the *Carlton Club*.

Available wherever paperbacks are sold, or order direct from the
Publisher. Send cover price plus 50¢ per copy for mailing and
handling to Penguin USA, P.O. Box 999, c/o Dept. 17109,
Bergenfield, NJ 07621. Residents of New York and Tennessee
must include sales tax. DO NOT SEND CASH.

DANGEROUS GAMES   (0-7860-0270-0, $4.99)
by Amanda Scott

When Nicholas Barrington, eldest son of the Earl of Ul-
combe, first met Melissa Seacort, the desperation he
sensed beneath her well-bred beauty haunted him. He
didn't realize how desperate Melissa really was . . . until
he found her again at a Newmarket gambling club—being auctioned off by her father to the highest bidder. So,
Nick bought himself a wife. With a villain hot on their
heels, and a fortune and their lives at stake, they would
gamble everything on the most dangerous game of all:
love.

A TOUCH OF PARADISE   (0-7860-0271-9, $4.99)
by Alexa Smart

As a confidence man and scam runner in 1880s America,
Malcolm Northrup has amassed a fortune. Now, posing
as the eminent Sir John Abbot—scholar, and possible
discoverer of the lost continent of Atlantis—he's taking
his act on the road with a lecture tour, seeking funds for
a scientific experiment he has no intention of making.
But scholar Halia Davenport is determined to accompany
Malcolm on his "expedition" . . . even if she must kidnap
him!